DANGER CLOSE

DANGER CLOSE

CAMERON CURTIS

Srishti
PUBLISHERS & DISTRIBUTORS

Srishti Publishers & Distributors
A unit of AJR Publishing LLP
212A, Peacock Lane
Shahpur Jat, New Delhi – 110 049

editorial@srishtipublishers.com

First published in India by
Srishti Publishers & Distributors in 2024

First published by Inkubator Books in 2021

10 9 8 7 6 5 4 3 2 1

Printed and bound in India

To Abby, who inspired me to return to writing.

1

FAYETTEVILLE, 2000 HRS THURSDAY

I'm superstitious.

Anyone who spends most of his career getting in the way of bombs and bullets learns. It's better to be lucky than good.

Best to be both, but no one survives without luck.

My best friend once told me, "Dumb luck can kill you."

I didn't argue, because he was right.

Kettle Creek Apartments, Fayetteville, is occupied by middle class folk from the city. Civilian employees, and military families from Fort Bragg. My place is one bedroom, seven hundred square feet. Big enough to be comfortable, not big enough to own me.

Perfect for a man trying to figure out what to do with the rest of his life.

I sit in the living room, sipping a beer. Watching the news. Every station is showing live footage of a New York City street. Jammed with emergency vehicles. Police cars, fire trucks, ambulances. The firemen wear oxygen bottles and breathing masks. They carry injured civilians from a subway. Dozens of injured people, a constant stream.

Paramedics give the casualties oxygen and first aid. There aren't enough gurneys. The injured are laid on the sidewalk and treated. The police stand behind wooden traffic barricades, blocking the street on either side of the subway exit.

Ominously, many bodies have been covered.

A reporter steps in front of the camera and speaks into a microphone.

"We're still learning what happened in the New York City subway around 6 pm today. Police have cordoned off an area two blocks square around 28th Street and Broadway. Witnesses on the scene have told us about an explosion on a subway train. There have been fatalities, but authorities haven't been able to tell us yet how many. We're hearing that numerous injuries resulted from the crash and derailment, and there are casualties from smoke inhalation. Firemen are working to extract the injured from the tunnel. This is proving extremely difficult in the smoke and darkness.

"The police commissioner will make a statement later this evening; we'll wait to see if he can comment on whether this incident was an accident, or the result of terrorism. All we can say is the city is paralyzed, worse than it's been since the events of September 11, 2001."

The situation looks bad. For the moment, nothing is clear. This could be an accident caused by a derailed train. It could also be a terror attack. Worse than the Boston Bombing, not as bad as 9/11.

Police wearing breathing apparatus pile out of a large black van. It's parked behind delivery trucks and cars lining 28th Street. Beat cops are trying to get drivers to move the vehicles out of the way. An impossible task. This is the Flatiron District. Tourist hotels, beauty shops, ethnic restaurants.

The police look like hazmat and forensic teams. They are carrying metal cases and heavy-duty flashlights. Single file, they enter the subway. You'd think they'd wait for the emergency crews to clear casualties. The investigators must be in a hurry to examine the wreckage for evidence. Before the firemen and stampeding civilians ruin it.

I sip my beer. The windows are open. A gentle breeze fills the apartment with fresh suburban air. The smell of grass and trees.

The camera switches to an aerial view of the city. A wide shot from a news helicopter. Throngs of people spilling from the subways. Snarled traffic. A total mess.

My phone buzzes. I lift it to my ear. "Breed," I say.

The voice on the other end is curt, economical. "It's Lenson."

Mark Lenson, one of my best friends. He owns a sporting goods and gun shop in El Paso.

I mute the television. "What's up? You see this mess in New York?"

"What mess?"

"Subway. An accident or an attack. Cops aren't saying which. I make heavy casualties. Hazmat and forensics teams on-site. They are not waiting for the dust to settle."

"Sounds like they have good reason to be worried." Lenson sounds distracted. He has more important things on his mind. "Breed, there's bad news."

"What is it?"

Lenson sucks a breath. "Keller's dead."

I sit bolt upright. "No."

"Murdered on his ranch."

"Mary and Donnie?"

"They're okay. Hancock and I are with them. We're staying at the hotel while the sheriff sorts things out."

"When did it happen? Who did it?"

"Keller was found yesterday. The sheriff doesn't know who

did it. Could have been illegals or coyotes, but right now it's a guess." Lenson hesitates. "Breed."

"Yes?"

"Breed—they cut his head off."

My stomach hollows. "They *what*?"

"They cut his head off. With a big knife, or a machete."

I get to my feet. Pace. "I'm coming down. First flight I can get in the morning."

"I have to go. Message me your flight and arrival. I'll meet you at the airport."

"Roger that."

"Lenson out."

Images of chaos and suffering continue to stream from the widescreen. What is more tragic. A mass casualty attack or the murder of a friend. The personal nature of Keller's death shakes me to the core.

The reporter's lips are moving. The television is still on mute, there is no sound. More bodies are laid on the sidewalk behind him.

There is a flash of light on the street, and the widescreen picture dissolves into a mass of jagged diagonal lines. When the picture resolves itself, the image is canted sharply to one side. An ant's-eye view of the street. The camera has fallen to the ground.

I switch the sound back on.

The street is an image from hell. Men and women scream and plead for help. Black smoke and dust fill the air. The pavement is a carpet of shattered glass, blown from shop windows and tall buildings on either side. Police and firemen—those who are able—stagger to their feet. Ghosts in the half-light, their clothing hangs in bloody tatters.

A woman's voice, a studio reporter, cuts in.

"There's been an explosion. We can't reach our reporter at the scene.

We're switching to aerial coverage. I think we have footage of the blast."

The image flicks to an aerial shot of the street before the explosion. The news helicopter is hovering, the cameraman holding the lens steady. There are four wooden barriers, two on each of 28th Street and Broadway. Each a block from the intersection. I can see police cars, fire trucks, and ambulances parked on the street. There is enough detail to identify first responders by their uniforms.

My eyes are drawn to movement. A man in civilian clothes emerges from one of the shops. A heavy backpack is strapped to his shoulders. With an air of purpose, he steps onto the street. The police are too preoccupied to notice him.

In slow motion, a flash of light consumes the man. The flare expands with the explosion and human figures are blown this way and that. The air seems to shiver as shock waves bounce from the buildings. The disturbance ripples sideways along the street. Silver shards of glass shower the pavement.

A second bomb. There must have been eighty pounds of explosives and shrapnel in that backpack. That bomb was not homemade. The flash, the black smoke, the terrific blast effect —all characteristic of a military-grade weapon.

The first bomber drew first responders to the 28th Street Station. Exposed, where the second suicide bomber could kill them.

Sophisticated terror tactics.

Elbows on my knees, I sit on the sofa. This is the United States. I am staring at an image of midtown Manhattan.

America under siege.

2

EL PASO, 1300 HRS FRIDAY

Duffel and garment bag in hand, I step into the arrivals hall of El Paso International Airport. A message stares at me from my phone. It's Lenson.

Traffic. ETA 1400.

Lenson's characteristic economy. I look for a place to while away an hour. Starbucks isn't crowded. The coffee shop has comfortable armchairs. Leather the texture of butter.

I was the last of the team to retire. Dan Keller, Mark Lenson, Bill Hancock. One by one, the others said goodbye to the army and the unit we called Delta.

1st Special Forces Operations Detachment - D. The army's elite counter-terror and direct action force. Created in the seventies as a response to high-profile terrorist attacks.

Keller had been the first to leave. Early. Sixteen years in the bank, and not a scratch on him. He said he wanted to watch his boy grow up. Hancock and Lenson left next, nursing their wounds.

The coffee shop's widescreen is tuned to the news.

Late last night, the police commissioner issued a statement. In a New York City subway car, a suicide bomber detonated an explosive vest. Just before the train arrived at the 28th Street platform. Killed sixty people. Injured hundreds of others when the train crashed deep beneath the city's streets. Many of the fatalities were from smoke inhalation. Survivors panicked, stampeded in the black, smoke-filled tunnel.

Thirty-seven more were killed on the street when the backpack bomb exploded. Eighty-six were maimed by shrapnel and falling glass. Most were police, firemen, and paramedics. They were cut to ribbons.

Smoke inhalation killed as many people as the blast on the street. I haven't seen such a diabolical attack since 9/11.

I sip my coffee.

The world expects the President of the United States to kill the Iran Nuclear Agreement. A deal negotiated by his predecessor to delay Iran's bomb program.

Delay. Not eliminate.

The talking heads speculate that the two events might be related. They might be, but the Iranians have never struck in the continental United States.

My entire career, I've fought jihadists. They are the most professional, committed enemies a soldier can face. Their religion and ideology are completely consistent with their warfighting. I've seen and done things no one should have to see or do. Understand this—if I didn't, *your* son or husband would have to.

I wake up most nights, sweating. Find myself standing barechested on my apartment's balcony, clutching a pistol. Not knowing how I got there.

Sometimes I feel like I'm losing my mind.

FIVE YEARS AGO, Keller and I conducted our last operation together.

The disaster was born in an air-conditioned Quonset hut in

KAF—Kandahar Air Field. A briefing room insulated from the stinking heat of Afghanistan. Insulated from the heat, but not the mix of dust and dung that choked the air and settled over everything.

Orin Scott, the CIA section chief, was fresh from Langley. He had arranged to meet Abu Massoud, a local Taliban leader. The Harvard boy wanted to make a name for himself with overtures of peace. The RV—rendezvous—was to occur a hundred miles north of Kandahar. A valley surrounded by low foothills. My Delta section and a platoon of Rangers were to provide security.

A Ranger captain and lieutenant had built a sand-table replica of the RV. The valley was as flat as a parking lot. The hills were arranged around it like a horseshoe open to the south. A click—one thousand meters—to the north, lay a whaleback ridge. A quarter click to the east, a low mesa scowled upon the crossroads. To the west, a saddle joined two peaks. There were gaps in the range of hills. Long roads stretched through the openings and into the distance.

Keller stood next to me. "You're not going in there," he whispered.

I gave Keller a faint shake of my head. Turned to Scott. "Sir, we should reconsider this RV."

Hands on hips, the Ranger captain stared at me. "What's wrong with it, Warrant?"

The sonofabitch knew damn well what was wrong with it. But then, he wasn't going. He wanted to make Orin Scott happy. I forced myself to hold a professional tone. "I can't protect Mr Scott in there. We should arrange an RV with more cover."

The section chief gave me a warm smile. "Thirty Rangers and Deltas can't protect me?"

Scott meant well, but he hadn't been in-country a year. White dress shirt, fraternity tie, glasses. He didn't know his ass from his elbow.

"Not in there, sir. It's a shooting gallery."

The Harvard man tried to sound confident. "There's no time to rearrange the RV, Breed. You'll have to make do."

The Ranger captain thrust out his jaw. "Mr Scott, the security force is adequate."

"I agree, Captain." Scott folded his arms. "Massoud is coming to talk, not fight."

I stepped away from the sand table. Keller, Lenson, and Hancock gathered around me.

"Hancock and I will go with the VIP," I told them. I half-turned and pointed to the sand table. "Keller, I want you and Lenson on that saddle by dawn. Set up a firing position on the north hill."

Keller didn't like it, but he was a good soldier. "Roger that." He looked at Lenson. "If we hit the road now, we'll get there by midnight."

I watched Lenson shoulder his M24 sniper rifle. The two men took their rucksacks and walked out of the air-conditioned Quonset hut. They would drive to within fifteen miles of the RV and hide their vehicle. Cover the remainder of the distance on foot.

Getting the two snipers situated for overwatch was dangerous. If I was right, there was a good chance the Taliban would occupy the hills. If Keller and Lenson ran into trouble, Scott would have to abort the meeting. If they didn't, Hancock and I would have two elite marksmen watching our backs.

AT MIDNIGHT, my radio crackled. It was Keller. "Seven-five Savoy, this is eight-eight. We are on the saddle, north peak."

"Seven-five copy. See you in the morning."

"Eight-eight out."

I closed my eyes, but didn't sleep.

Our convoy headed out of KAF at 0330 hours. A moonless

night. We filled five Humvees. The drivers wore helmets fitted with Night Optical Devices—NODS. I didn't like riding in Humvees. There was no protection from IEDs. Driving at night was safer. The bombs couldn't be armed all the time, or the batteries would run out. They were usually armed at first light.

With the restricted vision afforded by the NODs, we swapped the risk of a car crash for the risk of getting blown up.

A blood red sun rose over the mountains of the Hindu Kush and cast an angry glow over the barren terrain. We raced on flat ground toward the distant foothills. On either side of the road, endless grape fields stretched into the distance. Desiccated, many hid Afghanistan's main crop, poppies. The Taliban were awash in cash, all from the heroin they trafficked west.

I sat in the front passenger seat of our Humvee, in the middle of the convoy. Hancock and Scott rode in back with three Rangers and an Afghan interpreter. One of the Rangers stood at the fifty caliber mount. "Fifteen minutes," the driver told us.

My TAC radio crackled. "Seven-five Savoy, this is eight-eight."

"Go ahead, eight-eight."

"Three SUVs approaching RV from the northwest."

"Copy, eight-eight. Any activity on the hills?"

"Negative." Keller hesitated. "But that doesn't mean anything."

"Say enemy strength, eight-eight."

"Eleven. Three in lead vehicle, four in each following."

"Do you make Abu Massoud?"

"Negative. Cannot confirm."

"Keep us informed, eight-eight."

Keller would be tracking the Taliban with his spotter's scope. Lenson would have his M42 lined up, ready to fire. The figures in the valley were no more than three hundred meters from our snipers' position. Easy pickings if anything went wrong. It was the mesa and the whaleback that worried me. With the sun rising in the east, Keller and Lenson would have a good view. Enemy soldiers standing on the mesa would be silhouetted against the sun. But—the glare would conceal snipers hidden on the forward slope.

I had anticipated that situation. With the sun behind it, the mesa would look like a black mass to Keller and Lenson. Were a sniper to fire from the feature's forward slope, his muzzle flash would give him away.

That meant a sniper on the mesa would get one free shot.

The convoy slowed as we approached the RV. On the left stood the saddle with its two hilltops. From the southern approach, the whaleback and the mesa looked like a single ridge. An illusion. There was at least a quarter mile of space between them. A row of three white SUVs sat in the middle of the valley.

The Ranger lieutenant was riding in the lead Humvee. His voice crackled over the TAC radio. "Seven-five Savoy, this is five-one Charlie."

"Go ahead, five-one."

"We will fan into line and park with your vehicle in center. Your call to approach."

"Copy that, five-one."

The hairs stood on the back of my neck. I liked the situation less and less. Keyed my mike. "Eight-eight. Do you have eyes on Abu Massoud?"

"Negative, seven-five. Two Hajjis dismounting center SUV. Black turbans, black face covers. Man-jams. They all fuckin' look alike."

"Weapons?"

"Negative visual."

Our convoy drove up the road. The saddle was on our left, the mesa on the right. The lieutenant's Humvee peeled away and parked on the left flank, closest to the saddle. The rest of us parked in a straight line running from east to west, with my vehicle in the middle.

The lead SUV flashed its headlights.

Scott's voice was high with excitement. "It's him."

"Negative, Mr Scott. We're not sure."

"Breed, we have to make a move."

"Why? You don't want to go in there."

The section chief put his hand on our driver's shoulder. "Flash your lights."

Hancock tensed. The SUV flashed its lights in response to ours.

"This is my operation, Breed." Scott's voice was firm. "We'll pull up thirty yards from the SUVs and get out."

My orders were to support the CIA. I didn't like it, but there it was.

"Eight-eight, this is seven-five. We're going in."

"Copy that, seven-five."

Our driver inched forward.

"Lock and load." I pulled the charging handle on my M4 and released it. The bolt slammed home and chambered a round. Hancock and the Rangers did the same. The man on the big fifty cocked it and swung its long barrel to bear on the SUVs.

"Stop here," Scott commanded.

Thirty yards from the SUVs. A hundred ahead of the Ranger platoon. I felt buck naked.

Scott jumped out of the Humvee. Hancock and the interpreter followed him. I eased one boot to the ground and dismounted. Carried my M4 low-ready. "Eight-eight, this is seven-five."

"Go ahead, seven-five."

"Watch the hills."

With their optics focused on the men in the valley, Keller

and Lenson might miss snipers. By my measure, snipers were now the greater danger.

Scott and the interpreter walked side by side toward the SUVs. Hancock and I followed behind them. Hancock walked on my left.

The two turbaned figures strode toward us.

I held up one hand. "Stop!" To the interpreter: "Tell 'em to stop."

The interpreter jabbered in Pashto. The two Afghans halted.

"Abu Massoud," I called. "Which one of you is Abu Massoud."

Neither of those fuckers was Abu Massoud.

Thwack.

Orin Scott's head burst like a melon. Bits of wet bone and tissue splattered my face. Hancock cried out, clutched his right leg, and fell to the ground. An instant later, I heard the crack of a rifle.

The typical sniper round travels two or three times the speed of sound. One hears the impact of the bullet before one hears the gunshot. The time difference between the sounds indicates range to the weapon that fired. The Afghans liked Dragunovs. For that weapon, a half-second differential meant a range under three hundred meters.

I threw myself on Hancock. Hit by the round that killed Scott, he was holding his hand against his thigh.

Thwack.

The interpreter dropped like a rag doll.

Another shot. Less than half a second after impact.

A thousand meters or more, the whaleback ridge was too far away. The Afghan sniper was close.

"Eight-eight," I yelled, "he's on the mesa."

Crack.

The distinctive bark of Lenson's M42.

"Hit." Keller's voice.

Lenson had neutralized the sniper. Gunfire erupted everywhere. The Rangers and the men in the SUVs were firing. The two figures that approached drew AK47s from under their robes. The driver of their SUV threw the vehicle into gear and accelerated toward us.

I rose to one knee and raised my rifle. Fired a short, three-round burst. The first Hajji went down. I fired again, watched the second man drop.

The ranger on the fifty caliber hosed the SUV. Heavy slugs riddled the vehicle's hood and windshield. Killed the driver, cracked the engine block. I covered Hancock with my body.

The SUV exploded and the concussion blew me over. For an instant, my vision blurred. A hot torrent of earth, metal, blood and human remains roared over my head and pelted our Humvee. Engines roared. The other two SUVs charged the platoon's line.

I crawled back to Hancock, tore a field dressing open with my teeth. His BDUs were soaked in blood, but he was conscious. The look in his eyes. Determination.

Hancock was holding his hands so tightly over the wound I had to pry them off. Blood swelled from the black hole, but there was no arterial spray. I stuffed the battle dressing into the hole and placed his hands over the package. "Direct pressure," I yelled into his ear. "Don't let go."

There was another blast as the second SUV rammed one of the Humvees in line behind us. It was a suicide attack with truck bombs. The third SUV roared past, Taliban firing from open windows. I shouldered my rifle and returned fire. The vehicle slewed sideways. Carried by the momentum of its rush, it rolled on its side and tumbled toward the lieutenant's Humvee. The Ranger on the fifty caliber threw his hands up to protect his face. The SUV crashed into the Rangers and exploded.

The shooting faded and stopped.

"Seven-five Savoy, this is eight-eight."

I keyed my mike. "Eight-eight, this is seven-five."

"Seven-five, sitrep."

"Casualties heavy. Call immediate medevac."

Keller knew Hancock had been hit. "Copy, seven-five. QRF and medevac en route."

Piercing screams. The stink of burned hair and flesh filled the air. Mixed with the stench of burning fuel and rubber. Flames and greasy smoke poured from the wreckage and plumed skyward. Rangers from the three remaining Humvees struggled to recover their dead and wounded.

I turned to Hancock. His boyish features were twisted into a grimace. I tore the aid pack from his vest. Opened it and scrabbled for morphine. Found a syrette and made to stab him.

"Breed, no." Hancock gasped through gritted teeth. "I need to stay awake."

I hesitated. Stuffed the syrette back in his vest. Rotors thundered as the QRF and medevac helicopters approached and flared for landing. Clouds of dust swept over us. I cradled Hancock in my arms and waited for help.

THAT WAS FIVE YEARS AGO. Far from the civilization of a Starbucks coffee shop. To say Keller and Lenson saved my life that day would be true, but melodramatic. We saved each other's lives over and over during endless deployments. We became brothers. Somehow, we all made it home. For Keller to be murdered on his own land was the ultimate obscenity.

"Breed."

Mark Lenson strides toward me. Fit, broad-shouldered. A black patch covers his right eye. The IED that exploded in his face nearly blinded him. His broad features are marked with tiny scars. With his western shirt, Levi's and cowboy boots, the patch makes him look like a hard-case wrangler.

I get to my feet and we shake hands. Lenson picks up my garment bag, and I sling my duffel over my shoulder. "Car's this way," he says.

We walk together to the parking lot. A hundred degrees outside and the heat hits me like a sledgehammer.

Far West Texas.

An old line comes to mind.

"There's no God west of the Pecos."

I shiver in the heat.

3

SALEM, 1430 HRS FRIDAY

"Mary doesn't know how Keller died," Lenson tells me.

From the airport, Lenson drives to Washington Park, then dog-legs onto Alameda. The traffic moves freely, and Lenson does not hurry. He wants to use the drive to catch up before I meet Keller's family. Living in El Paso, he and Hancock have much more contact with the Kellers than I do.

"How can she not know?"

Air-conditioning at full blast, we drive south on Alameda Avenue, Texas 20. It runs parallel to I-10, the major east-west interstate. Because of El Paso's unusual position, both highways run southeast to northwest.

"We didn't tell her he'd been... disarticulated." Lenson looks miserable. "The sheriff wanted to keep the details out of the press. It's enough for her to know he was shot."

"What about the funeral?"

"Open casket. Dress blues. He looks good. The mortician told me it wasn't difficult."

The word *mortician* makes me cringe. We all think the same. *It won't happen to me.*

"Who do they think did it?" I ask.

"Sheriff thinks illegals, crossing his land."

Illegals don't want trouble. For the most part, they are people attracted to higher wages on the American side of the border. "What about their guides. Coyotes."

"I don't think so," Lenson says. "Keller must have stumbled onto a drug deal."

I stare at the Franklin mountains on Lenson's side of the vehicle. The range bisects the city. The heights are close enough for students to climb and watch the Sun Bowl.

Soon, we will be in Salem County.

"How's Mary taking it?"

"Hard, but she's a soldier's wife."

From the air, El Paso looks like a human colony on a distant planet. The city is a vast collection of dwellings planted in the middle of the desert. While dominated by mountains and foothills, the terrain on which we drive is flat.

This part of greater El Paso is a built-up area. Walmarts, gas stations, low office buildings, strip malls. The land between the Franklins and the Rio Grande has been desecrated by developers. To me, the city feels claustrophobic. I can't wait to reach open spaces further south and east.

I block the clutter from my mind. Think of the day Keller told me he planned to leave the army.

THREE DAYS after the debacle that cost Orrin Scott his life, we shipped Hancock home. The medics stabilized him at the field hospital in KAF. Flew him to Germany for orthopedic surgery. First, the doctors told us the good news—they could save his leg. Then they told us the bad news—Hancock would walk with a limp the rest of his life. They kept him in service long enough to get a medical discharge. The discharge entitled him to a pension and medical benefits.

Keller and I sat in the barracks, packing Hancock's personal effects. I had to backfill his slot. The squadron was in the thick of the fighting. Hancock's replacement would arrive in twenty-four hours, and we had to free up his bunk.

"Breed, this is my last deployment."

I couldn't believe my ears. "Say that again."

"I won't re-up." Keller looked me in the eye. "I'm going home to Mary."

"Dude, what are you—five years short of twenty? Think about it."

"I have. Dad left me the ranch, and Mary can't handle it on her own. Not with Donnie three years old." Keller paused. "I want to watch Donnie grow up. I want him to know his Dad."

"Is Mary pushing you?"

"No, Mary supports me. One hundred percent. This is about me owning up to my responsibilities."

Keller took out his wallet. Showed me a wrinkled photograph of Mary and three-year-old Donnie. I'd seen it before. Wondered if I would ever have a family of my own.

"We're good," Keller said grimly, "but it's always better to be lucky than good. That goat-screw cost Hancock his leg. Bad luck. The round that killed Scott had no business drilling Hancock, but it did."

"Are you blaming me for that?"

"Of course not. That's the point. We can cover all the bases, do everything right. Dumb luck can kill you. I'm going home before mine runs out."

KELLER WENT HOME. On leave, we visited him. Ranching was hard work, but Deltas always took the hard jobs. His Dad left him three thousand acres. Too small to be economical. He borrowed money, bought more. Hired two ranch hands to help him manage the livestock. They nurtured the grass, beat back the shrubs.

He'd grown up on the ranch. Told me how difficult it was for his Dad to make a go of the business. The only income they had was from the livestock they sold each season. When he took over, Keller supplemented the income by selling grazing rights. It was a hand-to-mouth existence.

The mountains recede as we drive further south and east. We pass Fabens, then Tornillo. A secondary border crossing to relieve congestion at the Bridge of the Americas.

"He had two men working for him," I say. "Did they see anything?"

"No. This time of year, they live away from the ranch."

The impossibility of the situation hollows my stomach. "What will Mary do? She can't manage the ranch on her own."

"I don't think she's thought that far. She'll probably have to sell."

"And do what? Her parents are gone. So are Keller's."

Lenson says nothing.

I feel restless with frustration. Mary is still in shock. In time she will face insurmountable difficulty.

Mary wanted to be a nurse. When she and Keller got married, she continued with her studies. When Donnie was born, she dropped out and never went back. Mary has no qualifications. Soon, this problem will have to be faced.

Keller was our brother.

Mary and Donnie have become our responsibility.

4

SALEM, 1500 HRS FRIDAY

I wonder what it's like to lose one's depth perception. Half of one's peripheral vision. We are visual animals. Our jobs place a premium on visual acuity.

"How's your eye," I ask.

Lenson shrugs. "Time heals. I'm ready to deploy, but they won't take me back."

The further south one drives from El Paso, the more arid and barren the landscape. The Franklins are behind us. Now all we see is flat land and miles of foothills.

"You've been out two years."

"Yeah. I did one deployment after my first rehab. My eye started to deteriorate again, so they sent me home."

"To William Beaumont?"

William Beaumont Medical Center is the military hospital in El Paso. After being shot, Hancock had been sent there.

"Yes. To stop the deterioration, I had more surgery. The doctors said there was a danger the procedure would blind me. But if I didn't risk it, I'd go blind anyway. It would just take longer. So I told them to go ahead. The surgery worked, my eye is fine. I applied for a second waiver, but the army said no."

"I always wondered. If I were with you in Helmand, I might have kept you from being blown up."

After Hancock was hit and Keller left, Lenson and I were assigned to different squadrons. We knew teams weren't forever, but it wasn't the same.

"Don't let it eat you," Lenson says. "You might have been blown up too."

"Two pairs of eyes are better than one."

After years of working together, each of us knew how the others moved. Our four-man team became a single animal. Each man covered gaps that rendered the others vulnerable. No matter how proficient, it took time for replacements to learn the idiosyncrasies of a team.

"The guy who tripped the mine was twelve feet in front of me," Lenson muses. "I don't know what triggered it. I play it over again and again in my mind. One minute he was there, the next he was gone. I saw his arms and legs fly off—then everything else disappeared. I felt like I'd been hit by a truck. Flat on my back, couldn't see. The first thing I did was check my legs and balls were still there."

"Shrapnel didn't hit your legs."

"No, the mine was buried and exploded upward. The angles worked so everything hit me from the chest up. My armor and rifle took most of the shrapnel. There were pieces in my arms, hands and face. Screws and wires, all the crap they packed into the IED. Rocks and dirt, the stuff they covered it with."

"The eye patch looks good on you."

"Yeah. Ladies love it."

Lenson slows and pulls off the concrete highway onto an asphalt road. A white sign announces we are entering Salem, Texas. Unassuming, the road is easy to miss. A lonely diner sits at the crossroads. The Dusty Burger's billboard is bigger than the city's.

The county seat, Salem remains a small town. Population of

three thousand, three-quarters Latino. Most live in low-rent housing between main street and the Rio Grande. The houses are separated from the river by the great border wall. On the north and east sides of town sit more upscale residences owned by small businessmen.

"Everyone is at the hotel," Lenson explains. "Mary didn't want to stay at the ranch house while arranging the funeral."

We drive past the sheriff's station. It's clean and modern. A single-story building with parking lots front and back.

Lenson notices my interest. "We can walk over tomorrow," he says. "Sheriff said the lab will finish with Keller's truck by then."

"I want to ask the cops some questions."

Most murders are solved within twenty-four hours. The more time passes, the less likely the killer will be caught. It has been seventy-two hours since Keller's body was discovered. By any measure, the trail has gone cold.

"We all do. The sheriff hasn't had much to say. To be fair, he's been busy. Choppers have been flying overhead for three days. No deputies in town. They have all been manning road-blocks and processing the crime scene."

Salem's main street is typical. A long strip of businesses. A Chinese restaurant, laundromat, and hardware stores. A drugstore. There, on the right, set off from the street by a wide driveway and parking lot, is the hotel.

It's not the tacky two-story motel ubiquitous in the United States. This is a converted mansion. It must have been built by a wealthy man in the nineteenth century. A rancher, or an entrepreneur. Sold off as the town and county evolved, converted from a personal residence to a business.

I read the sign over the driveway. "The Salem Inn," I say. "That's original. Sounds like we're in New England."

Lenson pulls into a parking space. Across the street from

the hotel squat a 7-Eleven and gas station. They are strategically located to serve travelers staying at the hotel.

We dismount the SUV and step into the oppressive heat. I take my garment bag and duffel from the back. Follow Lenson into the hotel.

The interior is frigid from air-conditioning. The walls and furniture are dark mahogany. The nineteenth-century tycoon who built the house had good taste. The structure and all its furniture could have been transported from Boston. The house and everything in it seems out of place in dry, dusty West Texas.

The foyer has been renovated to accommodate a front desk. Two large parlors on either side have been converted into a lounge and a restaurant. A pretty blond girl checks me in and hands me a modern key card with the number 205 stenciled on it.

"You want to take your bags up," Lenson says. "I'll order us some drinks and find Hancock."

"Roger that. See you in five."

I take a small, modern elevator to the second floor. Find Room 205. The key card works perfectly. The room is clean, the bathroom modern. There's a king-sized bed and a widescreen mounted on the wall. I hang my garment bag in the closet and set my duffel in a corner. Turn the light on in the toilet. I wash my face, lock the door behind me, and go downstairs.

Hancock and Lenson are waiting for me in the lounge. The girl from the front desk approaches with a cocktail tray and three frosted mugs of lager. She sets them before us on a circular table. A nice hotel, a family-run business. Light on staff.

"Breed, it's good to see you."

Hancock's aged twenty years in five. His boyish features are drawn, and he looks tired. Five years my junior, the hair at his temples has gone gray. He looks fit, but his right leg looks stiff as he reaches to shake my hand.

"Let's take a load off," I say. "How's the leg?"

We sit at the table. Hancock lowers himself into a chair, careful to keep his right leg extended. He grimaces. "Femur's healed," he says. "All the way from hip to foot, the hydrostatic shock fucked the nerve. Pain won't go away."

"They give you meds for the pain?"

Hancock takes a vial of pills from his pocket. It's translucent amber, with a white plastic cap. He holds the tube between his thumb and forefinger, rattles the contents. The bitterness and dissipation in his smile make me uncomfortable. "Oxycodone helps. And I get therapy at William Beaumont."

Lenson and I exchange glances.

"See this?" Hancock extends his right foot, pointing the toe of his dress shoe at the next table. "I can extend the joint. But—I can't flex it."

Hancock pulls his toes in the direction of his knee. Grits his teeth with pain. Relaxes.

"Does the physiotherapy help," I ask.

"Some. It maintains muscle tone." Hancock shakes a white pill onto the tabletop. Washes it down with a gulp of beer. "Bullet in your thigh fucks up your foot. Go figure."

"Can you sleep," Lenson asks.

"VA gives me trazodone," Hancock says. "Fucking horse tranquilizer. Yeah, I sleep."

Trazodone treats insomnia—associated with severe depression. How do I know? The medics offered it to me. I tore up the prescription two minutes after walking out of the hospital. When I came home, I decided I was off pills. It sounds like Hancock is a walking pharmacy.

"I do weed gummies," Lenson laughs. "You should try it, dude. Sleep like a baby."

"Might give it a try." Hancock looks skeptical. "The pain's worst at night."

I should have refused to go into that valley. Escalated the

issue through the Delta chain of command. Uncomfortable, I want to change the subject.

"Where are Mary and Donnie?"

"In their room." Hancock slips the vial into his pocket. "Mary's exhausted, we've been making arrangements all day. I don't think it's physical, she's under a lot of strain. Can't blame her."

Lenson looks up at the widescreen. The news is playing the same coverage of the New York City subway bombing. It's on a reel. "We killed them over there so we wouldn't have to kill them here."

"They're tough," Hancock says grimly. "And committed. They're not going to stay over there. It's like Whack-a-Mole."

"This war," Lenson pronounces, "is ideological. It'll last a hundred years."

I stare at him. "Unless we kill them all."

5

SALEM, 2100 HRS FRIDAY

Mary Keller's voice is gentle, but betrays her exhaustion. "It's your bedtime, Donnie."

"Mom, I'm not sleepy. Can't I stay up a bit longer with Uncle?"

"You go on to sleep, Donnie," I tell the boy. "I'll be here all week. We have lots of time."

"I miss Dad."

We're sitting in the hotel bar, sipping drinks after a long day. Donnie has finished his Shirley Temple, a 7-Up with cherry juice. Drowsy, he fights to stay awake.

"Come on, Donnie." I get up and pat his back. "I'll take you to bed. Tomorrow will be a busy day."

I look to Mary. "He got a room key?"

Mary fishes in her bag and holds a key card out to me. "Use mine."

The number 312 has been stenciled on the plastic. I leave Mary with Lenson and Hancock. Usher Donnie to the elevator.

The lounge is one of two converted parlors on either side of the front desk. The other is the restaurant. Above the bar hangs a widescreen. It is tuned to the news, but the sound has been turned off. Instead, captions for the hearing impaired scroll across the bottom of the screen.

We all attended Keller's wedding. The squadron wore full dress uniforms. The arch of swords is normally performed at officer weddings. Lenson took charge of borrowing a set of swords from the drill detachment at Fort Bragg.

After the ceremony, Dan and Mary emerged from the JFK Memorial Chapel. Two rows of Deltas raised their swords in an arch over the couple's heads. The couple walked under the arch. Mary's long blond hair shone in the sun, and her cheeks glowed. She was just twenty-two, beaming with the rosy blush of youth. At the end of the walk, Lenson and I lowered our swords to block their path. Mary looked surprised and Keller grinned.

"Give that man a kiss," Hancock yelled.

Mary melted into Keller's arms, and they kissed like there would be no tomorrow.

Lenson and I lifted our swords. "Welcome to Delta, ma'am," I said.

I push the button for the elevator, and the doors hiss open. Donnie and I get in and I push number three. The doors suck shut on the image of Mary, Lenson, and Hancock sitting around a table in the lounge.

"Uncle Breed." Donnie stares at me. The boy has his father's features. In ten years, he will look exactly like Keller. Will he follow in his father's footsteps. For this boy, everything is possible.

"Yes, Donnie."

"Mom told me Dad died in an accident."

Trapped in a steel box with a merciless eight-year-old.

Donnie's voice is matter-of-fact. "That's not true, is it?"

Should I tell the truth or back up Mary's lie. "No, Donnie. It isn't."

Donnie blinks back tears. "Don't tell Mom I know."

"Okay." I let out a breath.

We get off on three and follow the signs to 312. I slide the card into the key slot and turn the handle. The door opens.

Donnie says, "Are they going to find who did it?"

"I don't know. They're trying."

"Thanks, Uncle Breed." Donnie steps into the room and turns to face me. "I'll be okay now."

"Goodnight, Donnie."

"Good night."

The door closes and the lock clicks.

I walk to the elevator. Think of Keller and Mary cutting their wedding cake with a ceremonial sword. Serving each other the first slice.

I feel like shit. By the time I get back to the lounge, I want to punch somebody.

"Donnie's exhausted," Mary says.

"He'll be fine." I hand Mary her key card. Collapse into my chair and stare at my beer. Right now a bottle of Bourbon would better suit my mood.

Lenson and Hancock exchange glances. After years watching each other's back, we've become sensitive to each other. For years, we spent more time together than with our own families.

The sooner I finish my beer, the sooner I can order something else. I drain the glass in one long gulp.

I stick my head up, catch the bartender's eye, and wave him over.

"Double Bourbon," I tell him. "Maker's Mark if you have it."

The bartender smiles. "I'm sure we do."

I watch him walk to the bar. On the other side of the lounge, an attractive woman is staring at me. Slim, dark-haired, serious eyes. Polite, not embarrassed, she looks away.

"You know," Mary says, "I always feared Dan would be killed over there."

"Don't you hate the army," Hancock asks.

"No." Mary shakes her head. "Of course I wanted Dan to come home. But if he wanted to stay in the army, I would have supported him one hundred percent. I told him that. He wanted to come back."

"I know," I tell her.

"I was prepared for him to be shot while he was in the army." Mary looks helpless. "It's part of a soldier's job. Getting shot is not part of a rancher's job. Not this century."

The bartender brings my Bourbon, and I drink half. Fight the urge to buy the whole bottle.

Lenson and Hancock look thirsty.

"Did Dan have enemies," I ask.

Mary shakes her head. "Dan worked hard and was fair to everyone. The only enemies he had were *over there*."

Keller respected the Taliban and Al Qaeda. About the enemy, we had spoken many times. Delta were the best warriors the United States could field. Sent to kill fighters as committed to their ideology as we were to ours. Combat was simple. We met the best the opposition could send and put them down. Sometimes, they put one of us down. That was the merciless calculus of war.

"Did Dan mention seeing strangers on the ranch?" Hancock asks.

"I've been through this with the sheriff," Mary says. "Dan never mentioned strangers. Certainly not illegals. He would have told me if he had. Larry and Bo say the same thing."

The names are unfamiliar to me. "Your ranch hands?"

"Yes. The sheriff spoke with them. They're staying on. I need them more than ever."

Mary's voice trails off. Distracted, she stares at the wall. I straighten in my chair, prepared for her to break down.

Instead, Mary folds her hands in her lap. "It's *my* bedtime," she says. Looks at Hancock. "We have things to do in the morning, don't we?"

"Yes," Hancock says. "Some loose ends, but things are under control. It won't take long."

Mary stands up. "Be that as it may, I should get some sleep."

The three of us stand politely.

"Good night," Mary says.

We watch Mary walk to the elevator. Her body is lean and straight, her walk sure-footed. A soldier's wife.

I turn to Lenson and Hancock. Exhale through puffed cheeks. "Fuck this," I say. Signal the bartender to bring us the bottle of Bourbon.

The thin brunette is nowhere to be seen.

6

SALEM, 0900 HRS SATURDAY

Sheriff Garrick is a classic West Texas lawman. Fifty-five years old, lean and leathery. He wears a Stetson, cowboy boots, and dark tan pants. His sheriff's star is pinned over his left shirt pocket. His mustache is neatly trimmed. A tan man in a tan country.

Men like Garrick haven't changed in a hundred and fifty years. The only modern thing about him is the nine millimeter Glock he wears on his right hip. Garrick wears the holster high. Policing a town like Salem, I doubt he's ever drawn the weapon.

"County lab's done with the truck," he drawls. Holds the keys out to Lenson.

Lenson accepts the keys. "Did they find anything?"

Garrick shakes his head. "No. Come on, I'll walk you over."

The Salem police station is small. Enough for Garrick, two deputies, and an administrative assistant who doubles as dispatcher. The sheriff's office is at the rear. There is a public service counter for the dispatcher to sit behind, and a desk for each deputy. The dispatcher is a young woman in her thirties. One of the deputies, a clean-cut man in his twenties, sits at a desk, filling out paperwork.

"Where did they find Keller," I ask.

"Keller owns a small spread." Garrick leads us out the back way, and we step into the sunlight. "About ten thousand acres. Started out with three thousand, bought more. We found him right in the middle."

Ten thousand acres is over fifteen square miles.

"In the middle."

"Middle of nowhere."

There are three vehicles in the parking lot. A Ford Police Interceptor with a light bar stands next to an open-topped Jeep CJ-5. The Jeep has a Winchester 94 lever-action rifle clamped vertically in the front cab. The CJ-5 is an old model, long out of production, but the vehicle is well maintained. I'm guessing it's Garrick's Jeep. He's probably owned it most of his life.

My attention is drawn to the Ford F-150 two-door pickup parked across from the other two. It's been washed down. Drops of water glisten on its surface. They are evaporating in the heat. A good thing. The sun, shining through the water droplets, might damage the truck's glossy red paint.

Garrick and Lenson go to the cab, and Lenson opens the driver's door. I circle the truck and study the vehicle. A four-wheel drive, it's built for farm and ranch work. An eight-foot bed. Thirty-five-inch tires, eighteen-inch wheels, and six inches of lift. A glossy black grille protector and five-liter V8 engine. A practical, no-nonsense truck for a practical, no-nonsense man.

"Was he killed in the truck," I ask, "or outside."

"Outside." Garrick turns to me, hands on hips. "No blood in the truck. None in the bed. None on the outside. Lab went over it with a fine-tooth comb."

Mounted on a rack in the cab, a high-powered rifle and shotgun hang within easy reach. I know them well. "Either of those fired?"

"Neither one." Garrick shakes his head. "Your friend was

shot once in the chest with a pistol. Difficult to determine the caliber."

I open the passenger door. No frills in the cab. The showroom model would have had bucket seats. Those have been replaced by a long, nylon-upholstered bench that seats three. The kind of modification a practical farmer or rancher would make. Nylon surfaces are easy to wipe down if muddy. Or bloody.

"Lab go over the interior with luminol?"

"The works." Garrick's laconic drawl betrays a hint of offense. "There was no blood in the truck."

The pickup has a standard instrument panel, air-conditioning, and a wide glove compartment. I turn my attention to the gun rack.

The rifle is a World War I eight millimeter Mauser. Bolt-action. Keller bought it for two hundred dollars. I was with him when he sporterized it. Welded on a larger bolt handle, re-barreled the weapon, customized the stock. The Ernst Apel mount allows the scope to be swung out of the way of stripper clips. He shot half-minute of angle groups with this rifle at eight hundred yards. The scope is a 3.5-10x variable power optic. Keller kept the weapon in pristine condition.

I take the rifle from the rack and jack open the bolt. The rifle's empty. Keller kept his weapons clean, except for an optimal layer of copper fouling he left in the barrel. He knew a freshly cleaned barrel never fired true. Rifles are always most accurate with a certain amount of fouling. The regular army has strict cleaning routines. Delta allows its operators latitude to optimize cleaning for best results.

I meet Lenson's eyes across the cab. Replace the rifle, take down the shotgun.

Keller liked vintage weapons. This is a Winchester Model 1897. External hammer. They don't make 'em like this anymore.

Short combat barrel, heat shield, bayonet lug. I jack a round out of the action and examine the load. Two-and-three-quarter-inch twelve-gauge, double-ought buck, twelve pellets.

The United States Army took Winchester shotguns to Europe in World War I. Used them to clear trenches. The weapons were so devastating the Germans lodged a formal complaint. Claimed the American use of shotguns at close quarters violated the Hague Convention. Threatened to summarily execute American soldiers captured with the weapons.

The American response was simple. "You introduced poison gas and flamethrowers. If you execute a single American soldier, we will conduct reprisals."

Six months later, the Germans surrendered.

I pop open the glove compartment. Registration papers. A box of eight millimeter Mauser cartridges and four five-round stripper clips. Boxes of twelve-gauge shotgun shells. Keller kept the Winchester loaded, not the Mauser.

There is a small travel pouch stuffed in one corner of the glove compartment. Inside the pouch is a Kestrel anemometer and barometer. An infrared thermometer, a pocket calculator, a laser rangefinder, and a GPS. A small loose-leaf notebook with data tables for the Mauser. A pair of compact, sixteen-power Zeiss binoculars. A professional sharpshooter's ready kit.

"Can you show us where he was found," Lenson asks.

"If you like," Garrick says. "Not much to see."

"We'd sure appreciate it."

Garrick nods. "All right. Ride with me."

We pile into Garrick's Jeep. Lenson rides in front beside the sheriff. I sit stretched out in the rear bed, clinging to the roll bar. The engine catches with a throaty roar, and Garrick pulls out of the lot.

"Where does the investigation stand," I ask.

Garrick drives down main street, passes the hotel, and heads toward the highway. We pass the Dusty Burger, turn right, and head south.

"It's possible," Garrick says, "your friend happened on illegals crossing his land. Their transportation was waiting on the highway. When he spotted them, coyotes killed him."

Lenson looks skeptical. "How much progress have you made."

"Not much," Garrick admits. "Border Patrol checked the wall for six miles. No breaches, no sign of penetration. They covered the whole county with helicopters for three days. I called in extra deputies. Personally put up roadblocks on the main highway, both directions. Roadblocks on secondary roads, both directions. Nothing. I've called them off. Your friend was killed between twelve and sixteen hours before he was found. That amount of time, the killers could have been halfway to California or Florida."

"Coyotes like to cross here?" Lenson asks.

Garrick shakes his head. "Funny enough, no. Border Patrol keeps the stats. Salem County has the least activity of any section of the border for a hundred miles."

"Did sensors pick anything up?"

The Border Patrol have motion sensors buried the length of the wall. The sensors detect motion more than two feet above the ground.

"Nary a peep."

"Do *you* think coyotes murdered Keller?"

"No."

I drink in the mountains, north and east. If the killers were spirited away by truck, there's little chance of catching them. But I can't imagine Keller getting out of his pickup, unarmed, and accosting a group of illegal migrants.

"Let me tell you boys something." Garrick pulls off the

highway and drives across open range. "Coyotes might have shot him, but they wouldn't have cut him like that. Cartels would, but not this side of the border."

7

LAZY K, 1000 HRS SATURDAY

The murder scene is a corral. A patch of range thirty yards square, fenced with wooden posts strung with yellow police tape. Garrick stops the Jeep and we get out. The earth is dusty soil and parched grass. Clumps of mesquite and creosote. There are low foothills to the north and east, taller volcanic mountains beyond.

I turn to the sheriff. "Who found the body."

"Helicopter," Garrick says. "After Mrs Keller reported him missing."

The investigators have finished with the crime scene. I step over the police tape. "What time was he killed?"

"Tuesday. Between 8 pm and midnight." Garrick walks toward the center of the corral. "We found him noon Wednesday. Truck was right there. Body about ten feet away, lying face down."

Four hundred yards in the distance, a small herd of cattle graze. The breeze kicks up dust, rustles the brown range grass.

"Aren't you afraid those animals will disturb the scene?"

Garrick rests a hand on one of the corral posts. "We're done here. It'll be all right."

Keller's truck flattened the grass. Tracks in the dirt from his heavy, off-road tires make it clear he drove from the direction of the border wall. Painted white, wooden tent pegs have been driven into the ground in the outline of a headless man. Three more pegs form a triangle six feet away.

"No use marking with paint or whitewash," Garrick explains. "That's where he fell, that's where they left his head."

There is a patch of black earth above the headless corpse. Congealed blood, soaked into the dirt. "Not much blood," I observe.

"No." Garrick squats on his haunches. Points to the group of three pegs. "The shot to the chest killed him. His heart stopped pumping. They cut his head off, planted it over there. Some blood leaked out, not much. It soaked into the ground and dried up. Wind's scattered it."

Garrick turns his attention to the thick tar atop the shoulders of the headless corpse. "Heart wasn't pumping, but there was a lot of blood in the body. Some poured out through the arteries in his neck. The rest settled inside."

I scan the earth around the outline. "You find the brass?"

"Nope. Reckon the killer took it with him."

"Killer looked for it in the dark. Pretty careful for a coyote."

"They get smarter all the time."

Lenson strokes his chin. "You said it was a pistol shot. Did it go straight through?"

"Exit wound between the shoulder blades. We went over the ground with metal detectors." Garrick traces an arc with his hand. "Couldn't find the bullet. The medical examiner can't exactly determine the caliber."

"What do you mean?"

"The size of an entrance wound depends on the elasticity of the skin. Bone is something else. All he can say for sure is the bullet was smaller than a forty-five caliber. Because the bullet hole in your friend's sternum was smaller than a forty-five. Off the record, a nine millimeter or forty caliber, but he won't swear to it."

"Shot in the chest and fell forward," Lenson observes.

"Arms at his sides," Garrick points out. "I think he was pushed onto his stomach."

"That," I say, "is so a man kneeling on Keller's back could expose his throat."

I imagine the scene. The killer standing six feet from Keller, pistol extended. A nine millimeter would punch through and fall within the arc Garrick's hand described. A quarter-mile search should have located it.

"You should have found the bullet," I tell him.

Garrick shrugs. "We swept a quarter mile, a hundred and eighty degrees. The round may have buried itself. Too small and deep for a detector to pick up."

I look at the tracks to the west left by Keller's truck. More tracks stretch east toward the highway. Parallel to those of Garrick's Jeep. A heavy vehicle, with four tires in the back. "What made those?"

"Tow truck," Garrick says. Plants his hands on his hips. "The county lab boys photographed everything. Spent the whole afternoon and most of the evening taking samples. We weren't about to drive Keller's pickup, so we had it towed to the lab. We wrapped the body in a tarp and put it on the tow truck bed. Transferred it to the ambulance at the highway."

"Two vehicles," Lenson says. "Keller's pickup came from the direction of the river. The tow truck pulled it to the highway. Nothing else?"

"No, sir. Some boot prints, some running shoe prints. We took casts."

"How many pairs?"

"Half a dozen."

"You see them coming and going?"

"Ground's dry and dusty. Wind scatters them. A lot of faint prints around the scene."

Not much to go on. I blink sweat from my eyes. Scan the brown grass, the parched, scrubby mesquite.

With a grunt, I step over the police line and walk two hundred yards towards the highway. Turn right, walk a wide circle around the corral. My eyes sweep the dusty earth ahead of me. I cross the tow truck's tracks. The tracks left by Garrick's Jeep and Keller's pickup.

Sets of tire tracks extend from the highway. The same direction as Garrick's. Steel-belted radials, narrow-gauge. Sedans. Probably police and other investigators. No footprints in an arc a hundred and eighty degrees south. The ground a hundred and eighty degrees north looks like it's been trampled by a herd of elephants. Boot prints. Deputies searching for the bullet.

My eyes are drawn to a clump of dusty mesquite. Snipers are trained to track, and detect anomalies in a landscape. As much as they are trained to *not* leave tracks and anomalies in a landscape. This mesquite has been disturbed. Branches have been hacked off with a knife, leaving a section looking more regular than the rest. Regular outlines are not natural. They draw a sniper's eye.

Perhaps the deputies wanted to scan the earth beneath the clump.

Perhaps not.

I complete my circuit of the crime scene. No vehicle tracks to the north or south. Lots of boot prints to the north. No footprints of any kind to the south. No boots, running shoes or street shoes. The wind has erased all trace of illegals swarming across Keller's land. It has not erased the prints of deputies.

The deputies arrived a day later.

I make my way back to the corral.

"It doesn't make sense," I say.

Lenson squints with his good eye. "It sure don't."

"I'm out of ideas, boys." Garrick kicks at a scorpion with the toe of his boot. "If you think of anything, I ain't too proud to ask for help."

"If Keller wanted to head off illegals," I say, "he wouldn't leave the vehicle without a gun."

"Roger that." Lenson turns to Garrick. "Don't make no sense at all, Sheriff. Keller *wouldn't* head them off. What was he supposed to do with them?"

8

SALEM, 1130 HRS SATURDAY

"Why did you pull those roadblocks?"

We are back at the sheriff's station. Hands on hips, a big man has squared off against Garrick. Six three and two hundred eighty pounds, his bulk fills the reception area. He wears a cream-colored Stetson, a pale blue linen blazer, and cowboy boots. His white shirt has been buttoned up to the collar, fastened with a bolo tie. He might shop at Big 'n' Tall, but I have a feeling he has his clothes tailor-made.

"We kept 'em up three days," Garrick fumes. "Highways and secondary roads. If the killer caught a ride, he was gone the first night."

"He could have gone to ground," the big man says. "Waited you out."

"Where. It's flatter than a parking lot out there."

"There's hills north, south and east of the Lazy K. Hundreds of draws and gullies a man could hide."

"Border Patrol helicopters covered those hills." Garrick's tanned face darkens. "As for roadblocks, I don't have the budget."

Lenson and I approach the pair cautiously. The dispatcher, who had been struggling to look busy, flashes us a warning look.

"*You* authorize the over-run." Garrick stabs the man's chest with a finger. "In writing. Then I'll set the roadblocks."

The big man blinks. For the first time, he notices us. "Who are you?"

Garrick swallows hard, remembers his manners. "These gentlemen are friends of the victim," he says. "Mr Breed, Mr Lenson, this is Mayor Posner."

Posner takes my hand and squeezes it. A firm handshake from a man who isn't trying to impress me. He's thirty pounds overweight but wears it well. He turns, shakes Lenson's hand.

"I'm sorry." The mayor is in his fifties, with broad features. "Mr Keller was a respected member of our community."

"Keller was a good man," I tell him. "One of the best."

Posner grunts, turns on Garrick. "You get those roadblocks back up."

"I'll be happy to," Garrick drawls. "Once y'all authorize that budget."

Lobster red, the mayor stalks from the sheriff's station.

"Could he be right?" I ask. "Maybe the killers have gone to ground in the hills."

Garrick shakes his head. "No," he says. "Hills are too low for trees, and the mesquite don't grow tall enough for shelter."

"The Border Patrol have called off their helicopter search." A woman joins us. She's the one from the hotel last night, the one who checked me out. Her voice is husky. "The sheriff's right. If the killers made off in a vehicle, they are long gone. If it was a drug deal gone bad, the killers will not be hiking cross-country."

The woman is an attractive brunette, slim in a black pantsuit. I could cut myself on those creases. Her open-collared white blouse reveals a pale throat. Sensible, low-heeled office shoes. An Ivy League lawyer, a senior government or corporate executive.

Garrick introduces the woman as Anya Stein, from the Department of Justice. That can mean anything. She could be FBI or the Marshal's Service. From under her suit jacket peeps a SIG P226 automatic. A solid, reliable weapon. The SIG is favored by army CID, military police units, and some special forces.

"Sheriff," she says, "may I borrow these gentlemen?"

"That's up to them, ma'am."

Stein turns to us and smiles. "Help me get to know the victim."

I glance at Lenson. He nods, and I say, "All right."

The woman says to Garrick, "Can we use your interview room."

"Y'all may as well use my office." Garrick adjusts his belt. "I have things to see to."

He wants to cool down after his encounter with Posner. I don't blame him. The Salem County sheriff is an elected official. But Salem is the largest town, and the county seat. Garrick has a degree of autonomy, but the mayor wields the power of the purse.

Stein leads us to Garrick's office and motions us to seats in front of the sheriff's desk. Throws herself into his old wooden recliner and makes herself at home. She leans back, and the springs in the recliner squeak. The effect is not what she intended.

I suppress a smile. "What do you do at the DOJ?"

"I have a flexible mandate." Stein looks amused. "I was asked to look into your friend's death."

She chooses her words carefully. No indication which branch of the DOJ she works for. I bet she's from another service, seconded to the DOJ.

"How did you know Keller," she asks.

"We served together," Lenson says.

"I pulled his file." Stein folds her arms across her chest. "Ex-Delta. What one might call a very heavy dude. Are you two still in the service?"

"We're retired."

Stein looks like she is making a mental note. I glance around Garrick's office. Dented metal file cabinets stand beside the desk. There's a wooden gun rack with a neat row of lever-action rifles and pump shotguns. Winchesters, Marlins, Remingtons. Above the rack is the sheriff's trophy wall.

High on the wall are mounted plaques with deer and elk antlers. Pride of place has been given to an exceptional bull elk.

"When was the last time you saw him alive?"

Lenson shrugs. "A few weeks ago. I live in El Paso. Come down when I can. Sometimes, he comes to visit."

Stein shifts her gaze to me.

"Last year," I tell her. "We all came to visit."

"Why did he leave the army?"

"He said he wanted to watch his son grow up."

"What was he like?"

"That tells you what he was like." I cross my legs. "He was a good man. Loyal, patriotic, loved his family."

"Special Forces screen their people carefully."

"We don't recruit the best men," Lenson says. "We recruit the *right* men."

"That's a nice slogan. Is it still true? The number of special operators in the army and navy has exploded in the last ten years." Stein picks up a pencil from the sheriff's desk and twirls it absently. "I'm sure there is a broad spectrum of personalities in special forces units."

Lenson and I say nothing.

Rows of black-and-white photographs of Garrick have been plastered on the wall. Almost all are hunting photographs. Garrick with friends and animals he bagged. Photographs of

Garrick and friends at a hunting lodge. One winter photo shows Garrick and a friend standing at the gate of a ranch called El Diablo. Garrick is wearing his Stetson and a long sheepskin coat. The photo must have been taken high in the Rockies.

"Am I boring you, Mr Breed?" Stein jerks my attention away from the wall.

"No. I'm just admiring the sheriff's hunting photographs. Looks like he spends a lot of time in the Rockies."

Distracted, Stein looks at the photos. "Yes. Some people find slaughtering animals fun."

I want to ask Stein if she is a vegetarian. She has the look. Pretty and slender, like she doesn't eat. Probably does yoga.

Stein taps the pencil on the desktop. "I have a problem with this case."

"What might *that* be?"

"Sheriff Garrick's theory makes sense as far as it goes. Keller stopped a group of illegals making their way across his land. He got out of his truck, challenged them, and was shot for his trouble. But... Can you see a Delta walking into that? Would *either* of you have walked into that?"

The cold bitch *knows* we wouldn't.

Stein gives herself five measured beats of silence.

"I think Keller knew the man who shot him."

9

SALEM, 1230 HRS SATURDAY

The Ivy League lawyer stares at us.

"I think Keller knew the man who shot him."

In Garrick's ice-cold, air-conditioned office, my face flares with heat. I know exactly where Stein is going with this. Not once did I admit the possibility.

"Go ahead," I tell her. "Let's hear it."

"Breed." Stein's voice is soft. "This brings me no pleasure."

"Get on with it."

"All right. Keller had no reason to be there at night. Not in the middle of ten thousand acres of barren land. He must have gone to meet someone he trusted. Otherwise, he would have carried a weapon."

Lenson balls his fists on the armrests of his chair. "You think he was involved in smuggling."

"Trafficking, yes." Stein straightens and leans forward. Plants her forearms on Garrick's desk. "People, or drugs."

"Not Keller," I say firmly.

"Ranching is a difficult business." Stein adopts a soothing tone. "Especially here in the Trans-Pecos. The average ranch in Texas is fifteen hundred acres. Out here, it's twenty thousand.

By that standard, Keller's ranch is small. This is the most arid land in the southwest. Grazing supports fewer cattle per acre than ranches to the east."

My throat is clotted with spit. "Was Keller in financial difficulty?"

"My team is checking. I'll know soon. Did he say anything to either of you?"

"No." Lenson shakes his head. "Not a word."

"It's not the kind of thing one would speak to friends about," Stein says. "Greater El Paso is the only part of the Trans-Pecos that is growing. Salem County and City governments have merged. In time, El Paso County will absorb Salem. Property values, including Keller's land, are rising. But the value will be in development, not necessarily agriculture and ranching.

"If I had to guess, I would say your friend's business was tight on cash."

I take a deep breath, force myself to relax. First the muscles in my shoulders. Then my arms and the muscles in my stomach. "I don't believe it."

"I can't think of any other explanation for the facts," Stein says. "If you think of something, tell me."

"We need to go." I get to my feet. "We have a funeral to prepare for."

"I understand." Stein rises and offers me her hand.

Stein's grip is firm and dry. Cold. I lead Lenson from the office.

In the back lot, we get into Keller's truck. Lenson sits behind the wheel and starts the engine. With a throaty roar, the V8 springs to life. We give the engine a couple of minutes to warm up.

"Keller wasn't dirty," I say.

"No, but she's right about one thing."

"What's that."

"Keller knew the person he met. Otherwise, he wouldn't have dismounted without a weapon."

Lenson taps the gas, and the engine settles into a low rumble. He throws the truck into gear and pulls out of the lot. Drives the short distance to the hotel. We go inside and find Hancock in the lounge.

"Where's Mary?"

"She's tired," Hancock says. "We've arranged an honor guard unit for tomorrow. Command pulled a few strings."

"That's good." I settle into one of the deep leather chairs. Signal the waitress for three cold beers.

Veterans are entitled to military funerals. Honor guards have to be available and booked in advance. Veterans in attendance are permitted to wear their uniforms. All three of us came prepared.

Lenson throws himself down in one of the deep leather chairs.

I tell Hancock about our morning, and that Stein thinks Keller was dirty.

"I can see why she's exploring the possibility." I take a beer from the waitress. The mug is frosted. I pour the cold amber liquid down my parched throat. "You know how easy it would be for somebody from Delta to do serious damage here in the world."

Hancock pops an oxycodone. "Heard about a Special Forces medic at Bliss. CID busted him for stealing morphine."

"Uncle Sam spends two million dollars a head turning us into weapons," Lenson says. "Sends us home with nothing to do."

"The point is," I say, "Uncle Sam must be having trouble with operators going off the rails. Imagine the three of us deciding to rob a bank. Nobody could stop us. Stein figures Keller might have money problems, might be tempted."

"To do what." There is violence in Hancock's tone.

"Smuggle drugs and illegals across his land," I say. "She thinks he crossed the cartels, and they lopped his head off."

"Let's war-game the scenario," Lenson suggests.

"Okay." I stare at my beer and collect my thoughts. "First of all, he did *not* stumble on illegals. There were *no* personnel tracks arriving from the river, *none* leaving for the highway."

"The lady's right," Hancock says. "Keller didn't belong out there at night."

"So it was an RV." Lenson looks at me. "Who with?"

"That," I say, "is the question. Someone he trusted. We have to consider the possibility that Keller arrived with his murderer in the truck."

"Why take someone out to the middle of nowhere," Hancock asks.

"Privacy," Lenson says. "To avoid being seen together."

I shift my gaze from one man to the other. "We can't rule out the scenario. But then the murderer had to leave on foot. Or in another vehicle. And covered his tracks."

Lenson fixes me with a one-eyed stare. "There were only two vehicles at the scene. Keller's pickup and the tow truck. The tracks of the police vehicles were outside the cordon, on the highway side. You spent a lot of time out there, Breed."

"We can't rule out the presence of one or two more vehicles," I say. "There was mesquite cut from a clump of brush two hundred yards north. The killer could have fastened the mesquite to the back of his truck. Retraced the route he took into the RV. The brush would have covered his tracks."

"Which direction?" Hancock asks.

"No way to tell. The murderer left before everyone else arrived."

"Scenario number one." Lenson frowns. "Keller went out there to meet someone he trusted, who murdered him."

"Scenario number two." I meet Lenson's gaze. "Keller was

murdered somewhere else. The sheriff found neither the brass, nor the bullet."

"Murderer took the brass." Lenson strokes his chin. "The bullet is a needle in a haystack."

"A clearly defined two hundred and fifty thousand square yards." I drain my beer and signal the waitress for three more. "Garrick swept four hundred yards of a hundred-and-eighty-degree arc. Called up a hundred men, spent three days. From space, you can see the ground they trampled."

"That's a big haystack," Lenson says.

I shake my head. "Not if you do a sector search for the bullet. With a hundred men."

"It might have shattered."

"Unlikely, given the exit wound."

"All right," Lenson concedes. "Either way, there was a rendezvous."

"Yes. But—they should have found the bullet. Keller was killed somewhere else."

"What was the RV?" Hancock lifts his mug and stamps rings of condensation on the tabletop.

"A payoff or a ripoff," Lenson says.

Hancock stretches his game leg. Takes a long draw of his beer. "None of us would ever get involved in that."

I think of my long, dreamless nights.

My lack of purpose.

10

FORT BLISS, 1100 HRS SUNDAY

I have been to military funerals at a number of cemeteries, but none are sadder than those at Fort Bliss. The army bowed to the environmental movement and budget pressure. Over the years, it replaced the green grass over the graves with crushed red stones. Fort Bliss National Cemetery looks and smells arid. Where other cemeteries smell of fresh-cut grass, Fort Bliss smells of heat and dust.

The army takes care of the fallen. Transfers are dignified. All honors are rendered. For a soldier who fell in a foreign land, burial near his loved ones should bring comfort. If only a little more could be spent, to allow those who died in service to rest under fresh green grass.

Fort Bliss National Cemetery is truly a garden of stone.

The chaplain finishes his committal service, closes his Bible, and steps back. The honor guard stretches the flag taut across the casket. The seven-man firing party marches to the graveside.

In full dress uniform, Lenson, Keller and I stand with other mourners. On our shoulders, we wear the Delta insignia. A red

Airborne patch with a black Fairbairn-Sykes commando knife in the center.

Mary and Donnie sit on folding chairs.

I glance at Hancock. He was offered a chair because of his bad leg. Refused. Sweat glistening on his brow, he stands for the entire ceremony. The pain must be unbearable. Hancock is not the man I knew. His mind is warping from the pain.

Ready.

Rifles at high port, the firing party work the actions of their ceremonial M14s.

Aim.

The soldiers hold the rifles at a forty-five-degree angle, muzzles pointed skyward.

Fire.

Seven rifles crash as one. Mary flinches at the first volley. Mercifully, the next two volleys are fired in rapid succession.

The squad leader bends sharply and retrieves a spent shell casing.

A bugler plays "Taps." A forlorn, lonely sound. When he finishes, he lowers the bugle and the honor guard fold the flag. The leader of the firing party steps to the leader of the honor guard, hands him the shell casing, and withdraws.

The honor guard pass the flag to the sergeant at the head of the casket. He takes the flag in his white-gloved hands and inserts the spent cartridge into its folds. He marches to Mary, kneels before her, and presents the flag.

On behalf of the President of the United States and the people of a grateful nation, may I present this flag as a token of appreciation for the honorable and faithful service your loved one has rendered.

The sergeant rises to his feet and salutes Mary. The white-gloved salute is delivered in slow motion. Mary looks numb.

. . .

The ritual is over. We walk back to the drive where our vehicles are parked and waiting. I look back at the cemetery. It is a forest of white headstones in a red field. Eighty acres that look like they have been corralled from the desert. Aching, I say goodbye to my best friend.

Mary, Donnie, and Hancock get into a polished black Lincoln. I watch Hancock get into the car, his leg extended. He folds himself into the leather passenger seat. Once inside, his whole body sags with relief. Mary lays her hand on his forearm.

Lenson and I get into his SUV.

"Feels good to wear the uniform, don't it," Lenson says.

"Yes, it does," I tell him, "but I'm sick to death about the reason."

We follow the Lincoln down Texas 20 to Salem. The big limo lets Mary, Donnie and Hancock off in front of the hotel, and Lenson parks the SUV.

Hancock ushers Mary and Donnie inside. I scan the 7-Eleven across the street. I notice a pair of Latinos sitting in a blue Impala sedan. I wonder if they are watching the hotel. They start the car, back around to the gas pump, and the driver gets out. He twists off the gas cap and fills the tank. His friend studies a map.

Hard-looking guys. The driver is older than his friend. Long greasy hair over a pockmarked face and a thick mustache. Jail-house tattoos cover his arms like sleeves.

"What's up?" Lenson asks.

Wearing our green berets and dress uniforms, we stand in the parking lot. The Latino filling the tank checks us out, looks away.

I shake off the paranoia. "Nothing. Let's get out of this heat."

The sun has climbed to the vertical. I've lost my shadow. We go inside, agree to meet at the restaurant for lunch.

Upstairs, I take off my uniform and fold it carefully into my garment bag. Change into jeans and a loose shirt. Pack the jump boots into the bottom of my duffel and pull on my Oakleys.

I go to the window and look down at the 7-Eleven. The Latinos in the Impala have gone. My room is above the foyer and front desk. Looking down, I see Anya Stein walk across the parking lot and unlock her Civic. She drives down main street in the direction of the sheriff's station. DOJ lawyers don't carry SIGs. And if Stein were FBI or Marshal's Service, she would have said so.

Stein must be CIA, attached to the DOJ.

But why.

This situation is all wrong. Keller wasn't killed where he was found. Why would a killer move his body. Because there was something incriminating about where he was killed.

I go down to the restaurant. The table is subdued. No one wants to talk about the investigation. It is too uncomfortable, and Donnie is not supposed to know. Mary is making a mistake. Sooner or later, she will have to address the issue with the boy. Older than his years, he is being kind.

Donnie is dealing with his pain alone. No eight-year-old should go through this without support. Later this week, I *will* have a word with Mary. She cannot continue to lie to the boy.

"Are you sure you want to go back to the Lazy K?" Hancock asks Mary.

"We have to go back sometime," Mary says.

I meet her eyes over the table. "I'm not sure that's a good idea."

Lenson leans forward. "Ask Larry and Bo to move back into the bunk house."

"I have," Mary admits. "They'll move in tomorrow night."

"Stay at the hotel tonight, then," Hancock says.

Mary looks at Donnie. "What do you think, Donnie? You're the man of the family now."

Donnie frowns. "I want to go home."

"That settles it," Mary says. "We'll leave after lunch."

I should go with them, but inviting myself to the Lazy K would be inappropriate. I say nothing.

11

LAZY K, 0900 HRS MONDAY

The hotel feels oddly empty with Mary and Donnie gone. We watched them drive off last night. Sat in the lounge, beat back our apprehension with Bourbon. I couldn't sleep. Exhausted, I rose from bed and went down to breakfast.

Parked in front of the hotel, the hatchback of Lenson's SUV stands open. I swing Hancock's garment bag aboard. It's the last of the pair's luggage. I reach up with both hands and swing the hatchback shut.

"Let us know how Mary gets on," Lenson says. "One of us will come down next week."

The sun is climbing in the sky. Its rays bathe the white wooden walls of the hotel in a golden glow.

"She's thinking of making a go of it," Hancock says.

I grunt. "Not much choice. She's got two ranch hands. If she can hire one more and appoint a foreman, she might have a chance."

"Someone to do the work," Lenson says, "and someone to do the books."

"That's the easy part," I tell him. "The hard part is understanding the markets for cattle and grazing rights. Keller grew up on a ranch, Mary didn't. I don't know if she'll take to it."

Silent, we stare at each other. Ranching is a hard life, a challenging business for a strong man. West Texas is an unforgiving environment. Alone, a woman raising a young boy will struggle to survive.

"She's a strong woman," Lenson says. "She might surprise us."

It's oh-nine-hundred, ninety-eight degrees. Our shirts are stained with sweat. Skin exposed to the sun burns. Hancock glances at the SUV, longing for its air-conditioned interior.

"I won't keep you gents," I say. "Let's stay in touch."

We shake hands and the pair drive away. Feeling hollow and alone, I watch them head down main street toward Texas 20.

I decide to drive to the Lazy K. For the duration of my stay, Mary has loaned me Keller's truck. I walk the length of the hotel parking lot, get in the cab, and start the engine. The air-conditioning vents blast hot air in my face, and I wait for the cool to kick in. I throw the truck in gear, back out of the parking slot, and roar toward the highway.

On Saturday, we drove past the ranch access road. I have no trouble finding it—a wide, open gate. "Lazy K" worked in wrought iron across the top.

I turn onto the dirt road and race toward the ranch house. The truck throws up a plume of dust, visible in the rearview mirror. On either side of the road lie brown, rolling hills covered with mesquite and creosote. The terrain looks earthier than the rocky land fifteen miles south. The mesquite grows taller.

Movement atop a hill catches my eye. A pack of wild dogs are fighting over something. I take my foot off the gas, and the speedometer drops to twenty miles an hour.

The dogs are worrying an object. Like a soccer ball, their plaything rolls this way and that.

I allow the truck to roll to a stop. Pop open the glove compartment and fish out Keller's sixteen-power binoculars. I twist in my seat and raise the optics to my eyes. Looking through the side window, I focus and adjust the diopter. Survey the strange competition.

The dogs snarl and snap at each other. The animals are frothing at the mouth. My stomach flutters.

I lay the binoculars on the seat next to me and take a five-shot stripper clip from the glove compartment. I get out of the truck and reach for Keller's Mauser. I unlock the Ernst Apel and swing the scope ninety degrees. Lift the handle and draw back the bolt. I squeeze five rounds into the magazine, pocket the stripper clip, and lock the scope in place. In the heat, the smell of gun oil floods my nose. In my hands, the rifle feels heavy and familiar. I close the bolt, chamber a round, and turn to the hill.

The horizontal distance is two hundred yards. Keller zeroed his scope at four hundred and calculated tables of hold-overs. The reticle in the 3.5-10x variable-power scope is graduated in minutes-of-angle. One can either dial adjustments into one of the scope turrets, or hold-over using the reticle. I don't want to kill the dogs, so an eyeball estimate will do.

Whether one shoots uphill or downhill, one always shoots high. The horizontal distance to a target is always shorter than the line-of-sight distance. Gravity has less time to work on the flight of a bullet. One uses the minute-of-angle adjustment appropriate to the shorter range.

I raise the Mauser to my shoulder and aim slightly below the animals. Through the scope, the dogs look feral. The Mauser has a two-stage military trigger with four pounds of pull. I take up the slack and break the shot.

Crack.

The rifle slams into my shoulder. A foot from the dogs, the bullet kicks up a puff of dust. I work the bolt and fire a second time. The shot ricochets off a rock and nicks one of the animals. In a flash, the dogs disappear from view.

I eject the spent shell casing, chamber another round, and safety the weapon. I pick up the two empty shell casings and put them in my pocket with the stripper clip. Rifle low-ready, I climb the hill. In the stifling heat, I pace myself. I walk with a measured step and measured breath.

At the top, I cautiously approach the object. It's spherical, covered with blond hair, matted with earth and blood. The dirt, wet with the dogs' saliva, has turned to a muddy paste. The dogs have torn much of the skin from the object, denuding one cheekbone and the mandible.

I stare at Mary Keller's head.

12

LAZY K, 1000 HRS MONDAY

My mouth is dry as sandpaper, and my ears pound with every heartbeat. I sling the Mauser over my shoulder and carry the grisly discovery down the hill. My inclination is to carry the object by the hair. I cannot bring myself to do it. A storm rages inside me. I cradle Mary in the crook of my arm and hold her against me. When I reach the truck, I rummage under the bench seat and find a pair of oily rags and an Indian blanket. I wrap Mary in the weaved cloth and set her on the seat next to me.

I thought war had desensitized me to death. Thought wrong. I'd seen Islamic terrorists behead prisoners of war. Never seen it done to someone close. Never a friend.

I know what I will find at the Lazy K. I drive at a sedate pace, my breath shallow. When I reach the ranch house, I park on one side of the wide, brushed gravel driveway. The Kellers have a four-car garage, and there are no vehicles outside. I don't want to disturb tracks in the gravel.

The house has two stories. The ground floor spreads over eight thousand square feet. A wide front porch with metal furniture frames the entrance. The second floor, with the sleeping quarters, is a cozy four thousand square feet. Four bedrooms, a library, and a second sitting room. When I came to visit last year, Keller showed me around with pride.

I get out of the truck, take Keller's Winchester, and rack a shell into the chamber. I approach the house with the weapon at high port.

In front of the garage doors, a round, dark object sits on the gravel. It was tossed from the porch, scattering blood as it sailed through the air.

Donnie.

The front door is ajar. I push it open with the muzzle of the Winchester. A wide, carpeted foyer greets me. To the left, an open doorway leads to the main living room. Droplets of blood trail from the living room to the front door.

Both walls on either side of the foyer have been ventilated by shotgun pellets. Two patterns, close together. The patterns on the left are tight, the drywall shredded. The patterns on the opposite wall are more widely dispersed. Not all the pellets penetrated.

The door to the living room is in the center of the wall. A center-fed room. Two dead zones in the corners closest the door. An operator entering the room cannot see either corner without exposing himself. A corner-fed room has a doorway at one end of the wall. An operator has only one dead zone to cover. Center-fed rooms are inherently more dangerous.

I snap the shotgun to my shoulder, careful not to extend the barrel past the doorway.

In the middle of the living room carpet, Mary Keller's headless corpse has been thrown on its stomach. The back of her blouse is bloody, shredded by exit wounds. On the floor next to her lies a Mossberg Maverick pump-action shotgun. A spent shell case has rolled against one of the legs of the coffee table.

Clearing a room is a dance. It's balance and footwork. Especially if you are alone. With two men, I could cover one dead zone and leave the other to a partner. By myself, I have to assess each corner separately.

I short-stock the Winchester. With the stock flat *over* my left shoulder, I shorten the weapon's effective length by five inches. Weight on my left foot, I peer to the right. On the right side of the living room, in front of the widescreen, lies Donnie's body. Like his mother, he was shot with an automatic weapon, laid on his stomach, and decapitated. Incongruously, a bloody buck knife lies on the floor between Donnie and the doorway.

Stepping to the right, I short-stock the Winchester over my right shoulder and peer left. Capture as much of the left corner as I can. I know it is a cramped corner. Crowded by a sofa and a bookcase. Anyone waiting to ambush me is more likely to hide in the dead zone to the right. Flat against the wall, deep in the cut, weapon extended.

I shift the shotgun to my left shoulder. Leading with my left foot, I barge into the room and snap the muzzle to cover the cut.

Empty.

A lethal ballet. I turn, cover the opposite corner. Alone, I have only the dead for company.

Blood spatter stains the wall next to the entrance. The same patterns I saw from the foyer. One pattern of drops blown from a body, the height of a man's face. They hit the wall at an angle. Another pattern the height of a man's chest. On the floor, a brown puddle has begun to congeal. Number four birdshot. Keller would have selected that load for Mary. Inside the house, it was less likely to over-penetrate.

The birdshot had more than enough power to punch through a grown man and an interior wall. I doubt the man survived.

The floor around the buck knife is littered with spent brass. AK47 ammunition.

I have no Salem numbers stored in my mobile phone. I shift

the Winchester to high port and go to the landline. Eye on the entrance, I lift the handset and dial 911.

THE DISPATCHER at the sheriff's station promises to send Garrick right away. I hang up and go outside. Take one of the rags from the pickup. I stare at Donnie's head. In my heart, fury builds.

I cover Donnie and examine the gravel. At least three sets of tire tracks. One set of off-road tires, Keller's truck. Two sets of steel-belted radials. One set terminates at the garage door. The other set terminates in the driveway. It traces a curved V where the vehicle backed around to leave. Both sets are sedans. One from Mary's car, the other driven by the killers.

Squatting on my haunches, I examine the second set. On the outside, the right-hand tread is worn. The wheels are out of alignment.

Plumes of dust rise from the access road. Garrick's Jeep leads two police cruisers. I stand at the entrance to the driveway and hold up my hands to stop them.

Garrick climbs out of his Jeep. "All right, Breed," he says. "What happened?"

I tell him Mary and Donnie have been killed. "There are tracks from the killers' vehicle in the drive," I say. "You'll want to secure the crime scene and let the lab boys do their thing."

The sheriff directs his deputies to set up a perimeter around the house. They will need a lot of posts and yellow tape.

"You coming?" Garrick starts toward the front door.

I shake my head. "I've disturbed the scene enough," I tell him. "The lab boys need to take exclusionary samples from me. You too, if you go inside."

Garrick stares for a full ten seconds. He grunts, goes inside alone.

I watch the deputies string crime scene tape. Wait for Garrick to return.

Fifteen minutes inside the house, and Garrick comes straight to me. “Same ones who murdered Keller.”

“I think so.”

A blue Civic sedan pulls up behind the police cruisers. Anya Stein gets out and strides toward us.

“What do you think,” she says to Garrick.

“Well, good morning to you too, Miss Stein,” the sheriff drawls.

“Nothing good about it so far.” Stein plants her hands on her hips. The motion brushes back her suit coat. Her weapon is indeed a SIG P226 Legion in a leather skeleton holster. Three hundred dollars more than a standard P226, the Legion is expensive and sexy.

Not standard issue. She bought it herself.

Doesn’t the woman sweat?

Stein’s heart beats twice a minute.

“They killed the woman and boy,” Garrick says. “Breed here found the woman’s head on a hilltop down the road. The boy’s is over by the garage. Same bunch who did the husband. Looks like the woman hit one of the killers.”

“What with?”

“Shotgun.”

Impatient, Stein strides to the front door and pushes through.

Lab boys will need to take another set of exclusionary samples.

Silent, Garrick and I stare at the house. I shudder, turn to look at the hill. Think of the dogs dragging Mary’s head.

Stein emerges from the house and does a circuit of the driveway. Examines the gravel. When she has finished her inspection, she marches to us.

“Number four birdshot,” she announces. “Home defense load. Enough to stop an attacker but not so powerful as to over-penetrate. The boy stabbed the first man to come through the door. Bought his mother enough time to get off two rounds. One pattern got the attacker at the edge of his face. Blood spattered at an angle against the wall. The other pattern got him center mass. Tight enough to penetrate his body and one interior wall. Blood and tissue embedded in the material."

Stein is good. So far, her conclusions match mine.

The woman shifts her attention to me. "You saw the brass on the floor."

I meet her gaze. "An AK47. The second man to enter shot her dead. Turned the weapon on the boy."

"How many do you think?"

"Three or four. Probably four. You saw the tire tracks. Three men and a driver in a sedan."

"The first man was wounded."

"No, he was killed." I think of Mary's second shot. The pattern that caught the attacker center mass. "His friends carried him out. The blood trails look like they came from heads that were thrown onto the drive."

"You found the woman's on a hill."

"Wild dogs dragged it away."

Stein wrinkles her nose. "Where is it?"

"I gave it to one of the deputies."

Stein's coldness angers me.

Garrick stares into the middle distance. "They wouldn't have carried away their friend if he was dead."

"They might have, to make our job more difficult." Stein takes a leather-bound notebook from her handbag. With a Montblanc ballpoint pen, she scribbles notes. "They were in a hurry. They didn't pick up their brass, they didn't wipe the place down for prints."

"They weren't expecting resistance," I tell her. "A soldier's wife and a soldier's son. You'll find blood from at least three people, a lot of fingerprints. Prints on the brass, prints on the knife. You may trace some to cartels south of the border. You'll have to exclude us and the two ranch hands."

"The killers panicked," Stein says.

"Not all of them." I shake my head. "*One man* beheaded Mary and Donnie. The same man who beheaded Keller. He was stone cold."

I SIT in the interview room at the Salem sheriff's station. Smaller than Garrick's office, it is one hundred percent utilitarian. The laminated plywood tabletop is clean and functional. I review my statement once, then sign it. A sheriff's deputy witnesses the document.

The crime lab technicians came and took hair samples. They didn't need fingerprints or DNA. Mine are in the army personnel database.

"Wait outside," the deputy says. "Sheriff might want to talk to you."

I stretch and lead him out of the interview room. Opposite the dispatcher's counter, a row of chairs have been set against the wall. A pair of cowboys sit there, waiting. Keller's ranch hands, Larry and Bo. The men look leathery and capable. The deputy directs them to the interview room.

I pace.

Strident voices are audible from behind the closed door of the sheriff's office. Male voices. Garrick and Posner.

"I want those roadblocks up," Posner says. "You said whoever murdered Keller was in LA or Miami by now. Admit you were wrong."

"The roadblocks went up as soon as we found the bodies. Don't tell me my job."

"I will tell you your job when I think you're not doing it."

"I'm telling *you* I want that budget authorization. *In writing.*"

"Budget over-runs happen all the time. They are resolved at the next council meeting."

"In writing, Goddamnit. Or the *Salem Gazette* will have a story about our underfunded sheriff's office."

"I'll give you the damn authorization," Posner snarls. "But council will review the budget, and we'll have an audit of your office."

The door opens and Posner storms out. He's red-face pissed. When he sees me in the waiting area, he stops and takes a breath.

"Mr Breed, I'm sorry for your loss."

Garrick comes out of his office and joins us.

"It's clear the people who killed Mary Keller are still in the area," I say. "These aren't illegals or coyotes. These are cartel *soldados*."

Garrick hooks his thumbs in his belt. "Stein is operating on the assumption the killings are drug related," he says. "She's calling in the FBI and Border Patrol."

Posner looks skeptical. "To do what?"

"The FBI will help with forensics. The Border Patrol will help us set up roadblocks on main and secondary roads."

"You had roadblocks up for three days last week." I look Garrick in the eye. "You didn't find anything because the killers never left. They are right here."

Garrick's tone is defensive. "You don't know that."

"It's obvious," I tell him. "The killings are related."

Two minutes ago, Garrick and Posner were at each other's throats. Now, to mollify me, they join forces.

"The sheriff, the FBI, and the DEA are doing everything they can," Posner drawls. "Mr Breed, why don't you leave this to the professionals. We'll keep you posted."

"I'm in town for the week," I say. "Someone has to make arrangements for Mary and Donnie."

"Well, that sounds right reasonable, Mr Breed." Posner

smiles. "The sheriff here will let you know when the medical examiner has finished."

I glance at the interview room. The deputy is taking statements from Larry and Bo. I leave the station and walk back to the hotel.

One thing is certain—Salem is no longer the most peaceful sector of the border.

13

BLEDSOE, 1300 HRS TUESDAY

The thermometer on the dash of Keller's truck reads one hundred and four degrees. I have the air-conditioner on full blast. The interior of the cab is as cold as a refrigerator.

I want to look into Keller's murder. Instinct tells me to start where soldiers always start. The battlefield, the topography, the road net. Routes for ingress and egress.

Next to me on the bench seat is a map of Salem and the Keller ranch. Trust Keller to keep maps in his glove compartment. This map outlines the major roads and topographical features. Perfect for initial reconnaissance.

Keller's ten thousand acres are south of Salem. The land is immediately adjacent the border wall and the Rio Grande. The ranch house is on the northern edge, with a paved road leading to the main highway. A dirt road runs around the perimeter... along the border wall, the stream, past the hills, and along the highway.

I've driven the border, looking for breaches or fresh signs of penetration. Clothing hung up on the barrier, discarded water bottles and litter. Nothing. Garrick told me the Border Patrol inspected six miles of wall in either direction.

Across the stream, Bledsoe Meats owns the adjoining property to the south.

There it is. A set of squat adobe-colored buildings behind a high chain-link fence. Keller's perimeter road forks. The right fork crosses over a bridge, onto Bledsoe land. The left fork runs east toward the hills.

The Bledsoe fence is constructed of evenly spaced pipes fifteen feet high. At the top, the last three feet are bent outward at a forty-five-degree angle. Chain-link is stretched between the pipes for the first twelve feet. The last three are strung with strands of razor wire.

The fence makes the buildings look menacing. Large signs are hung on the fence every two hundred yards.

BLEDSOE MEATS LTD.
PRIVATE PROPERTY
NO TRESPASSING

This is West Texas, folks protect their privacy.

There, on a low hill overlooking the plant. A flash of sunlight glinting off something shiny. Metal or glass. I drive east, my eye on the hill. *Another* flash.

The road dog-legs north, skirting the base of the hills. I follow the road, part company with the stream. My view of the Bledsoe plant swings from the right passenger window to the rearview mirror. I follow the road until the plant disappears behind the hills.

My eyes search the terrain for a break in the alluvial plain. There, at the base of the hills, is a series of draws formed by the erosion of centuries. Storms deluge the hills with rain. Water pours down, seeking routes of least resistance. Enough to carve natural cover into the earth. Dry stream beds deep enough to conceal a vehicle.

I pull off the road and park the truck in a shallow draw. Open the door and step onto dry earth. Centuries of silt, washed down the mountains by rain. Spread over the surface by overflowing streams, then dried and baked by the sun. There are tire tracks on the stream bed. It's a natural place to stop if one is inclined to climb the hills.

The heat is overwhelming. It sucks the air from my lungs. When I take my next breath, I have to work to fill my chest. I reach into the truck and take a two-quart plastic bottle of water from behind the seat. Drink half.

In the desert, a soldier can sweat five gallons a day. The secret to combat effectiveness is hydration. One drinks six quarts of water before a patrol, then a quart every hour thereafter. Medics monitor intake.

I cap the bottle and put it back in the cab. Take Keller's Mauser from the gun rack and a stripper clip from the glove compartment. I fired two rounds yesterday, leaving three. I work the bolt and empty the rifle. Swing the scope out of the way. Squeeze five fresh rounds into the magazine, pocket the clip and three extra bullets. I lock the scope in place, chamber a round, and safety the weapon.

Five minutes climbing the hill and I'm drenched in sweat. A slick, greasy film covers every inch of my body. My shirt and jeans cling to my flesh. I wish I'd borrowed one of Keller's hats.

The physical exertion feels good. I'm close to the spot where I reckon I'd seen the flash of light. I slow my pace and carry the Mauser low-ready, trigger finger safe on the stock.

A woman lies prone on the hilltop, scanning the Bledsoe plant with a pair of binoculars. It's a great view, I'll give her that. From here, one can see the full length and breadth of the plant. It's three-quarters of a mile wide at the border wall. Two miles long. The buildings are huge, industrial facilities. On the side closest the stream lie vast cattle holding pens. One gate opposite the pens opens to a wide yard where trailers unload feedstock. On the other side spreads another yard where tractors and eighteen-wheelers park and load product.

To the south, outside the fence, sits a vast gravel parking lot. Must be fifteen football fields long by twenty wide. Like the yards, crushed flat by a steamroller. Parking slots have been painted white and numbered. Long, endless rows. There must be a thousand cars and trucks parked out there, and the lot isn't half full.

"You should put those away," I tell the woman.

She twists sharply, staring at the rifle in my hands. "It's a free country."

Defiant and hostile. There is something else in her tone... Fear. I understand all three. I can make it easier for her.

"It is." I put up the rifle, a peaceful gesture. "But you need to know people can see sunlight off those lenses two miles away. I did."

"What is it to you?" Her voice trembles. Awareness of her mistake has shaken her confidence.

I like what I see.

Thirty years old and tiny. No more than five-two or three. Long black hair, smooth skin the color of brown chocolate. Her small breasts strain against a white t-shirt soaked in sweat. No bra, everything to see. Long legs in proportion to her frame.

I squat and hold the rifle across my knees.

"You wouldn't be glassing Bledsoe from up here unless you wanted to hide your interest. I am also interested."

The woman sits up and draws her knees to her chest. Reaches over and stuffs the binoculars into a black canvas rucksack. She frowns, as though working a puzzle. "Why *are* you interested?"

There's intelligence in her eyes. Shrewd and street-smart,

but unfamiliar with fieldcraft. A city woman. Blundering around, liable to get herself killed.

"My friend Keller owns this land." I wave my hand north in a sweeping gesture. Far away, the Lazy K's ranch house is a tiny speck. "He and his family have been murdered."

"I heard." She looks at me with suspicion. "How do you know him?"

"We were in the army together. What's your name?"

"Mirasol Cruz." Her features soften. "And you?"

"Breed."

"You have a first name, Mr Breed?"

"Yes." I smile. "How did you get here?"

"My car is parked at the foot of the hill."

"Let's get out of here," I say. "It's possible I'm not the only one who saw your glass."

Mirasol chews her lip. She's uncomfortable she made a mistake. Smart enough to admit she doesn't know everything. "Do you know Salem?"

"A bit."

"We may be able to help each other. There is a diner just off the highway to El Paso. Let us meet there in an hour. The Dusty Burger will be cooler than this wretched pile of rocks."

I don't think she'll run. If she does, she won't leave town.

"All right." I get to my feet. "Walk with me."

Mirasol adjusts the straps on her rucksack and sets a Stetson on her head. I sling the Mauser over my shoulder, and we walk down the hill.

We approach the draw where I parked Keller's truck.

"Where did *you* park," I ask her.

"A place like this one," she says. "A hundred yards further along the trail."

"Great minds think alike."

We approach Keller's truck, and Mirasol freezes. Her chocolate skin lightens as blood drains from her face. She stares at me with confusion. She looks ready to run.

"What's wrong?"

In time to hers, my heart quickens. If she runs, I'll sprint to catch her.

Mirasol squints at me. "Is this *your* truck?"

"No," I tell her. "It was my friend's. His family loaned it to me while I'm in town."

Mirasol allows herself to breathe. "We have much to talk about, Breed."

"More now than fifteen minutes ago?"

The moment has passed. I feel as though some crisis has been averted. I'm conscious the woman's nervous system and mine have become synchronized.

"Yes. Your friend was here last week. In this very spot. A few days before he was killed."

14

SALEM, 1500 HRS TUESDAY

The Dusty Burger is a long prefab building at the junction between Texas 20 and the road to Salem. It looks clean enough, with a big billboard advertising its custom.

I pull Keller's truck into the asphalt parking lot. Stride twenty feet to the Diner's air-conditioned interior. I'm conscious hot tar is sticking to the soles of my Oakley desert boots.

"What can we bring you today?" a pleasant waitress says. She wears a white shirt, black pants, and a green apron. A little pad and pencil stuffed in the pocket.

"Coffee, please," I tell her. "Black."

I take a window seat and stare at Keller's truck. The confusion in Mirasol's eyes said it all. She thought it was *my* truck. That I had been to the hills last week. But I hadn't arrived in town yet. And Keller was still alive.

The waitress pours my coffee.

Mirasol pulls up in her Camaro and parks on the opposite side of the lot, next to a local vehicle. A transparent effort to prevent curious passers-by from associating our vehicles. She takes her rucksack from the back seat and hurries to the diner.

I get to my feet and motion for her to sit opposite me. She pushes her ruck all the way to the window. Crowds into the booth next to it.

"What do you want," I ask.

"Coffee's fine."

I signal the waitress to bring another cup.

Mirasol is all business. "Why should I trust you?"

"I warned you not to give yourself away with that glass."

"After you and everyone else spotted me."

"Perhaps not everyone else. Had Bledsoe people spotted you, their security force would have wasted no time getting up there. I didn't."

"Unless you're with them."

She's careful. "Mirasol, do you know how my friend died?"

"No."

"They shot him. And cut his head off. Yesterday they did the same to his wife and son."

Mirasol looks ready to lose her lunch. Before she can respond, I carry on. "Were I one of them, we would not be sitting here. You would be gone, buried in the desert."

Mirasol swallows hard. "All right, I'm sorry."

"You saw Keller's truck last week. Tell me."

The waitress brings Mirasol a cup and pours for her. Mirasol carefully measures sugar and cream into her coffee. Waits for the waitress to leave.

"I arrived over a week ago. Found the spot on the hill. Every day, to watch the plant, I drove up there. Last Monday, I arrived to climb to the lookout. I saw your truck—Keller's truck. Parked exactly where you parked today. I didn't want to be up there unless I was alone, so I left."

"Did you ever see it again?"

"No. I only went back on the weekend. Friday, I heard a

rancher had been found murdered. There were no details. I had no reason to think it was his truck I saw."

I believe her. "Why are you interested in the plant?"

That is the question. Mirasol shifts in her seat. Sips her coffee to buy herself time. I wait patiently. She looks like she wants to tell me.

"I'm a journalist," she says at last. "There is a story here. I believe Bledsoe is involved in human trafficking. Running prostitutes from Mexico to the United States."

"What makes you think that?"

"Not just prostitutes, Breed." Mirasol's eyes bore into mine. "Children. Girls thirteen, fourteen years old. I have met them in Los Angeles, Boston, and New York. They all say they spent a day in a refrigerated trailer with carcasses and meat product. They were shipped from Texas."

"They pointed you to Bledsoe."

Mirasol shakes her head. "No. They were too frightened to say more. They would not say how they came across the border. I correlated their dates and places of arrival in the big cities. Traced the tractors. The shipments originated here, in Salem. Bledsoe Meats."

"That's good detective work."

"Trafficking is common," Mirasol says. "These people come here for a better life. The hourly wage in El Paso is equivalent to the daily wage in Juarez. What would you do?"

I shrug.

"If a woman decides to sell her body for a better life, that is her choice. But not children." Mirasol's face darkens. "Not children."

The woman's anger unsettles me. The nerves in my arms strain like taut guitar strings. Mirasol's interest is personal.

I sip my coffee. Force myself to relax. "All right."

Mirasol calms herself. "I have made enquiries," she says.

"Among Hispanics. They are good citizens, but they know things they will not tell police."

"What do they tell you?"

"The man who owns that business. Paul Bledsoe. He likes children. He does not find what he wants here in the USA. He goes to Ciudad Juarez."

I drain my coffee. Motion to the waitress for another.

"Keller may have seen something."

"I am sure he did. For more than a week, I camped on the hilltop. Every day, they ship girls. In the early hours after midnight." Mirasol takes a deep breath. "Very well, Breed. It is your turn to tell me what you know."

"Keller was found dead next to his truck. In the middle of his ranch, with nothing around him. Shot once in the chest, then beheaded with a sharp blade. Something like a Bowie knife."

"He must have been at my lookout," Mirasol says. "Perhaps they saw him."

"I'm sure he saw something." I shake my head. "But they didn't see him."

"How can you be sure?"

I look at her kindly. "I can't rule it out, of course. But Keller was a soldier. He would not have made the mistake you made. You see… It is what we do."

Keller would never have glassed the plant without protecting his lenses.

"What exactly did you and Keller do in the army?"

"We killed bad people who attacked our country." I stare out the window. "On September 11th, I watched innocent people jump from buildings rather than burn alive."

Mirasol's eyes are wet. "So you and Keller went?"

"Yes, and others. My squadron was the first into Afghanistan."

We are silent a long time. It is a comfortable silence. I decide to bring us back to the matter at hand.

"You saw Keller's truck Monday. His body was found Wednesday. He was killed Tuesday night. When did you return to the hilltop?"

"Saturday." Mirasol looks miserable. "I was frightened when I saw Keller's truck hidden the way I hid my car. I decided to stay away for a few days. I was at the hotel when I heard a rancher had been killed. I didn't know it was him."

"The manner of Keller's death raises questions." I stare out the window. There isn't a cloud in the sky. "The gunshot killed him. Cutting his head off was... extravagant."

"The cartels do it."

"Not this side of the border. And they did it to Keller's wife and son."

"You are right," Mirasol says at last. "It makes no sense. Let us say a cartel is responsible for trafficking with Bledsoe. Why draw attention to themselves here? They could have simply made him disappear."

"Keller was a prominent local citizen. Had he disappeared, the search would have become national in scope. Now that he has been found murdered, the investigation is strictly local."

"Why kill his family?"

"Keller was at your lookout, and he saw something. The killers had to assume he told Mary. They had to assume Donnie overheard. They beheaded Keller to frighten his family into silence. Came back for them later."

"But why wait a week to kill them? Why not kill them the night they killed Keller?"

"I'm not sure. Maybe they were busy with their shipment, finished close to dawn. The killers missed their chance. Mary and Donnie moved to the hotel. As long as they stayed with us, they presented hard targets."

Mirasol rests her fingertips lightly on my hand. Her touch is electric.

"Breed. Help me find evidence Bledsoe is trafficking. His crimes are connected to your friend's death."

Mirasol's eyes are all pupil. Kissing eyes, I call them. She can't consciously turn them on and off.

I have to maintain objectivity.

"I need to think," I tell her. "Promise me you won't go up there alone."

Mirasol frowns. Withdraws her hand. "I can't promise," she says. "You have your war, and I have mine."

In those hazel eyes, anger smolders.

"Going up there alone would be very foolish," I tell her.

For the moment, something has been lost.

I wish she hadn't taken her hand away.

15

BLEDSOE, 1800 HRS TUESDAY

I watch Mirasol's hips sway as she strides to her car. Wide hips, rich with feminine promise. She moves with the ease of a woman confident of her sexual power.

She backs the Camaro out of its parking spot, drives through the exit, and turns onto the road to Salem.

I review the data in my mind. Mirasol's revelations have changed everything. I drain my coffee, pay the bill, and leave. Start Keller's truck, crank the air-conditioning to the max, and peel out of the lot. In the opposite direction to Mirasol's. She's heading to town. I'm going back to the lookout.

The roads around Salem are becoming familiar. I race down the highway toward the Lazy K. Miles of tan ranch grass, mesquite and creosote flank the road. The mesquite trees are stunted. Barely shrubs. In the distance, the hills and more distant mountains are warped by the rippling shimmer of heat. To a trained eye, that mirage indicates wind speed and direction. The single factor most likely to affect the flight of a bullet.

I pass the gate to the Lazy K. Note my odometer. Fifteen miles, and I arrive at the hills. I lean forward in the seat and look for Keller's perimeter road. There it is, a dirt path running parallel to the paved highway. Without slowing, I pull off the concrete and drive onto the dusty track.

This morning I drove counterclockwise and approached the hills from the west. Skirted Bledsoe's fence. Now I drive clockwise and approach from the east. No chance of being spotted from the plant.

The hillsides crack into dozens of broad wadis and shallow draws as I pass. I wonder how I'll ever find the place I parked. How the fuck can a road look completely different than it did in the rearview mirror three hours ago.

Features are reversed.

Out for six months and I'm slowing down.

There's the draw Mirasol used. I spin the wheel and pull off the road. The Ford bounces on its raised suspension. I drive to where Mirasol parked, stop the truck, and get out. Drink, take down the Mauser. Walk a hundred yards west to the draw I used.

Knowing what Mirasol told me, it looks different. Imbued with significance, details spring out.

Two sets of tracks from rugged off-road vehicles. Keller's truck and one other. I take my phone from my hip pocket and photograph them. There, at the mouth of the draw, another set of tracks. I hadn't noticed them earlier. Steel-belted radials, worn on one side. A street sedan out of alignment, the same one parked in front of the Lazy K.

I photograph the sedan's tracks. Take close-ups of the tire wear. Maybe I can compare them to casts Garrick's men took at the crime scene.

There's no doubt in my mind this is a second crime scene. I squeeze the phone into my hip pocket and climb the hill. There is nothing casual about my approach. I carry the Mauser at high port.

I reach Mirasol's outlook. Take my shirt off and drape it over the rifle, shrouding the barrel and telescopic sight. The sun scorches my back. I hold the rifle under the shirt, finger safe on the stock.

On closer inspection, the outlook is a dusty rock shelf. Mirasol had lain prone at the edge, overlooking a steep, rocky slope. At the foot of the slope is the stream and the alluvial plain occupied by the Bledsoe plant and the Lazy K. The contrast is stark. The ranch grows organically from the earth. It is almost indistinguishable from the plain. The plant is distinctly foreign. Its squat, industrial buildings are built on the dark gravel of the parking lot and loading yards. They look like they have been transplanted from another planet.

The footprints Mirasol and I left earlier are gone. The shelf is too hard and windswept to preserve tracks.

I turn a slow hundred and eighty degrees. Behind me are boulders and jagged rocks. Drab shrubs, stunted by the heat, thrust between them in a futile effort to shoulder them aside.

The rock shelf extends around the hilltop. First narrowing, then widening, it struggles for space with the rocks and vegetation.

Shrubs that extend over the shelf look like they have been pressed back. Men have passed that way. I hold the Mauser at my hip and slowly edge around the narrow path.

I come upon a horseshoe clearing on the reverse side of the hilltop. Fifteen feet square and sheltered from the wind. The shallow dust has preserved faint boot prints. I photograph them. It is hard to tell how many men stood there. At least three. Maybe as many as five.

Close to the rock wall is a faint dark patch. Blood. It dripped on the rock, and someone blotted it up. Removed most of it, but enough remained to stain the surface. Dust has begun to obscure it. With the passage of time, it will become barely noticeable. I photograph the discoloration. Decide against trying to sample it.

Tiny running shoe tracks cross the shelf, disturbing some of the boot prints.

Mirasol.

Her tracks lead to a corner of the clearing, and a big creosote bush. Behind it, I find her spoor, desiccated and crumbling. A second mistake Keller would not have made. We have gone for days with spoor wrapped in plastic, buried in our rucks.

Tracking and being tracked. To stay alive, one must not leave a trace.

I turn back to the clearing. Squint. The victim had his back to the wall. The killer stood between him and the edge, leveled his pistol and fired. I estimate the height of Keller's chest and examine the rocks. One of the boulders has been chipped. A deep scar an inch and a half long. Shaped like a comet with a tail.

Following the tail, I see faint chip marks on boulders further along the rock wall.

Bullet splash. The nine millimeter round penetrated the victim's body, hit the rock, and broke up. Fragments splattered and chipped the wall. A forensic team might find pieces, but I doubt much remains.

More photos.

I walk to the edge, turn, and face the wall. Imagine myself staring at a victim. Point a pistol, pull the trigger. The slide snaps back, extracts the spent shell casing, chambers another round. The spent brass flies to my right, rattles on the stone, and rolls—to Mirasol's bush.

I walk to the bush and squat. With the rifle barrel, wrapped in my shirt, I push aside the narrow branches of shrub.

There, on the bare rock, sunlight glints off a shiny object.

An empty nine millimeter shell casing.

16

SALEM, 2000 HRS TUESDAY

To the west, the sky glows blood-red. The border wall is a thin black line rising from the ranch and farmland. I drive at a sedate pace. Salem is fifteen minutes away, and I must decide what to do. Should I tell Garrick and Stein what I know. Do I have enough?

The nine millimeter casing lies in my shirt pocket. I picked it up with a ballpoint pen, careful not to smudge any prints. I have enough evidence to prove Keller was shot on the hilltop.

I can't prove a motive. All I have is Mirasol's story about Paul Bledsoe's sexual preferences and a smuggling operation.

More to the point—I don't want Garrick and Stein to arrest them.

The killers don't deserve to live.

Last night, I spent half an hour speaking to Lenson and Hancock. It was all I could do to convince them to wait in El Paso.

Leave it with me. When I'm sure, I'll call.

Sure of what.

The identities of the killers. There were at least four, though I feel certain only one man wielded the knife. It takes a particular savagery to behead a victim. At a minimum, the killer has divorced himself from human emotion. At worst, he seeks personal gratification. Jihadists did it to express their ideology. Their will to power. Cartels mutilate victims, but not for ideological reasons.

It's dark. The truck's headlights pick up the white Salem sign, and I pull into the turnoff. The lights of the Dusty Burger look warm and inviting. I drive past, go straight to the hotel.

At the very end of the lot, Mirasol's Camaro sits dark and brooding. It is as though she is deliberately separating herself from others.

I take my phone and search for Mirasol's number. Punch the call button.

Mirasol's voice is cautious. "Yes, Breed."

"Where are you?"

"In my room at the hotel."

"I'm going back to the hilltop tonight. Do you want to come?"

"Of course."

"Meet me in the parking lot at eleven o'clock."

I end the call, pocket the phone. Get out of the truck, go into the hotel. The same young woman stands behind the front desk and smiles. "Hi, Mr Breed."

Blond hair, blue eyes. Fetching. With an open look, she invites me to take the time and trouble.

"Hi." The girl's no more than twenty-five. Probably closer to twenty-three. I return her smile, keep my options open. "I'm going into the lounge. Can I get a beer?"

"You sure can. I won't be but a minute."

The lounge is dimly lit. At a table by the window, a slender figure sits, staring at the street. Stein's leather-bound notebook lies open next to a glass of wine. I lower myself into the chair opposite her.

"Care to join me?" Stein asks.

I smile.

"Where have you been all day, Breed?"

I shrug. "Drove over the Lazy K. Checked out the border wall. Looks secure. No breaches, no signs of penetration."

"The Border Patrol checked it thoroughly."

"I like to do my own homework."

"So do I." Stein picks up her Montblanc. Glances at her notebook. "I had your records pulled."

"Why so curious?"

The girl brings my beer. Flashes Stein a look of annoyance.

Stein watches the girl leave. "Didn't take you for a cradle robber, Breed."

"I never take anything doesn't want to be taken."

"You and your friends are quite the crew, Breed. Elite sniper unit, the first into Afghanistan. Served together fifteen years. Until Hancock was shot and Keller retired. Lenson got blown up. Both Hancock and Lenson were medically retired. They get the benefits of twenty and a day, without serving the full term."

"That's standard for medical discharges," I tell her. "They deserve every penny."

"They do," Stein agrees. "You re-enlisted, then retired before your contract was up. You get half pay and half a percent for every additional year you served. Four thousand dollars a month won't win many small wars."

"I'm a simple man, Stein."

"It's the reason you left that interests me."

My throat is dry. I reach for my beer. "Why is that?"

"You shot Afghan women. The army almost court-martialed you."

"The women flayed American POWs. Dragged them through the streets."

"So you shot them."

I force myself to hold Stein's eyes. "You've got the file."

"You claimed the POWs were still alive."

"My spotter confirmed it." I cross my legs. "I would have welcomed a court-martial."

"The army preferred you resign."

"Whatever." I am tiring of the exchange. "They discharged me honorably. I was happy to go."

"Hancock was referred for counseling last year." Stein changes tack. "His colleagues at William Beaumont considered him a suicide risk."

I didn't know that.

"He didn't show up for work one day. A friend went by his place to see if he was okay, found him sitting with a loaded Glock 21 on his desk."

"Constant pain does things to you."

"The prognosis for his nerve damage is not good." Stein turns a page of her notebook. "Lenson runs a sporting goods store. It's close to bankrupt."

"Do you have a point to make?"

"Four veterans, good friends. All in difficulty."

My fist clenches. "Keller wasn't in difficulty."

"We checked his finances. The ranch was cash poor." Stein draws a line under a figure in her notebook. "He had a five million dollar life insurance policy, with his wife as beneficiary. It will clear the mortgage on the Lazy K. Provide working capital."

The amount staggers me. "Five million."

"Keller was by no means wealthy. I told you his ranch is small by Trans-Pecos standards. Further east, a ranch the size of the Lazy K would be worth twenty-five million."

"You think we're involved."

"I have to consider all the possibilities," Stein admits. "My central scenario is that Keller was involved in trafficking drugs or illegals. He was killed in a falling-out with the cartels. You and your friends are very close to him, so I can't exclude the possibility you are involved."

"That's ridiculous."

"No, Breed, it's not." Stein leans forward. "Give me a reason not to suspect you."

"Fifteen years and more serving our country."

"Not good enough."

I think of the hilltop, the nine millimeter casing in my pocket. "I can't help you."

"You will."

The sixth sense that kept me alive in combat kicks in. Mirasol, drawn to Bledsoe. Keller's murder. Stein coming to town. Lenson, Hancock and myself. All of us at the Salem Inn, all in the space of a week. *There are no coincidences.*

"What about you, Miss DOJ? You aren't FBI. You aren't a marshal. Lawyers don't carry SIG Legions. You're a spook."

"What if I am?"

"You arrived Johnny-on-the-spot. That means you're here for something bigger than Keller. When you level with me, I'll level with you."

Stein shakes her head, sips her wine.

17

BLEDSOE, 2300 HRS TUESDAY

The moon is waning. High enough in the sky to provide some light for our trek. I've followed this path twice, and that's enough for me to lead the way. I climb with Keller's binoculars about my neck, his Winchester low-ready. I move slow and smooth. Two yards behind me, Mirasol follows in my footsteps.

We reach the hilltop. Below us, the Bledsoe plant sprawls across the landscape. The buildings are dark aside from a handful of lights along the perimeter fence.

I motion for Mirasol to wait at the lookout. Obediently, she sets down her pack and lowers herself to a prone position. Watches as I continue along the path to the other side of the hill. Check to ensure we are alone.

When I return, she stares at me. "You've been back," she whispers.

"Yes." I drop my ruck next to hers and lower myself. In a quiet voice, I tell her what I found.

"I was there yesterday and the day before," Mirasol says. "I saw nothing."

"You didn't know what to look for."

"You make me feel stupid, Breed. I don't like it."

I take Keller's binoculars and glass the plant. There isn't much to see. Without night vision, I strain to see details. There, in the wide yard next to the factory building, is the long bulk of an eighteen-wheeler. There is no activity. The plant is quiet.

"There's more." I lower the binoculars and look at Mirasol. She looks childlike in the dark. "You're the reason Keller was here."

"What?"

"Think about it. How many times did you see his truck?"

"Once."

"Yes. The morning of the day he saw something—after midnight."

Mirasol's brow furrows. "Oh my God."

"Keller didn't climb up here by accident. Why would he wait all day and night? Because he saw *your* car parked below *all day and night*. On several occasions. He saw it in the morning and drove off. Came back in the afternoon, and it was still there. Drove by late one night—there again. He watched you come and go at least once. Then he decided to find out what was so interesting about Bledsoe."

"You're guessing."

"Informed guesses. He deliberately left his truck where you would see it. He assessed your threat level. If you came up while he was there, he would speak with you. If not, he would stake out Bledsoe himself."

"Yes, and he saw a shipment of girls."

I glass the plant again. Cattle rustle in the pens closest the stream. I imagine the concentrated smell of animal hide and dung drifting on the breeze. A night watchman paces the length of the east fence. I speak to Mirasol while looking through the binoculars. "That much is certain. But it doesn't explain what happened the next day."

"What do you mean?"

"He came back." I make the statement as a matter of fact. "He saw the same thing, and they killed him."

"Why?"

"That isn't the question," I tell her. "The question is... how did they know he was up here. At this point in our narrative, the only person who knew he could have been up here was *you*."

I lower the binoculars and look Mirasol in the eye.

"You think I told them he was here?" Mirasol looks ready to explode.

"That would be a logical absurdity. But someone else found out he was here. Someone who didn't know about you."

"Why do you think that?"

"Whoever killed Keller thought he was the only person who knew about this lookout. Otherwise, they would have posted a guard here the day after. There would be a guard up here now."

"I have told no one about this place, Breed."

"I believe you."

We fall into a moody silence. Mirasol asked Latino townspeople about Paul Bledsoe's attraction to pubescent Mexican girls. Word might make its way back to Bledsoe, but those inquiries are not directly related to the lookout.

Hours pass. Mirasol and I take turns glassing the plant.

"Breed."

Like a switch has been flipped, floodlights blaze to life. They are mounted on the roof of the main factory building and on four towers the length of the cattle pens. Together, the floods bathe the yard in a cold, silver glare.

Two men march from the factory to the eighteen-wheeler. One gets in the tractor's cab and starts the engine. The other checks the power cables connected to the trailer. More men emerge from the factory, open the back doors of the trailer, and lower a lifting platform.

"Now the meat," Mirasol whispers.

Men in long white coats and helmets emerge from the factory. They drive forklifts piled high with pallets of meat product.

I check my watch. It is almost three in the morning.

Stacks of pallets disappear into the cavernous maw of the refrigerator truck. No need for night vision devices here. Every detail of the process is lit with the brilliance of daylight. In the floodlights, stones in the yard sparkle like diamonds. I imagine Keller lying in this spot, a week ago. These binoculars held to his eyes. My stomach flutters with the excitement of the hunt.

When they have finished loading the trailer, the men drive the forklifts back into the factory.

Two men wearing jeans and Stetsons emerge. One is mid-sixties and distinguished. He wears an air of privilege.

"That's Paul Bledsoe," Mirasol whispers.

The other man is big and rawboned, with long blond hair. A caricature of a cowboy, he stands next to Bledsoe with his arms folded.

I turn the binoculars on the loading bay doors. Another cowboy leads a dozen Mexican girls to the truck. They are dressed in street clothes and carry pitiful bundles of belongings. Mostly nylon backpacks. A few small suitcases. The oldest looks sixteen. Most look much younger. They wear sweaters and jackets, but even so, the interior of the trailer will be dreadfully cold. I don't know if they will survive the eleven hour drive to Los Angeles, let alone the thirty-six to New York.

My heart skips a beat.

A swarthy man emerges from the factory. Five-eleven. Long, wavy black hair. Sharp, aquiline features. He wears a dark shirt and black Levi's. Sensible boots. He's lean and fit. Walks with the confidence of a predator.

"Have you seen him before," I ask Mirasol.

"No."

The man checks his watch, confers with Bledsoe. Turns and signals someone inside the factory.

Three more men file through the loading bay doors and go to the trailer. They are all dark and clean-shaven. They wear jeans, boots, and expensive North Face jackets with hoods. They carry their belongings in heavy rucksacks.

All three wear gloves.

"They're dressed for it," I observe.

"Yes," Mirasol says. "Unlike the girls."

The three men get on the cargo lift. The driver's assistant works the controls, and they disappear into the trailer. The trailer doors are closed and dogged shut. The big cowboy mouths something to the driver. The second cowboy speaks into a walkie-talkie.

The plant's east gate opens. The portal's two big doors slide apart, and the eighteen-wheeler's lights spring to life. The driver's assistant gets in the passenger side of the cab and slams the door. The big tractor-trailer rumbles out of the plant toward the highway.

Almost four o'clock.

Followed by the cowboys, Bledsoe and the dark man walk back into the factory. The loading bay doors slide shut. Someone flicks a switch, and the plant is plunged into darkness.

My pupils were constricted by the glare of the floodlights. The instant the switch is pulled, my world goes black. I take the binoculars from my eyes and stare at Mirasol, willing my night vision to return.

"I have never seen that man," Mirasol says. "Men have never joined the girls in the truck."

"As far as you know."

"Correct." Mirasol frowns. "As far as I know."

18

SALEM, 0400 HRS WEDNESDAY

"It's a tunnel," Mirasol tells me.

"You've thought that all along, haven't you."

"Yes," Mirasol says, "but proving it is something else."

Traffic is light as we drive back to Salem. We're quiet, lost in thought. I'd thought of a border tunnel when Mirasol first told me her story. In fact, the existence of a tunnel was a given.

"Where do you think it comes out?" I ask.

"Ciudad Juarez."

I find Mirasol's Latina accent irresistible. Force myself to concentrate on the road. "Juarez is a big place."

White-line fever, they call it. Miles pass before we see another car. In the middle of the road, an endless string of broken white lines flash by. Hypnotic, shining in my headlights, drawing me. I squint, fight to stay in the right lane.

"Why do you need to know where it comes out? We need to get into that plant. Find evidence girls are being smuggled across. Then the police can arrest Bledsoe."

"You want Bledsoe. I want the men who killed my friends."

"You think they are in Juarez."

"A tunnel has two ends. You said yourself Bledsoe goes to Juarez for girls."

Mirasol looks thoughtful. "All right, Breed. Are you good at arithmetic?"

"I can hold my own."

"The Rio Grande is not so big. The banks are about three hundred yards wide."

"Go on."

"The border is full of tunnels. The Border Patrol search for them all the time. The longest they have found is one thousand yards long. Do you see?"

Sexy *and* smart.

"The plant's built right up to the border wall," I say. "We draw a circle with a radius of a thousand yards centered on Bledsoe. The Mexico end will be in the area between the chord of the far bank and the circle's edge."

"The tunnel could be anywhere from three hundred to a thousand yards long."

"Shit." I touch the brake and pull over.

"What are you doing?"

"Come on." I turn on the ceiling light, reach over, and open the glove compartment. I take Keller's map and get out of the truck.

I kneel and undo the lace on my left boot. Spread the map on the hood of the truck, turn on my phone's flashlight, and hand it to Mirasol. "Hold this."

Mirasol holds the flashlight over the map. I take the bootlace and my ballpoint pen. Find the scale and measure a thousand yards. I push the nib of the pen through the fabric, hold the free end over the Bledsoe plant, and stretch the lace taut. With one deft swipe, I draw an arc that spans the Mexican riverbank. Finally, I cap the pen and measure the length of riverbank covered by the arc.

"That chord is eighteen hundred fuckin' yards." I kneel and

re-lace my boot. "What's it like over there?"

"I don't know," Mirasol says. "I never looked too closely."

She suspected a tunnel from day one, but didn't think to look at the Mexican side. An intelligent woman. Not a soldier.

"What do you remember," I ask. "Is it farmland, ranchland, or buildings."

"Buildings," she says. "Juarez is a big city."

"Unlucky for us." I get up, fold the map, and take my phone back. "We'll take a closer look tomorrow. Right now, we need to get a few hours' sleep."

"I don't think I can sleep," Mirasol says.

I need to sleep. In the field, one learns to grab food and rest whenever one can. In combat, one cannot predict the next time one will be able to sleep or eat.

We get back in the truck and I pull onto the highway. "That's a lot of ground to cover on the Mexican side," I say. "Talk to me. Is there any way to make our job easier."

Mirasol shrugs. "It costs money to dig a tunnel. The profit the cartel makes must pay for its construction. The cheapest route is three hundred yards west to east."

"Because in this sector, the river runs south to north."

"That is where I would start." Mirasol looks at me. "Sometimes, the cartels dig north to south to confuse the Border Patrol."

"You know an awful lot about tunnels."

"I interviewed the Border Patrol. America built a wall eighteen feet high." Mirasol shakes her head. "They are digging tunnels eighty feet deep."

"Eighty feet."

"At its deepest point, the Rio Grande is sixty feet deep. The river is almost dry, so that doesn't matter. Ground-penetrating radar is ineffective below forty feet. The Border Patrol has sensors the length of the river. To capture the sounds of digging. Earth and rock have to be removed. The sensors capture the sound of trolleys carrying the earth from the tunnel. The sound of dump trucks carrying the earth away."

"Dump trucks."

"The thousand-yard tunnel required four hundred dump trucks full of earth. The Border Patrol creates heat maps of sounds vehicles make as they travel over bumpy roads. They can tell the difference between a family car and a dump truck."

"Why hasn't the Border Patrol detected this one?"

"The water table in this area is eight hundred feet, so the cartels can tunnel as deep as they like. Last year, Bledsoe expanded the plant. The sound of excavation and construction would have confused the sensors. The project also provided an excuse to use dump trucks to carry earth away."

"That must be one expensive tunnel."

"During the Cold War, the CIA dug a tunnel from West Berlin to East Berlin. It was a quarter of a mile long and cost fifty million in 1955 dollars. The thousand-yard tunnel the cartels dug cost many times that. Bledsoe is a wealthy man, but he could not finance the tunnel himself." Mirasol sounds bitter. "He is an American, yet he made a deal with the cartels."

"That's the other question," I say. "Who are his partners."

"Cartels vie for power all along the border. It is impossible to keep track."

I shake my head. "The dark man you hadn't seen before. He acted like he was Bledsoe's superior."

Mirasol looks skeptical. "You think?"

"Yes. One picks up behavioral cues. He had an attitude of entitlement. An attitude of command."

"It is hard to tell from a distance," Mirasol says, "but I don't think he is Mexican."

Neither do I.

Bledsoe looks soft.

The dark stranger, on the other hand, looks capable of beheading a victim.

19

SALEM, 0800 HRS WEDNESDAY

It's not the first time I've gotten by on three hours' sleep, and it won't be the last. I dress, go down to the dining room, and take the table by the window. The aroma of fried bacon and eggs revives me. I load up on the buffet, chow down, and go back for seconds. When I've finished, I carry a pitcher of freshly squeezed orange juice back to my window table. Pour myself a glass and lean back. Enjoy the air-conditioning. Outside, the sun climbs higher in the sky. The light in my eyes is blinding.

A hundred Latinos stand outside the 7-Eleven, baking in the heat. A handful have found shade, but the rest wait stoically in the sun.

Anya Stein approaches, takes the chair across from me. "You're not shy, are you," she says.

"Look who's talking."

"He takes the whole pitcher of juice," she observes. Pours herself a glass. "Some nerve."

"There's more where that came from. Besides, that's what we do."

Stein smiles flirtatiously. "What, hog the orange juice?"

I feel like a reptile has winked at me. "Take things from people. Fuck anybody gets in the way."

"You and your friends must have been something."

I'm not in the mood. Today I'm going to get inside Bledsoe Meats.

"Help me, Breed."

Two big yellow school buses pull up in front of the 7-Eleven. Three men pile out. Two cowboys and a Latino. The same two cowboys we saw at the plant last night. The big blond guy and his buddy. The Latino carries a clipboard. Stands by the front door of the first bus and takes a pen from his shirt pocket. The Latinos waiting in the heat gather around him.

"I don't see how I can."

I drain a glass of orange juice, savor the flavor, and pour some more.

"It's obvious you know more than you're telling."

Mirasol stands in the group of Latinos. She's got gumption, I'll give her that.

"Is it?" I shake my head. "You think I'm involved."

"Less and less likely. You only left the army six months ago."

Mirasol looks uncomfortable. Like she can't make up her mind if she should stay or leave. She recognizes the cowboys, but there's no reason for them to recognize her. Unless one of the Mexicans she asked about Bledsoe finked on her.

The man with the clipboard begins reading names. One by one, the Latinos get on the bus, and he crosses their names off the list.

A waitress takes my plate and stares disapprovingly at the pitcher of orange juice. She's not the pleasant girl from the front desk. Too young to be the girl's mother. Hired help.

"What's going on there," I ask her.

"Day workers," the woman says. "They fill the quota over at Bledsoe."

"How's it work?"

"Bledsoe has employees to do the regular work. Fewer than he needs, so he doesn't over-hire. Those beaners put their names on a list. Every day, the truck comes down and they hire enough to make up what he needs. Looks like he wants two busloads today."

"Don't they need experience?"

The waitress sniffs. "Most of them have."

With my plate in her hand, she walks away.

I look back at the Latinos queued up at the buses. Squint. Mirasol is in line. Skintight black T-shirt, jeans and running shoes. Passionate, committed, stupid.

"Help me, Breed." Stein leans across the table. "Let's trade."

I pour myself more orange juice. I'm tempted to drink from the pitcher, but Stein couldn't handle it.

Mirasol is at the door of the first bus. The blond cowboy shakes his head and takes her by the arm. His friend takes her other arm. Together, they hustle her away from the bus.

I get up, slide a twenty under my glass.

Stein folds her arms. Scowls. "You *are* a piece of work."

"You have no idea."

I stride from the restaurant, through the lobby, and onto main street. I cross the 7-Eleven's gas station and parking lot. The cowboys and Mirasol disappear behind the building. The Latinos watch them go and mutter. Continue boarding the bus.

A woman grunts. It's the belch of someone who has been hit high in the gut, under the solar plexus. I round the corner in time to see Mirasol collapse in a fetal position. Her hands clutch her midsection, her mouth open in a silent scream.

"That's enough." I close on the men.

The blond cowboy gets between me and Mirasol. He's helping me. Two-on-one, they should split and attack from either side.

"Mind your own business, mister."

"Two strong men beating on a little girl. That's my business."

The blond man steps in to push me. "Fuck off."

Before the words are out of his mouth, I bunch my fingers at the second knuckle and punch him in the Adam's apple. His eyes bulge and he staggers, clutching his throat. His mouth works silently, like a fish out of water. He drops to his knees. His Stetson topples from his head.

The second cowboy swings a roundhouse right at me. An amateur. I block the punch and grab his sleeve with my left hand. Twist my right in the collar of his shirt, drag him over my hip, and put him down. Before he can get up, I stamp on his face. His nose flattens under my heel, and blood squirts out the sides—I popped a blister of ketchup. I stamp on him again. His front teeth—top and bottom—give way.

He'll live. I'm not sure about his blond friend, whose face is turning blue-green.

Mirasol gets to her knees. I grasp her elbow and help her to her feet.

We round the corner of the 7-Eleven.

"That was stupid," I tell her.

"We have to get into that plant." Mirasol clutches my arm. Together, we walk back to the hotel. She's in pain, leans against me for support.

I put my hand over hers. "I'm going this afternoon."

"How are you going to do that?"

"I'll knock on the front door."

20

SALEM, 0830 HRS WEDNESDAY

I see Mirasol to the elevator. She promises to rest, and I promise to keep her posted on what I learn. I warn her to watch for unusual bleeding. Two men beating on a tiny girl with all their strength can cause serious internal injury.

The elevator door hisses shut, and I return to the restaurant.

"Who's your little friend?" Stein asks. The spook is where I left her, sipping a cup of coffee.

I settle myself in the opposite chair. "A girl who got in trouble with a pair of jackasses."

"I saw that. The question is how."

"Doesn't matter." I wave my hand, a gesture of dismissal. "You want to trade, let's trade."

"*What* do you have to trade."

Again, Stein adopts a flirtatious manner. She's no good at it.

"I know where Keller was killed."

Stein straightens in her chair. "The murder scene was staged."

"Yes."

"Of course it was. Where."

I shake my head. "I want something from *you*."

"I'm listening."

"I need your help to search a place."

"Private property, obviously."

"Yes. Your word—you'll get me inside."

"Only if what you give me is enough for a warrant."

"If *you* get in, I get in."

"All right, it's a deal."

Stein finishes her coffee.

I wave to the waitress. "Bring the whole pot."

"Can't take you anywhere," Stein grumbles. "Okay, Breed. Cough it up."

I take the pot of coffee from the waitress. Fill Stein's cup, pour one for myself. Set the pot on the table.

"He was killed seven miles from where he was found," I tell her. "On a hilltop overlooking Bledsoe Meats."

I tell her everything I know, but leave out the shell casing and Mirasol's involvement.

"How did you find the lookout?" Stein asks.

"Educated guess. Keller was a sniper, we're drawn to high ground. Those hills present the only elevated positions south of the Lazy K."

Stein looks skeptical. "What made him suspicious of the plant?"

"Maybe he wasn't. Those hills cover his land and Bledsoe's. He may have been hiking, surveying his property. Looked in the wrong direction, saw something he shouldn't have."

"Random chance?"

"Wrong place, wrong time. Dumb luck can kill you."

"We'll have the lab go over the scene," Stein says. "But it's not enough to get a warrant to search the Bledsoe plant."

"Last night I saw a dozen girls, some as young as twelve, go into a freezer truck with three men. Fifteen illegals."

"It'll be your word against Bledsoe's."

"There's a tunnel under that plant."

"Prove it."

"Get me in. Then I'll prove it."

"Breed, you are accusing a prominent Texas businessman of colluding with cartels. Smuggling prostitutes and God knows what else into the United States. In a tunnel that could have cost a hundred million dollars. Purpose-built, integrated into an American factory. Do you have any idea how crazy that sounds?"

"It's not crazy when the end justifies the means."

"Tell me more about the men you saw."

It's not my imagination. Stein is more interested in the men than little girls smuggled into the United States. "Not much to tell. Dark complexioned, not black. Well fed, fit. Unlike the girls, dressed for the trip. Thick North Face jackets, hoods, gloves, dressed in layers."

"Could they have been Middle Eastern?"

There it is.

"Your turn, Stein. Why are you here."

"I think you've guessed."

I shake my head. "I want to hear it from you."

Time to put up or shut up. Stein folds her arms, exhales through puffed cheeks.

"All right. On Monday, the United States will go to the UN. Under the Nuclear Agreement, we will impose an international arms embargo on Iran. Our intel indicates the Quds Force is planning attacks across the border."

The Quds Force. The unconventional warfare arm of Iran's Islamic Revolutionary Guard Corps, the IRGC. The Quds are tasked with the sponsorship and execution of global terrorism.

"I thought the US withdrew from the Iran Nuclear Agreement."

Stein smiles. "We did. But—the US remains a signatory to the United Nations Security Council resolution. Under the terms of the Nuclear Agreement, a sunset clause will terminate the weapons embargo on Monday. *Unless* a signatory to the resolution tables a motion to extend. The extent of Iran's uranium enrichment violates the agreement. We will impose the embargo."

"Will the Security Council let us do that?"

"They have no choice. We have a veto. The other parties want to pretend the deal is alive. On Monday, we will drive a stake through its heart."

I shake my head. "The Iranians aren't going to like that."

"Quds have been active in Latin America for years. They refrained from attacking because they did not want to jeopardize the deal. Now all bets are off. They sent us a message. If we kill the deal, they will hit us harder than we were hit on 9/11."

"What kind of message?"

"When we withdrew from the deal, it was obvious the embargo would be our next move. The Iranians warned us through covert channels. If we try to renege, they will make us pay in blood.

"The Quds can attack in different ways. We have teams responsible for each avenue. My team has been working the border for a year. Two thousand miles to guard. Airplanes, boats, tunnels—it's a sieve. No idea where to start. Until last Thursday."

"The New York subway attack."

"Yes. A dramatic escalation. They were telling us to stay in the deal or else."

"The deal's that good."

"You know it is. The sweetheart deal of the century. Our last president guaranteed them a path to the bomb in ten years. Gave them one-point-eight billion in small bills. Three different currencies. Dollars, Euros, Swiss Francs. The currency markets are so unstable. We probably paid for that damn tunnel."

"A joint venture of sorts."

Stein nods. "It must be. The Quds and the cartels have put up most of the financing. If you're right, Bledsoe put up the land and cover for the operation. The Quds smuggle terrorists, the cartel smuggles everything else."

"We digress. What led you to Salem?"

"We were all over that subway attack like stink on cheese. They made their first mistake. The battery in one of the bomb assemblies survived the explosions. We traced it to the general store right here in Salem."

Stein smiles and tips her head toward main street.

"You got lucky," I tell her.

"I boarded the first plane to El Paso. Drove into town Friday morning and heard a rancher had been murdered days before."

Stein arrived mere hours before I did. "There are no coincidences."

"No." Stein fixes me with a cold stare. "There *aren't*. One phone call, and I was seconded to the DOJ, in charge of the federal investigation."

"All that, and you can't get a warrant."

"Political correctness, Breed. It's a new world."

"So?"

"Greyhound won't allow the Border Patrol to search its buses. The ACLU and migrant rights groups are filing lawsuits all over the country. The constitutionality of searches is being challenged. Racial profiling, violation of the Fourth Amendment. One of those cases will go to the Supreme Court. That's why we can't search trucks leaving Bledsoe without a warrant."

"What do they want us to do, fight a war with one arm tied around our balls?"

Stein raises her eyes to the ceiling. "Breed, *please*. We have to navigate the new reality. If I am turned down, I will lose credibility with management."

"That's bullshit, Stein."

"Breed, I've spent ten years sucking cock and dealing with

sexist crap you cannot imagine. This is my break. Forgive me for not wanting to fuck it up."

Stein's vulgarity shocks me. "We have a deal. I expect you to make good."

She takes out her notebook and Montblanc. Makes notes. "And I shall. I will need help from you and Sheriff Garrick."

"He's out of his depth."

"Of course he is." Stein frowns at her notes. Her penmanship is immaculate. "With you and me to guide him, it won't be a problem. He has the local relationships."

Stein puts her pen down, explains her plan.

"It could work."

"Thank you."

"I have something else for you."

Stein lifts an eyebrow.

I reach into my shirt pocket and take out a small plastic bag. Inside, the gleaming nine millimeter shell casing. I push it across the table. "A gesture of good faith."

"Is that what I think it is?"

"That's from the round that killed Keller. I'll bet the killer's prints are on it."

For a long moment, Stein contemplates me. She takes the shell casing and puts it in her pocket.

"All right, Breed." Stein gets up. "Let's go."

21

SALEM, 1030 HRS WEDNESDAY

"I want to see this crime scene myself," Garrick says.

Stein and I sit across from the sheriff. He sits behind his scuffed desk, leans back in his squeaky wooden recliner. My eyes take in the dented metal filing cabinets, the gun rack, the trophy wall, the photographs. Once again, I feel like I am facing a caricature of a sheriff. A man from a bygone age. He is the kind of man I would go hunting with, the kind of lawman Salem County needs.

"After we visit Bledsoe," Stein tells him. "We don't want activity on that hilltop to stir things up."

"I don't know." Garrick strokes his chin, stares at me. "What were you doing up there?"

"I tried to put myself in Keller's place. Do what he did, go where he went. Those hills are the only high ground south of the Lazy K. They also overlook Bledsoe. Keller may have been surveying his land. Looked the wrong way, saw something he shouldn't have seen."

It's a flimsy story, but I have Stein and the truth on my side. The bottom line is... it's more important *what* I know than *how* I know it. The more I shove it in people's faces, the more likely I am to provoke a reaction.

"You stayed up there all night."

"Yes. Keller must have seen what I saw."

"This isn't enough for a warrant," Garrick says. "The judge will throw us right out of court."

"We're not asking for a warrant." When she wants to, Stein can be smooth as silk. "No respected American businessman would have a tunnel to Mexico built right into his factory. Yet Mr Breed, poking around the hills, saw what he saw."

Garrick snorts. "What he *thinks* he saw."

"*Exactly*." Stein leans into the sheriff for emphasis. "We are humoring him and politely request Bledsoe do the same. When Breed sees the plant is innocent, this will all go away."

"This is West Texas, Miss Stein." Garrick folds his hands behind his head and leans back. The recliner squeaks. "Folks around here don't take kindly to people who invade their privacy."

"Even the law, Sheriff?"

"*Especially* the law. I won't be any more welcome over there than you will."

"You won't help us."

"I didn't say that. All I'm saying is... I'm not the man to make the call."

"Who is?"

"The mayor's right close to Paul Bledsoe. They both belong to the same clubs in El Paso. Chamber of Commerce and all that."

"Will he make the call?" Stein asks.

"Let's find out." Garrick reaches for his phone.

"Wait," Stein says. "He's not to know more than we intend to tell Bledsoe."

"Breed saw something, we think he's nuts, let's humor him."

"That's about it."

Garrick looks me in the eye. "I won't be lying. Breed, the heat's gone to your head. I think you're seeing things."

I shrug.

The sheriff puts his phone on speaker and dials a number. Posner's hearty voice rumbles from the box. "Well, well, Sheriff Garrick... wants to speak with me. What can I do for you, boy?"

Garrick gives Stein a look that says, *You owe me for this*.

"Mayor," Garrick says. "You are on speakerphone. I got Agent Stein and Mr Breed with me. We got us an *issue*."

"An *issue*. My, my. Tell me all about it, Sheriff."

Garrick details our request.

"Sheriff, you done taken leave of your senses. Breed, what kinda Mescal you been swilling out in them hills. You get the worm, boy?"

I suppress a smile. Watching these two old boys thumping their dicks amuses me. If only the stakes were not so high.

"Mayor," Garrick cuts in. "If you persuade Paul Bledsoe to give us a tour of the plant, I am sure this will all go away."

"No promises, Sheriff. I'll call you back."

Garrick disconnects the call.

"I've done my part," Garrick says. "What do you expect to achieve?"

"There is a tunnel under that plant," I tell him. "We are going to look for evidence it is there. We are going to find where they are hiding it."

"If we find nothing, y'all will let it go."

"No promises, Sheriff." Stein shakes her head. "It depends what we find, and what the circumstances are."

Garrick looks miserable. He was enjoying Salem County until Keller's murder disturbed his quiet life. I doubt he writes many traffic tickets.

"In what sort of business does Martin Posner engage," I ask the sheriff.

"He's made his money," Garrick says. "Partner in one of the

biggest law firms in El Paso. Moved out here years ago for the peace and quiet."

Posner has a lucrative career. It makes sense that he would enter local politics in the town he decided to make his home.

We stare at each other for fifteen minutes. The phone rings. Garrick punches the speakerphone. "Garrick."

"I've spoken to Bledsoe, and he wasn't happy." Posner pauses for effect. "Afraid I had to throw you under the bus, boy."

Garrick grits his teeth. "Will he do it?"

"Be outside the plant at one o'clock. Bledsoe will show you around personally. Sheriff, you owe me."

"Thank you, Mayor."

Posner laughs from deep in his belly. "Don't thank me yet, boy. You don't *know* what you owe."

22

BLEDSOE, 1300 HRS WEDNESDAY

I stop Keller's Ford next to Garrick's Jeep in the Bledsoe parking lot. We're at the back of an ocean of cars, two hundred yards from the fence. Next to me, dark hair in a bun, Stein stares at the plant through designer sunglasses.

"Any thoughts before we go in?" Stein asks.

Garrick dismounts, hitches his belt, and waits for us to join him.

"I think we should go in with independent eyes," I tell her. "Neither of us should prejudice the other. We can compare notes after."

I open the driver's door and step onto Bledsoe land. My boots crunch on gravel. Sticky with sweat, I follow Garrick to the plant's east gate. Dressed in her signature black pantsuit and designer glasses, Stein walks beside me. She wears sensible, flat-heeled dress shoes, polished glossy black. The faintest touch of dust is visible at the edge of her soles. I imagine her sitting in her hotel room, wetting a finger and swiping the shoes clean.

Two security guards wait at the gate. Garrick signs a log, and one of the men leads us to the main building. Two refrigerated eighteen-wheelers stand parked at the loading bay. Scores of pallets are disappearing into their gullets.

The guard takes us to the office block and leaves us in the reception area. The decor is clean and modern. White walls, white leather sofas, broad glass coffee tables. There is a desk with two attractive Latina receptionists. They offer us seats, bring us tall glasses of iced water. I'm struck by their understated sensuality.

Handpicked.

Bledsoe makes us wait half an hour. An obvious power play. Comes downstairs looking exactly as he appeared last night. Stetson, crocodile boots, jeans, brass rodeo belt. His embroidered western shirt is fastened at the throat with a bolo tie. Black cord, silver bolo tips, a turquoise stone set in a silver arrowhead.

Garrick shakes Bledsoe's hand and introduces us. I'm surprised by the man's flaccid grip. His baby-soft hands. I say nothing, wait for him to make the first move.

"Mr Breed," he says. "Mayor Posner says you think you saw something unusual last night."

"I saw young Mexican girls loaded into one of those trucks."

The receptionists occupy themselves with matters on their desks. The state of their fingernails. Their ears are cocked, straining to hear every word.

"We did load a shipment some time before sunup," Bledsoe says smoothly. "You may have seen some of our staff taking inventory of the contents. We take inventory and check the temperature before a truck is factory sealed. The seal is not broken until it arrives at its destination."

"I know what I saw. They didn't look like staff. Neither did the three men who joined them."

"How far away were you, Mr Breed?"

"Half a mile. Up on that hill." I step to the wide picture windows of the reception area and point to Mirasol's lookout.

"Well, that's quite a ways, Mr Breed. At that distance, how can you be sure?"

"I used binoculars."

"I see." Bledsoe looks skeptical. "What were you doing up there at such an hour?"

"I was hiking in the hills and got lost. If you hadn't turned on the lights, I'd still be up there."

Bledsoe looks at Garrick, then at Stein. "Mayor Posner assured me this was an informal visit. You have no warrant, and you are looking for nothing specific. Under those conditions, I agreed to show you around."

"We'd sure appreciate it, Mr Bledsoe." Garrick strives to convey the right amount of obsequiousness.

Bledsoe looks at me. "Mr Breed, you didn't see what you think you saw. No hard feelings. I'll take you on a private tour of our plant. It's brand new, and we're right proud of it. Fair enough?"

The man steps to the reception desk without waiting for my reply. He singles out one of the girls. "Have Frank meet me at the restraint line in twenty minutes."

"Yes, Mr Bledsoe." The young girl's accent sounds like Mirasol's.

Bledsoe smiles and the girl lowers her eyes.

"Let's start in the loading yard," Bledsoe says. He opens the door and we step into the heat.

"We employ around two thousand people in this plant." Bledsoe sweeps his arm like a Roman emperor. "That's more than half of Salem's population."

We walk past the two eighteen-wheelers. The air spilling from the loading bay is chilled, a stark contrast to the hot air that surrounds us. The cool breeze brushes my cheek. It smells like plastic and packaged food.

"I think we'll skip the loading bay," Bledsoe chuckles. "Reckon Mr Breed got an eyeful last night."

On the other side of the loading bay are the holding pens and east fence. Beyond that, the foothills and Mirasol's lookout. Between the pens and the fence is another gravel yard. The space is empty.

"The cattle arrive in trucks," Bledsoe explains. "They back up to those gates, and the cattle are loosed into the holding pens. They run down a chute with a slip-resistant surface. We treat those animals with tender loving care, let me tell you. Don't want no bruising. Don't want to waste no meat."

Bledsoe leads us toward the factory building, points out features of the pens. Water pipes are suspended over the chutes. They are used to shower and disinfect the animals before slaughter.

"The animals come through the chute and into our restraint unit," Bledsoe says. "This is where we stun them."

He opens a door and we enter the building. Workers in white coats and helmets recognize him. Careful to stay out of his way, they go about their work.

Next to the cattle chute stands the blond cowboy I met this morning. He's wearing the same clothes, but has a red kerchief tied around his neck. Must have quite the bruise. Wonder if he talks.

"Frank," Bledsoe greets him. "Good to see you. This here's Frank, my right hand."

Frank shakes our hands, saves me for last. I prepare myself for a crushing grip, find his handshake dry and firm. His eyes are malevolent.

"Explain the stunning process to our friends," Bledsoe says.

"Yes, sir."

Frank ushers us to a raised wooden platform. "Y'all want to see, you have to come up here."

We climb the steps and line up at a rail constructed of two-inch lead pipe.

My mind races.

Bledsoe and Frank knew Mirasol had been asking questions. Probably turned in by one of the Latinos she approached. This morning, Frank did not know me. Now he does, and they know Mirasol and I are associated. We're *both* in danger.

"The cattle come through one at a time," Frank says. "That there is the restraining device."

Two men stand on either side of a narrow pen at the end of the chute. A contraption of bars and levers sits at one end. A cow sticks its head into the pen, and one of the men pulls a handle. The restraining device closes on the cow's neck, holding it tight.

"The animal is restrained. We don't waste no time—watch."

The second man reaches down with what looks like a nail gun. Presses it flat against the forehead of the animal and fires. The animal slumps.

"That there's the stunning device," Frank drawls. "See, that gun there destroys a steer's brain."

Frank turns and leads us down a flight of steps on the other side of the platform. "That all right, Mr Bledsoe?"

"You can go, Frank." Bledsoe smiles. "I'll take it from here."

I'll bet you will.

I watch Frank go. Bledsoe could have handled that demonstration himself. He wanted Frank to identify me. Of course, Frank's buddy is undergoing reconstructive surgery.

Bledsoe turns to Stein. "Hope y'all ain't *squeamish*, miss," he says. "I promise you from here on, these animals ain't feeling no pain."

We're indoors, and Stein has not removed her sunglasses. If Bledsoe is unnerved, he gives no indication.

Men with long knives stab the cattle in the chest to sever the arteries leading from their hearts. "Stunning destroys the animal's brain," Bledsoe explains. "This process kills the animal."

The process of slaughtering cattle is interesting, but not what I came to learn. "You said this plant is brand new."

"This is part of the original plant," Bledsoe explains. "We expanded the production lines towards the back of the building. Doubled the processing capacity."

"How could you double the processing capacity," Stein asks.

"We added a second stunning line. I'll show you."

The cavernous plant is dominated by conveyor belts and meat hooks. We watch as carcasses are skinned, gutted, and sawn in half. Spinal columns are removed in compliance with Mad Cow Disease regulations. There is no escaping the sickly sweet stench of gore.

We move deeper into the plant. By now, we are very close to the Rio Grande. We are in a large room where two uniformed men in blue coveralls are marking carcasses. Marked carcasses are pulled aside and dragged to a separate chamber.

"This is the new part of the plant," Bledsoe says.

We are still above ground. I don't know how much of the plant is below the surface, but it can't be much.

"These men are US Department of Agriculture inspectors," Bledsoe explains. "Regulatory standards are strict. If there is any question about the quality of a carcass, it is stored in that room. The USDA Retain Cage. More testing is performed. If a carcass is rejected, it's used for fertilizer. Only USDA inspectors have keys to the cage."

I step to the Retain Cage, poke my head in. It is larger than I thought. A hundred and fifty feet square. Rows of racked carcasses hang like giant bats. The floor is concrete, with drains in the middle and along the edges. On the far side of the room is another set of locked doors.

"Mr Breed," Bledsoe calls. "Will y'all join the group, please. This is a dangerous work environment."

We're led through a door and up a long corridor.

"Y'all been through the harvesting plant. This here's the fabrication plant."

Bledsoe leads us into a factory the size of an airplane hangar. Hundreds of men and women stand at conveyor belts as slices of meat roll past them. They inspect, slice, and trim the product. Machines plastic-wrap the cuts of beef, sorted by type and grade. Then the meat is packed into cardboard boxes and palletized.

"This here's one floor." Bledsoe beams. "We have another two, underground. It's cooler down there, more efficient for our air-conditioning."

"What's below us," I ask.

"That's where we make hamburger, Mr Breed." Bledsoe laughs. "Grinders big as box cars. Grind and test, grind and test. Keep that lean-fat ratio in line. Kind of like people."

I think of the *soldado* Mary shot.

Wonder if people are eating him with their French fries.

23

BLEDSOE, 1500 HRS WEDNESDAY

Stein wrinkles her nose. “I can still smell it.”

“You’ll smell it for a year,” I say. “When you think you’ve forgotten it, it will come back at odd times.”

“How do you know that?”

“It smells like a battlefield.”

We walk with Garrick to the parking lot.

“I want to see that hilltop,” Garrick says.

“Follow me,” I tell him.

The sheriff gets in his Jeep. Stein and I go to the pickup.

“Satisfied now?” Stein looks annoyed. “No evidence. That was a whole lot of nothing.”

“I wouldn’t say that.” I open the driver’s door, start the engine, and wait outside while the air-conditioner kicks in.

“Oh, you wouldn’t. Bledsoe practically laughed in our faces the whole time.”

“Get in,” I tell her. “I need to make a phone call.”

Stein gets in the truck, slams the passenger door.

I take out my phone and dial Mirasol.

“Breed,” she says. “Where are you?”

“Bledsoe.”

"Did you get inside the plant?"

"Yes. Stay in the hotel, stay around other people. We're both in danger."

"What happened?"

"I'll explain later."

I put the phone away and get into the truck. The air-conditioning has filled the cab with blessed cool air.

"We're sitting on the evidence," I tell Stein.

"What?"

I smile. "Look around you. What do you see."

"Cars. A parking lot."

"The whole plant," I say, "is built on crushed gravel. Tailings from the tunnel. A couple hundred dump trucks full."

Stein looks out the passenger window as though seeing the parking lot for the first time.

"A thousand-yard tunnel spits out four hundred dump trucks of earth," I tell her. "This tunnel coughed up at least that much. The plant's foundations are two levels deep under the fabrication plant. It's big, but that's not enough to account for four hundred dump trucks."

I pull out of the parking lot and speed back to the highway. Keller's truck kicks up rooster tails of dust in Garrick's face.

"Bledsoe and his partners had to be careful. The project is too important to blow through overconfidence. They decided they could explain away half the tailings by excavation. The rest they laid down on the parking lot and loading yards. Under the newly constructed sections of the harvesting plant. Crushed it flat with road rollers. Compare it to the earth everywhere else on the alluvial plain. The gravel is a different color, a different consistency."

"How long have you known this?"

I slow down, turn the wheel, and bounce the truck off the highway and onto Keller's perimeter road. This is familiar ground. I tear toward the hills. I want to show Garrick the murder site and get back to Mirasol.

"I only put it together after touring the plant," I say. "When we get to the lookout, it will be plain as the nose on your face."

"Where's the tunnel?"

"Big plant. Two thousand employees. Can't have someone stumbling on it."

"Come on, Breed. Where is it?"

"It's in the newly built section of the plant, in a spot very few people have access to." I wink at Stein. "Only one place fits that bill—the Retain Cage."

"Only USDA inspectors have keys to that cage."

"Bledsoe has a private key. His crew has the run of the place after hours."

"There must be rules. Controls."

I shake my head. "Bledsoe has a key. If he doesn't, he can bribe an inspector easily enough."

When we reach Mirasol's draw, I park, get out, and take Keller's Winchester.

"Expecting trouble?"

I stare at my reflection in Stein's sunglasses. "They've killed three times, and they know we're onto them. You should lock and load, Stein."

"I always keep one in the chamber."

"Good to know." I look at her shoes. "You'll ruin those."

"I have spares at the hotel."

I am sure she does.

Covered in dust, Garrick catches up to us. Eyes the shotgun with suspicion.

I lead them to Keller's draw. Point out the truck's tire tracks. The tracks made by the second ATV and the sedan with the worn right-side tread. "Those steel-belted radials are the same as those at the Lazy K. Whoever killed Mary and Donnie were here for Keller's murder. At least two cartel *soldados*."

"How do you know that?" Garrick asks.

"I saw two Latinos parked at the 7-Eleven across from the hotel. Blue Impala sedan, front end out of alignment."

Stein sniffs. "Aren't you full of surprises."

"They weren't alone," I tell her. "Those off-road tires carried another killer or two."

Winchester low-ready, I turn on my heel and climb the hill. Garrick follows me, and Stein brings up the rear. When we reach the top, Garrick is breathing heavily. Stein looks chill. Probably does four triathlons a year.

"Nice view," Stein says.

"Already seen it." I smile. "Come on. I'll show you where it all happened."

I move slowly and deliberately. Lead Garrick and Stein around the shelf to the back of the hilltop. I carry the Winchester with a shell in the chamber, external hammer cocked, safety on.

"Stand here," I instruct them. "You don't want to disturb any remaining tracks. That dark spot on the rock—blood. If there's enough for DNA, the lab boys will prove it's Keller's. The bullet fragmented on the rock wall behind. You can see the chips and scars from the splash."

I lead them back to the lookout.

"I'll call the crime scene team," Garrick says. He starts back down the hill.

Stein and I stare at the plant. "It stands out, doesn't it," she says.

"Sure does. When I first saw it, I thought it was remarkable how the Lazy K sprang organically from the earth. Bledsoe looks like it's from another planet."

The plain sweeps from the foot of the hill, under the plant, to the border wall. Beyond, the dry ravine of the Rio Grande, the Mexican bank, and a seemingly endless sweep of dirty buildings.

"Imagine eighteen hundred yards—a mile." I point to the Mexican bank, trace a chord with my finger. "The Quds you want are there."

Stein's voice is pensive. "I can't kill them in Mexico."

"That's why they won't come until they are ready."

I carry the Winchester with the barrel exposed to the sun.

"Aren't you supposed to shroud the barrel?" Stein says.

"It doesn't matter anymore. They know where to find us."

"Doesn't that worry you?"

"I'm counting on it."

24

CHIHUAHUA DESERT, 1600 HRS WEDNESDAY

I leave Stein and Garrick at the lookout. Deputies and crime lab technicians are on their way. When I reach the truck, I replace the Winchester in its rack. I get in, drive east, and pull onto the highway.

The blue Impala swings into position a hundred yards behind me. The heads of two *soldados* are visible through the windshield. The driver has long hair and a thick mustache. The same pair from the 7-Eleven. Parked on the shoulder, they sat and waited for me to drive back to town.

Light bar flashing, a sheriff's department cruiser speeds toward me. Heading for the lookout. Behind him, a plain sedan with red and blue lights mounted behind the grille. Driver and four passengers—the forensic team. Another sheriff's cruiser brings up the rear. They roar past, the sound of their engines fading with the Doppler effect. In the rearview mirror, they dwindle to the vanishing point.

A hundred yards back, the Impala holds position.

The *soldados* will make a move well before we reach Salem.

How are they armed. If past experience is any indication,

the ubiquitous AK47. Nine millimeter automatics. If I'm lucky, machine pistols.

It is possible to fight from a vehicle, but I can't do it alone. Neither the Mauser nor the Winchester will be any good. Aimed fire will be impossible with the Mauser, and it is a myth one cannot miss with a shotgun.

The Winchester's buckshot will scatter at a rate of half an inch for every yard. If the *soldados* pull up next to me at a range of five yards, my pattern will measure two and a half inches across. In a moving vehicle, firing with one hand, that's not much better than a Mauser.

Fighting from vehicles, the *soldados* have the advantage.

I need to fight them in the open.

The Lazy K's gate flashes by on my left.

The Impala surges forward. One moment, it is a hundred yards back. The next, it's tailgating me. The man in the passenger seat is carrying an automatic rifle. The muzzle pokes from his open window.

Right now, my most effective weapon is the truck.

The driver swings the Impala into the left lane and pulls even. I'm staring into the muzzle of a rifle.

I stamp on the brakes and the Impala overshoots. The gunman twists in his seat, leans as far as he can out the window, and opens fire. Spinning the wheel, I pull off the highway and take off cross-country.

In the rearview mirror, I see the Impala swerve to give chase.

Keller's truck, with its five-liter V8, is built for this. The Impala, with its low ride and V6, is not. I open up a healthy gap of a hundred yards. In the distance lies a line of foothills. Beyond, the more imposing peaks of mountains.

I step on the gas and race ahead of the Impala. Keller's truck tramples creosote and sage. Dodges between cacti, yucca trees, and clumps of mesquite. The Impala bounces and lurches from side to side. This is no contest. The *soldados* fall behind with every mile, but they refuse to give up.

A plan has formed in my mind. Combat is a string of decisions, often made in the moment. One can spend weeks preparing a target deck. Fancy PowerPoint presentations to sell mission proposals to commanders. Once in the field, it is about execution.

I've opened up a half a mile on the *soldados*. If the Impala shakes itself apart on the rough terrain, I'll change the plan. I need a bigger lead. Faster and faster, I push the truck toward the hills. Behind me, the Impala becomes a dark speck. Lost in the shimmering mirage.

The hills rear up in front of me. They are taller and rockier than I thought.

My lead on the Impala has grown to more than a mile.

The ground has become so rocky I cannot drive further without damaging the pickup. I stop twenty yards from the base of a hillside. I open the glove compartment, take out two stripper clips, and pocket them. Scrabble for Keller's laser rangefinder. I dismount the vehicle, grab the Mauser, and jog to the base of the hill.

The slope is not steep, but it is rocky and hard going. My legs burn with the effort of the climb. The breath rasps in my chest. Behind me, the Impala eats up my lead. I am filled with exhilaration and the joy of the hunt.

I stop for breath. Sling the rifle, fix the rangefinder on the truck, take a reading. Two hundred and eighty yards. The Impala is heading straight for me. The *soldados* decide I've nowhere to run. They're right. I turn and keep climbing.

My legs grow heavy.

I hear the splatter of bullets against the rocks above me. I see rock chips flying as AK47 rounds strike the boulders. The sound is like rain on concrete, magnified a hundred times.

Gasping, I flatten myself against a boulder. Look back.

The Impala has slowed to a stop next to the truck. The *soldados* have gotten out and raised their AK47s to their shoulders. They're firing at me, but their shots sail high over my head.

Not a surprise. In trained hands, the AK47 is reasonably accurate to three minutes of angle at four hundred yards. These *soldados* are not trained marksmen. They are not adjusting their sights for the slope of the hill. They are used to fighting in a phone booth.

I pin the laser on the Impala and take another reading. Four hundred thirty yards, line of sight. I push a button on the rangefinder and switch to inclinometer mode. The device calculates the cosine of the angle made between true horizontal and my line of sight. The digital reading is zero-point-eight-seven, equivalent to about thirty degrees.

A quick mental calculation gives me the range adjustment. The horizontal range is three hundred and seventy-five yards. Keller zeroed his scope at four hundred yards. With Mauser ammunition, the twenty-five yard difference is worth three-quarters a minute of angle.

The *soldados* stand exposed in full view. Drop their mags and reload. Their next burst of fire is closer. They don't understand external ballistics, but they know enough to walk their fire into me. I take the Mauser and shift position to the other side of the boulder. Chamber a round, take aim through the telescopic sight.

Keller's optic is a rugged 3.5-10x variable power scope calibrated in minutes of angle. I set the scope to 10x, but don't bother to dial in the adjustment. I lay the cross-hairs on the chest of the younger man. Reading off the scale on the vertical reticle, I lower my aim by three-quarters an MOA.

I normalize my breathing. Take up the slack on the trigger. Exhale. At the moment of natural respiratory pause, I break the shot.

The Mauser slams into my shoulder and the muzzle jerks skyward. When the sight picture stabilizes, the *soldado* is flat on his back. The front of his shirt is crimson and he is coughing blood from shattered lungs.

I lift the bolt handle, eject the spent shell casing, and chamber a second round. Search for the mustached *soldado*.

He's ducked behind the driver's door of the Impala.

Without lifting his head, he raises the AK47 over the driver's side window and sprays the hill. He empties his entire magazine into the hillside a hundred yards below my position.

Below the car door, the *soldado's* feet are visible.

I lay the cross-hairs on one of his ankles. Drop the sight by the angle-of-fire adjustment, break a second shot.

The round shatters the man's ankle and he screams. The shriek is so loud it echoes from the hillside. The man's foot hangs by a thin strap of skin and tendon. He drops his rifle and crawls behind the wheel. Starts the engine.

I cycle the action, chamber a third round.

The man struggles to get the car moving. He's lost all rational thought. His head is exposed behind the glass of the windshield.

I lay the cross-hairs on his chin and pull the trigger.

With the three-inch adjustment, I should hit him in the middle of the face. The slope of the windshield deflects the round—the top of his head vaporizes in a bright pink mist.

I take a breath and walk down the hill.

The young guy I shot in the chest is still alive, bleeding out from his chest and lungs. He coughs blood. It bubbles from his mouth and drips from the sides of his face. I kick his rifle aside and search him. Take a Glock from his waistband and stuff it in mine.

The man's wallet holds a Mexican driver's license. I compare the photograph to the face of the man at my feet. His eyes are wide and staring. I'm not sure he can see anything.

Alejandro Ruiz.

The other *soldado* is sitting behind the wheel of the Impala, his head rocked back. The man's scalp and the top of his skull are gone. The back of the car is messier than Bledsoe's abattoir. The lobes of the man's cerebral cortex have slopped onto the floor of the rear passenger compartment. His face has been distorted like a rubber Halloween mask.

Grotesque, but not the worst I've seen. I've killed High Value Targets with head shots. Photographed them to provide evidence they were neutralized. Pieced their heads together to get useful images.

I reach in and search the Mexican. Relieve him of a second Glock and a spare magazine. I turn his pockets inside-out. Take his wallet. Mexican driver's license. Jaime Rodriguez.

From his front pocket, I take a folded bar napkin. I spread it on the hood of the Impala. In black ink, someone has scribbled a phone number. In the middle of the napkin is printed the name of the establishment:

LA CUEVA
Ciudad Juarez

The keys are still in the Impala's ignition. I shut the engine off and take the keys. Unlock the trunk. No spare. They would have been in some fix had they blown a tire. A nylon tarp has been spread across the bottom of the trunk. There is a large brown spot on the sheet. This is how Keller was transported from the hilltop to the staged murder scene.

A quick inspection of the Impala's tracks confirms the story. The tires on the right side are worn.

I go to Keller's truck. I stuff the two driver's licenses in my hip pocket. Lay the Glocks on the bench seat. They are both nine millimeters. One at a time, I eject their magazines, check their chambers, and reload them. Both mags are full. Neither pistol has been fired.

Neither weapon was used to murder Keller. These men were involved. They transported Keller's body. They transported other killers to the Lazy K to kill Mary and Donnie. But —they did not shoot Keller.

I place one of the Glocks, the rangefinder, and the stripper clips in the glove compartment. The second Glock, I stuff into my waistband. Pull my shirt over it. I take three loose rounds of Mauser ammunition, top up the rifle's magazine, and replace it in the rack.

Alejandro Ruiz turns his head to look at me. I guess his optic nerves are still firing, transmitting images to his brain. His lips move.

The wounded *soldado*, I leave to die. I hope it takes a long time. I hope the animals get him.

I need to trace a phone number.

25

SALEM, 1800 HRS WEDNESDAY

Garrick's Jeep is parked in front of the sheriff's station. I drive past and continue to the hotel. At the far end of the lot, Mirasol's Camaro occupies its usual spot.

I park next to Stein's Civic. Go inside, greet the pleasant blond girl at the front desk. She smiles.

Maybe, when this is over.

"May I take one of those?" I ask.

"Of course," she says. "As many as you like."

The girl pushes a small stack of hotel business cards toward me. I take one and copy the phone number from the napkin onto it.

"Thank you." I pocket the card.

The girl tries to hide her disappointment. "Anything I can do to help," she says. "Anything at all."

Stein is in the lounge, staring at a laptop. She wears reading glasses. Probably the pair she wore through Harvard Law. She looks up at me. "Where have *you* been?"

Can't blame her for wondering. I left before them, but she and Garrick beat me back. I'm dusty and sweaty. Like I've been on a month-long hike.

"Killing people," I tell her.

"Be serious."

"I need your help with this." I hand her the phone number. "We need to trace it."

"Where'd you get it?"

"The man on the other end of that number," I tell her, "could be the murderer."

"Have you tried calling it?"

"Why would I tip him off?"

Stein takes the number and types furiously. "There."

"There, what?"

"I messaged my team in DC to run the number."

"What about the shell casing?"

"We lifted good prints." Stein looks satisfied. "If there are matches in our database, I'll know tonight."

"What are you up to."

"Preparing a presentation."

I'm not surprised. The military and intelligence agencies are no different from any corporate bureaucracy. The government spends two million dollars a head teaching Deltas to kill. Management makes them piss around for hours harmonizing fonts in PowerPoint.

Stein is ambitious, but she is not your run-of-the-mill careerist. She's single-minded. On the ground, doing the work. I wonder how long she'll last before her fire winds down. I hope it doesn't.

"The plant."

"Yes," Stein admits. "We still don't have enough to get a warrant, but the clock is ticking. Monday afternoon, the United States *will* kill the nuclear deal. We don't know exactly what the Quds have in mind. The New York City subway attack was only a taster."

"Why can't the Border Patrol search for a tunnel?"

"I've briefed the Border Patrol. They search private property all the time. But those are usually range land, culverts, or rights of way. Not inside a factory. The owners are happy to cooperate. In this case, Bledsoe's lawyers will resist."

"This is a case of national security."

Stein shrugs. "Can't fight city hall."

Annoying phrase.

"What's going on there?" I jerk my head toward the lounge widescreen.

The image is an overhead shot of a large warehouse. The building is surrounded by dozens of vehicles with flashing lights. Police cars, ambulances, fire trucks.

Stein gasps. "Oh no."

Silent, I read the captions scrolling across the bottom of the screen.

This hour, terrorists struck a Los Angeles nightclub. Three gunmen armed with automatic rifles, wearing explosive vests, entered and opened fire. For thirty minutes, they shot people indiscriminately. When police attempted to break into the club, the gunmen resisted. There are reports of police casualties. Moments ago, the three men detonated their suicide vests. As yet, there has been no official statement, but we expect loss of life to be high.

"It takes eleven hours to drive from El Paso to Los Angeles," I say. "Those were the three I saw get on the truck last night."

Stein's laptop and mobile phone ding. Again and again.

"Your people are going crazy," I observe.

"Wouldn't you? This is the second attack in two weeks." Stein frowns. "Every station is vying for attention. The whole board is flashing red."

"Yet *you* have the only real piece of evidence," I say. "The battery."

"Mexico City station reports Faisal Hamza has been sighted

in Chihuahua. He's the number one Quds Force operator in Latin America."

"Chihuahua's not far from the border, is it."

"This may be the United States, but we are sitting in the Chihuahuan desert." Stein takes her phone and taps it. Turns the device's screen toward me. "This is Faisal Hamza. Made his bones in Lebanon, Syria, and Iraq. We have intel he's been summoned to Venezuela to coordinate Quds operations in the field."

The photograph is of a swarthy man in his early forties. Close-cropped hair, chocolate-chip camouflage uniform, badges of rank. The three blooms of an Iran Revolutionary Guard Corps colonel. From the screen, his cruel eyes stab the viewer.

It's the man I saw with Bledsoe.

"He's not in Chihuahua."

"How do you know?"

"I saw him at the plant last night. He acted like Bledsoe's boss."

"Are you sure?"

"He's grown his hair out—long and wavy. Looks more Latin. It's him."

"Would you swear to it?"

"I'm a sniper, a trained observer. I know what I saw."

Stein shivers with excitement. "Hamza made his name fighting the Islamic State. He outdid them in savagery. He massacred whole villages whose only crime was paying tax to IS. He captured IS fighters. The ones he didn't behead immediately, he tortured to death. He turned the same tactics on our people."

"Faisal Hamza is an Arabic name," I observe. "Not Persian."

"He's Shia Lebanese." Stein stares at the photograph as though hypnotized. "Qasem Soleimani's most ruthless enforcer.

Soleimani personally recruited Hamza as a weapon. A pure killer. He murders for fun."

"Has he moved up since we took out Soleimani?"

"Apparently so. Soleimani knew how to control Hamza. Without Soleimani, the Quds are starved of leadership. They need to *do* things to retain the initiative. Hamza is viewed as the answer to their problems."

"His Quds masters sent him to Venezuela to take the war to the Great Satan."

"The Quds and Hezbollah have been active in Latin America for a long time," Stein says. "But they have been shy of attacking the United States. They did not want to fuck up the nuclear deal. Hamza was sent to shake the box."

"A maniac."

Stein's laptop dings. She scans the email. "We've identified the phone," she says. "A burner, purchased in El Paso. Paid for with cash, topped up with cash. It's been turned off, so we can't trace it."

"Damn."

"Come on, Breed. Where did you get the number."

"I can't tell you, Stein. Not yet."

"Breed, I *cannot* work like this. You cannot keep me in the dark."

"Do you like what I'm bringing you?"

Stein slaps her hands flat on the table. She's ready to leap to her feet. "Yes, but—"

"Stein." My voice is hushed. "You have to let me help you —*my* way."

"You think this is Hamza's phone?" Stein settles back in her chair.

"I think it *could* be Hamza's phone. Have your people stay on it. The minute it is switched on, they *have* to tell you where it is."

Stein stares out the window for a long moment. Turns back to me. "All right, Breed. Let's trade."

"Oh hell." I lean back in my chair. "Trade *what.*"

"Your little friend." Stein's eyes glitter. "You tell me where you got the phone, and I'll tell you what I know about Mirasol Cruz."

My stomach hollows. "How do you know anything about Mirasol?"

Stein leans forward, her smile crafty. "She used her real name at the front desk—you knew I'd check. Those cowboys beat the shit out of her for a reason."

In fact, I didn't stop to think Stein would check. I was too preoccupied with Bledsoe. "No deal, Stein."

"The young lady has an interesting past," Stein teases.

I cannot tell Stein about the men I killed. Not yet. "I said, no deal."

Stein leans back, disappointed. "Suit yourself."

The woman is a piece of work. But then, she's said the same about me. I stare at the widescreen.

The widescreen shows images of stretchers and gurneys being carried from the club. The camera pans over the sidewalk, where corpses are lined up in neat rows. The camera blurs the faces of the dead. Limbs have been blown from bodies along with clothing and shoes. In an explosion, a powerful shock wave expands rapidly, destroying everything in its path. Viewers are witnessing the impact of high-velocity, military-grade explosives.

"Breed, I am going to act on your intel. Your sighting is going in my presentation. If you're wrong, my career is over."

"Is that all you care about?"

"Breed, I love my country. I can't do any good filling out forms in Anchorage."

Stein means it. I exhale through puffed cheeks. "Okay, what are you asking for?"

"I want to go into Bledsoe with a fucking hit squad."

"You have to get the timing right, Stein. If you don't, you *will* lose Hamza."

26

SALEM, 2000 HRS WEDNESDAY

I go to my room. Take the Glock from my waistband, lay it on the bed. In the bathroom, I shower and change my shirt.

When I have finished, I close my eyes and gather my thoughts. Wonder what Stein learned about Mirasol. Her interesting past. Do I trust Mirasol? More than most, and now—I need her.

I pick up my phone and call Mirasol. I am surprised how glad I am to hear her voice.

"Breed. Where have you been?"

"Killing people."

Mirasol hesitates. "Who?"

I smile.

"*Dos soldados*," I tell her. "They were involved in the murder of Keller and his family."

"You said we are in danger."

"We are. One of the men who beat you up was at the plant and recognized me. The bad guys know who we are, they have connected us. The *soldados* were sent to kill me. I need your help."

"What do you want?"

"Do you have a laptop and access to the hotel internet?"

"Yes."

"We can't go downstairs. Stein is pulling an all-nighter in the lounge. Your place or mine?"

"Mine."

I slip the Glock into my waistband and walk barefoot to Room 210. All this time, Mirasol has been right around the corner. I knock on the door.

"Who is it?"

"Breed."

The door opens and Mirasol lets me in. She is dressed much as I. Blue jeans and a cream shirt untucked at the waist. Barefoot. Her long hair is loose about her shoulders.

She has set up her laptop on a table by the window. I turn off the light, step to one side of the jamb, and peer outside. My room faces onto main street, Mirasol's faces the back yard and lane. The houses on the other side of the lane are lit.

"We have to stay away from the windows," I tell her.

Together, in the dark, we rearrange the table and chairs. We will sit in the corner.

When we are done, I turn the lights back on. "Have you had dinner?"

"Yes."

"If you don't mind, I'll order a sandwich from room service. I haven't eaten since breakfast."

"All right," she says. "I'll join you for a drink."

I call downstairs and have them send up a burger, fries, and beer. A young man delivers the food. He bears a striking resemblance to the girl at the front desk. A family business.

We sit together at the laptop, and I open a beer for each of us. I spread the napkin I took from the *soldado* and show it to Mirasol. I tell her what happened at the plant. How I met Bledsoe and Frank, how I took Garrick and Stein to the hilltop.

I tell her how the two *soldados* tried to kill me, and how I left them in the desert. Everything but the part about Hamza and the Quds terrorists.

"La Cueva," I say. "We need to find it."

Mirasol fires up her search engine and types in "La Cueva," &" Juarez".

The search engine spits up a dozen hits on the first page. The top three hits all refer to the same establishment, a nightclub in Ciudad Juarez. One is the club's website, the other two are travel rating sites. One of the sites rates it four stars, the other gives it one star. Apparently for the same reason. Mescal, drugs, and slutty women.

The website is amateurish, barely finished. It features pictures of men and women drinking together, enjoying live bands. It provides an address.

I need to understand the ground. "Call up Magellan Voyager."

The Magellan Voyager is an online application that constructs a three-dimensional map of the globe. It uses a combination of satellite imagery, aerial photography, and GPS data. Users can navigate to any location on the planet by searching for place names, street addresses, or latitude and longitude coordinates. In most cases, street views are supplemented with strips of actual photographs. The level of detail varies by location, but it remains an excellent tactical tool.

Mirasol's fingers fly over the keys. A map fills the screen, with a little arrow pointing to La Cueva. "It's right on the river."

"I don't believe it." The brazen move stuns me. I expected the tunnel entrance to be located inland. "They've put it the first place anyone would look."

"Wait," Mirasol says. "This map only shows Mexico. We must see the United States as well."

Of course. We need to see its location in relation to Bledsoe.

Mirasol zooms out to display both sides of the river. La

Cueva is north of the plant, almost at the edge of the eighteen-hundred-yard chord I drew on Keller's map. It is a thousand-yard tunnel.

"I need to see more," I tell her. "I need to see the battlefield."

"There are photographs."

I scarf down the burger and wash it down with a beer. Open another.

Mirasol zooms in to view the neighborhood around La Cueva. Clicks on a ribbon of images below the map. The club occupies the ground floor of a large brick building. Dirty neon signs hang in frames bolted to the walls. Heavy drapes obstruct the second floor windows.

"This is the interior," Mirasol says.

Color photographs show a dance floor with a tacky crystal globe hanging from the ceiling. Men and women dancing. A long zinc bartop. I like zinc bartops. Tables where customers can drink and dine while they enjoy live performances. A staircase to the second floor.

I reach for the touch pad.

"Let's see the street outside."

I navigate to the exterior view, a photograph of the entrance. There is a panel with left and right, up and down arrows at the bottom of the screen. Click the arrow to the right and the pictures show what you would see if you turned right forty-five degrees. Click left to see the opposite. Keep on clicking and you turn in a full circle. If you click high in the middle, it is as though you walk forward. Clicking low in the middle causes you to retreat.

The feature works until I try to 'walk' into an alley to see the back of the building. I get hopelessly lost.

"There are no photographs of the back," Mirasol says. "This is in Mexico. The feature is not as developed as it is in the United States."

"How old are these photographs?" I ask.

"There is no way to tell unless you have been there before. I would not rely on them being recent."

"The street and buildings might have changed."

"That is not unusual."

I drink deeply and lean back in my chair. I am conscious of Mirasol sitting next to me. Her shoulders are slender, and her breasts swell against the cotton of her shirt. Her right knee brushes against my thigh. She holds it there.

The chemicals are working as nature intended. I clear my throat. "Mirasol, I have no right to ask you this."

"Ask me," Mirasol says.

"I am going to Juarez," I tell her. "I want you to come with me."

27

SALEM, 2130 HRS WEDNESDAY

I stare at Mirasol. "I am going to Juarez. I want you to come with me."

Mirasol jerks as though slapped. "Are you crazy?"

"No. Can you leave the country?"

Mirasol stiffens. Her face is ghastly pale in the glow of the laptop's screen. "Do you think I am illegal?"

"I don't know," I tell her. "I don't mean any offense."

The sexual tension from a moment ago is gone. Mirasol radiates anger. "I have a green card, Breed."

"All right."

Mirasol is young to have a green card. The waiting list is twenty years long. The only way I know to beat it is to win a lottery. I'm conscious of Stein's offer to trade information about Mirasol. Is Mirasol using forged documents?

"When are you planning to go?" Mirasol asks.

"Right away."

"You *are* crazy." Mirasol shakes her head. "Do you have any idea what it is like over there?"

I drifted through Fort Bliss. Visited my friends in El Paso. But—I'd never been to Juarez. "I reckon I'll find out."

"There is no law in Juarez." Mirasol's voice bears a hard edge. "The cartels, police and army kill each other. For control of drugs and women. There is so much money in the drugs, the cartels bribe everybody. Those they cannot bribe, they kill. The army murder everybody, including the police. It is a war—you do not know whose side anybody is on."

Mirasol pauses. Runs her hands through her hair.

"Why do the army murder police?"

Mirasol shrugs, a gesture of futility. "Because the police are corrupt. Because the army is corrupt. Police can increase their income *five times* working for the cartels. Put it this way. If a policeman has a reasonable income, three-quarters to eighty percent of his compensation comes from moonlighting. That means he is paid to be a bodyguard, contract killer, drug mule, or to look the other way."

"All right," I say. "I'll go alone."

We are quiet for a long time.

Exasperated, Mirasol says, "You don't know your way around."

"You do?"

Mirasol swallows. "Yes. Breed, why do you want to go to Juarez?"

"La Cueva. I have to be sure."

"Sure of the tunnel?"

"I need to be sure Keller's murderers are there."

Mirasol twists in her chair, puts her hand on my forearm. I am overwhelmed by her touch. "What then, Breed? You give them to Stein and Garrick?"

I haven't thought about what I'm going to do. Autopilot carried me this far. I've never articulated my plans to myself or anyone. Now I think there was never a question, never a choice. At a primal level, I have always known what I have to do.

I shake my head. "Stein and Garrick can do nothing in Mexico."

"I promise you the Mexican authorities will do nothing."

"I don't expect them to."

Mirasol's eyes widen. Hard enough to bruise, her grip tightens. "You *can't*."

I stand and pace. "Those animals killed a mother and an eight-year-old boy. Cut their heads off. You think I'm going to have them put in jail? So they can work out all day and bitch about not getting their ice cream? Think again."

Hands flat on her thighs, Mirasol looks up at me. "Breed. They are an army."

It's my turn to be angry. Mirasol says she's legal to travel. Why is she active in the United States, but not Mexico. Is she committed or not. "Yesterday you told me you were fighting a war."

Mirasol clenches her tiny fists.

"All right. I'll come."

I GO BACK to my room and stuff the Glock into my duffel bag. I'm not ready to risk the border with a weapon. Not yet.

Sitting on the bed, I pull on my socks and Oakley desert boots. Wonder about Mirasol's visceral reaction to Juarez. Everybody knows it has a crime problem. It's one of the battlegrounds on which the drug wars are fought. But—that's like saying there is a war in Afghanistan.

To know what it is really like, you have to have been there.

Mirasol made it clear Juarez is a city of confusion. The kind of city in which no one is safe. She knows what's going on.

The DOJ has a file on her.

28

JUAREZ, 2230 HRS WEDNESDAY

Mirasol navigates the late evening traffic of El Paso. We are on South Stanton Street, approaching the border crossing at the Puente Rio Bravo.

"All the films show the Bridge of the Americas," Mirasol explains, "but there are many border crossings. This one is operated by the city of El Paso. It is open till midnight."

The line leading to Customs & Border Protection is not long. There are two cars ahead of us. I watch the Border Patrol procedures. The agents wear forest green uniforms, utility caps, and patches with yellow trim. We are queued on a screening lane. Off to one side is an inspection area.

I worried that the Border Patrol would bring out dogs and scan every vehicle. Apparently not. At this hour, they must reserve that treatment for those who arouse suspicion. I mention this to Mirasol.

"Drugs and people are smuggled north," she tells me. "Weapons and money travel south. The Border Patrol are less concerned with southbound traffic."

"And the north?"

"The drugs, women, and illegals get through. We watched

them load people and boxes of meat on the trailer at Bledsoe. Do you think that was meat on the pallets?"

"They continue to smuggle drugs through these crossings."

"Yes," Mirasol says. "They bribe Border Patrol agents to wave them through. The best time to slip under the radar is when traffic is heaviest. This is not the best time to smuggle. In a strange way, crossing at this hour makes us *less* suspicious."

One car ahead of us.

Mirasol continues. "Most cartel profits come from drugs. Illegals count for little. Prostitutes a little more. *Mestizas* with light skin and European features are expensive. Blond girls from Eastern Europe bring top dollar. Children, especially those with light skin, bear no fixed price. Customers bid for them."

The Border Patrolman at the booth is of Mexican descent. He speaks flawless English. "Documents, please."

Mirasol hands him a Mexican passport and her green card. I pass over my passport and Department of Defense ID. The man scans them into a device. Studies the data that scrolls onto his screen.

"Where y'all off to tonight?"

"We are going to Juarez center."

"What's the purpose of your visit?"

"Pleasure."

"How are things working out for you, Miss Cruz?"

Mirasol doesn't miss a beat. "I am well, thank you."

The Border Patrolman returns our documents. "You folks have a good time. Watch yourselves over there."

The system obviously spat up chapter and verse on Mirasol's green card.

"What was that all about?" I ask.

Mirasol shrugs. "Nice guy."

I stare ahead at the Mexican border police kiosk. Two border guards, one with an M16 assault rifle.

"Not long ago," Mirasol says, "a car with four men drove to a US border crossing. Three were dead, including the driver. The man in the passenger seat held his foot on the gas until the car rolled to a stop. Then he died too. Welcome to the border."

The Mexican border guards examine our papers. Ask Mirasol to open the trunk. They look inside, slam it shut, and wave us on. They are careless. At a minimum, I would have used a mirror on a stick to inspect the underside of the vehicle.

Mirasol turns right, drives the short distance to the city center.

"Over here," she says, "we avoid police and army at all costs. We assume there are no good guys."

In the distance is a cathedral, at the end of a broad square. Mirasol tells me it is the Catedral de Nuestra Senora de Guadalupe. It is the central landmark of Juarez. The city looks clean, with throngs of people going about a busy nightlife. The lampposts are dirty. They have been plastered with paper handbills that bear photographs of young girls. The handbills are wrinkled and peeling. Many have been defaced.

"Thousands of young women have gone missing from Juarez over the years," Mirasol says. "The disappearances go back to the nineties. Their mothers, their relatives, post their photographs here. Pray for information."

"Have any turned up?"

Mirasol's voice drips bitterness. "No one has been found alive. Bodies are found in garbage dumps, or in the desert. Sometimes they can be identified. Frequently, they are mutilated beyond recognition. There was once a high-profile case. Families had to be told the mutilated bodies they buried did not belong to their loved ones. Imagine the number who have not been told."

Mirasol turns off the main avenue and into a side street.

"This part of the city is called the *Mariscal*. At one time it was the red light district, full of prostitutes and transvestites.

There are still many, as you can see. But it was worse. Now the City of Juarez is buying properties to redevelop the neighborhood. Slowly, they are pushing illicit activity out of the center."

We cruise past a derelict building. Three stories, built of hollow cinder blocks painted yellow. The second floor is surrounded by a wide balcony. The railing and posts of the balcony are green. The colors have faded. The glass windows on the second and third floors are broken. The windows on the ground floor have been boarded up. From one end to another, the walls are plastered with photos of missing girls.

"That is the Hotel Verde," Mirasol tells me. "It was the headquarters of the Los Aztecas cartel. Los Aztecas smuggle drugs into the US by bribing the Border Patrol. They kidnap young women, many underage. The top floor was a factory and warehouse for drugs. The second floor was a whorehouse, where they held girls captive. When the girls became docile, they were permitted onto the ground floor."

"This close to the center?"

"In Juarez, nowhere is safe." Mirasol dismisses the Hotel Verde with a shrug. "When the hotel was closed by a scandal, Los Aztecas moved."

"What kind of scandal?"

"The corpses of dead girls were discovered. In garbage heaps, in the desert. Arroyo del Navajo, eighty miles south. Several were traced to the Hotel Verde."

Through moderate traffic, Mirasol turns south.

We approach an intersection. A soldier steps onto the road and raises his hands to halt the traffic. Three cars separate us from the man with a rifle.

"Shit." Mirasol's knuckles are white on the steering wheel. "If they stop us, let me do the talking."

Ahead of us, two green Humvees loaded with soldiers pull into the traffic. Once they have cleared the intersection, the soldier jumps into the second vehicle.

Mirasol relaxes and we continue on our way.

"Years ago, the president sent the army and the federal police to battle the cartels. The killings increased. People disappeared, taken from the street in broad daylight. The people demanded the army be withdrawn.

"The current president pledged to fight the cartels with reform and economic development. He is naive. The killings continue, and he is viewed as weak. By everyone, not only the cartels. Now he sends the army and the *Federales* again. A small start, but a start. Soon the city will be at war once more."

The Humvees are new and well maintained. Each has a fifty caliber machine gun on a pintle mount. The troops are clean in digital camouflage uniforms. Kevlar helmets and body armor. M16s and M4 carbines.

"Trained by the United States army." Mirasol's observation conveys her cynicism. "For years, America has been supplying and training the Mexican army to conduct the war on drugs. The Mexican army does just enough to satisfy its sponsors. The corruption goes on."

Mirasol deliberately lags behind the other cars in the column. She gives the army plenty of room.

"Years ago, the Americans trained and equipped the Zetas to fight the cartels. They were a special branch of the army. An elite force. The best weapons, American military tactics. Thoroughly professional. The corruption took over and they plied their trade on their own time. Finally, the Zetas became what they are today. Another cartel."

Mirasol's litany of corruption is depressing. "Aren't we doing any good?"

"Not in Juarez. The cartels hired ex-US Army Special Forces to upgrade their communications networks."

I heard about that. Chalked it up to desperate operators hired out of *Soldier of Fortune* magazine.

No wonder Stein suspected us. I might be attracted to

mercenary employment. Retired operators make excellent money working as contractors.

The Mexican army Humvees turn right. As if by unspoken agreement, the traffic speeds up. The relief on the road is palpable.

"You know an awful lot about Juarez."

"It's my job." Mirasol sighs. "In El Paso, people say things have improved in Juarez. That the city is safe for tourists again. The reality is very different."

The street is splashed with color. The sidewalks are lined with vendors. Bare light bulbs hang from the corners of their makeshift booths. Their wares are charming. Pottery, toys, colorful clothing and fabrics. The aroma of chicken and beef grilled in the open air is appetizing. Rolled into tacos and burritos, more so.

"People must live," Mirasol says. "The city wears the clothing of normality. *Fiestas*, bars, shopping centers. The people play music, dance and drink. They dream of romance, while all around them gangsters kidnap girls, butcher each other in the streets. People make love on nights like this. Outside their windows, cartels burn their enemies alive in barrels. This is all regarded as normal."

Mirasol turns left onto a side street. Drives in the direction of the river. Three blocks and she turns right onto another brightly lit drag. Busier than the last. Street vendors, bars. On the left, with its back to the river, a two-story building. I recognize it immediately.

"There it is," Mirasol says.

La Cueva.

29

JUAREZ, 2300 HRS WEDNESDAY

The target is built like the Hotel Verde. The ground floor is cinder block, painted the color of tanned flesh. A garish green neon sign spells *Bar Cueva*. The second floor is wood frame and drywall. There is no balcony, no third floor.

Windows on the second floor are shuttered. The shutters are of thick wood, painted green. The windows on the ground floor are clear glass. They offer an unobstructed view of the dim interior, where people dance with abandon. The music is so loud the windows shake.

"Assume La Cueva is what we think," Mirasol says. "They will hold girls and store drugs on the second floor. There may be rooms where customers pay for sex.

"I doubt there is a drug factory on the premises. For this, the cartels have purpose-built labs. They hire professional chemists. They call them black-and-whites. Because they wear white Tyvek suits and black masks over their nose and mouth. I interviewed a woman. She financed her PhD working for a cartel. When she finished her doctorate, the illegal work was so lucrative she made it her career."

I digest the information. Hamza and his terrorists will occupy the second floor. Drugs and fair-skinned prostitutes are valuable. Underage girls are valuable. What is the price for Quds Force killers. What devil's bargain did Bledsoe make with Hamza and the cartels.

"Where would they place the entrance to the tunnel?"

"Like any bar, there will be a basement. There, they store wine, liquor, and kegs of beer. It is the logical place to dig the tunnel."

"Stairs leading to the basement," I say.

"Yes." Mirasol meets my eyes. "Or a trapdoor."

"Let's drive around the building."

Mirasol pulls into the traffic. Cruises past the club. I scan the people on the sidewalk, looking for sentries. There are hard guys at the corners. Nondescript clothing. Concealed handguns. Nothing heavier than a nine millimeter. I'm sure they have automatic rifles inside.

This street is lined with kebab shops. One or two have tables and chairs set on the sidewalk. Diners with Middle Eastern features smoke *shisha*. Suck up carcinogenic toxins.

Mirasol notices my interest. "Many people from the Middle East, Asia, and Eastern Europe come here. To cross illegally into the United States. Most of these people are waiting to pay their money to coyotes."

Quds will feel at home. It will be easy for them to blend in.

Two blocks past the club, Mirasol hangs a left into a dark alley. Ahead is the dry gulch of the Rio Grande. Beyond that, the US riverbank and the border wall. All shrouded in darkness.

The alley leads to a narrow road that runs parallel to the river. More like a lane, lit only by bare bulbs mounted on the walls of buildings. There are no other cars in the lane.

"They will notice us," Mirasol says.

"We can get away with it once."

Mirasol creeps forward.

To preserve my night vision, I avoid looking at the brightly lit street we left. Instead, I focus on the backs of the buildings, the river valley.

The back of La Cueva is dark. There is a rear entrance. Against the wall, bolted to the cinder blocks and supported by steel posts, are fire stairs. There are two bare bulbs, each protected by wire mesh. One is above the back door. The other hangs over the fire door at the top of the stairs.

A man lounges under the light, smoking a cigarette. He looks up at us.

He is an amateur. An experienced sentry would not stand in the light. He would stand in the shadows.

Late twenties. Short, spiky hair, angular features. The man flicks the cigarette away. His hand goes behind his back, reaching for a pistol.

I hear Mirasol suck breath. She takes her foot off the gas.

"Keep going," I hiss. "Don't. Slow. Down."

The *soldado* is frozen in our headlights. We drive past.

"*Dios mio.*" Mirasol is shaking.

"Easy." I put my hand on her shoulder and squeeze gently. "We're all right. Turn left."

We turn left into another alley two blocks past La Cueva.

"Park here."

Mirasol stops the car, shuts off the engine.

"What now, Breed? Have you seen enough?"

"No. I need to get inside. I need to see the second floor."

"How are you going to do that?"

"You said they keep women there."

Mirasol stifles a laugh. "You are crazy."

"Just another dumb *gringo* looking to get laid."

Mirasol stares at her hands for a long moment. When she lifts her face, she has come to a decision. "Breed, we are now fighting the same war."

"What do you mean?"

"Bledsoe comes to Juarez to indulge his appetite. I think the girls they keep here are young. You saw the ones they loaded into the truck."

"Yes."

"Bledsoe may have a private room on the second floor." Mirasol's voice quivers with excitement. "The way to get up there is to negotiate for a young girl."

"You mean act like a pervert."

"It may be the only way. These men are so depraved, the sickest preferences are normal to them."

"If you think it will work."

"I do. How much cash do you have?"

This is Mexico. In Latin America, credit and debit cards are only beginning to see use. Everywhere, cash is the accepted medium of exchange. That's why stickups and robberies are common. Fortunately, I came prepared.

"A thousand dollars."

"Big spender," Mirasol sniffs. "I have two hundred."

"Will it be enough?"

"It might be. If they have a short, brown, ugly girl like me."

She's fishing for a compliment. I say nothing. Reach for the door handle.

"Breed." Mirasol puts her hand on my arm. "We're doing this to get upstairs. Nothing else."

I smile.

MIRASOL LOCKS THE CAR, and we walk to the brightly lit street. I put my arm around her shoulders, and she hooks hers around my waist. I'm struck once again by how tiny she is. As we walk, she leans against me. It's a pleasant sensation.

We come to the corner, and I identify the *soldados* on guard. One at each corner. Hard looking guys with tattooed arms and earrings. Intelligence does not gleam in their eyes. These are blunt instruments.

My eyes sweep the interior as soon as we enter. The club is busy. A live band is playing popular dance music. Not well. I spot an empty table in an ocean of tables and guide Mirasol to a seat.

"What do you want?" I ask.

"A red wine."

I go to the zinc bartop. Find myself hobbled by my lack of Spanish. *"Una cerveza."* I hesitate, groping for words. *"Y... un vino rojo."*

The bartender's thirty, with a short beard and mustache. He sneers at the dumb *gringo* and brings me a large glass of amber liquid. Rows of goblets are held inverted in a wooden stemware rack above the bar. He retrieves one, sets it on the bar, and pours from an open bottle of red.

"Four hundred twenty-five pesos." The bartender smiles like he's asking me to grab my ankles. The little shit has a gold incisor.

It's about twenty dollars. I draw a wad of cash from my front pocket, peel off a twenty, and slide it across the bar. *"Gracias."*

The bartender's eyes follow the wad back into my pocket.

I pick up the glasses and turn my back before he can respond.

"Well done, Breed." Mirasol smiles mischievously.

"From now on, you do the haggling," I tell her.

"In Mexico, women are not welcome in bars. Close to the border, establishments are more liberal. We should not have trouble here, but attitudes are ingrained."

"Sounds like a chauvinistic society."

Mirasol sips her wine. "In Mexico, women are worthless. Their utility is limited to beer commercials. Liberals in America rally for women's rights, but they have no idea what it is like here. Once, every five years, they do a story on the women who disappear from Juarez. To be found murdered, or not to be found at all. Then the righteous Americans forget."

As we speak, my eyes rove about the club. I take out my phone and snap Mirasol's picture, careful to capture the sweep of the room behind her. The staircase leading to the second floor. I hand her the phone. "Take one of me."

I take the phone back and review the photographs. The picture of me captures the bar in the background. I push the phone back into her hands. "More. Take more."

Mirasol snaps more photographs. Me and the bar, me and the dance floor. I sit next to her, with our backs to the entrance. Raise the camera, snap a string of selfies.

When I am done, I have a panoramic collection of photographs of the ground floor. Three hundred and sixty degrees. I put my arm around Mirasol, pull her in, and kiss her. She stiffens. I hold her close, take my lips away for a moment, and kiss her again. I feel her begin to melt. Her lips part and she surrenders. Her fingers run through my hair, and she returns the kiss.

I close my eyes, enjoy the intimacy.

When I let Mirasol go, her eyes and lips are shiny.

She reaches for her wine and takes a gulp. My beer tastes like water, I've been ripped off. Mirasol's scent and taste overwhelm me. I force myself to switch on.

The bartender and a number of Mexicans are staring at us.

I pretend not to notice. Take in the men and scantily clad women dancing in front of the band.

Pensively, Mirasol stares at me.

Two men descend the staircase behind her. Lean and swarthy, clean-shaven. Their faces are more tanned than their jaws. One man is bald, the other has short, neatly trimmed hair.

With confidence, they walk to the bar and engage the bartender in conversation. He leads them to a back room. He shuts the door behind them and returns to the bar.

Quds. Preparing to infiltrate the USA.

They do not want their beards to give them away, so they shave. Shaving leaves their faces half-tanned.

"We should do this," I say at last.

"Yes," Mirasol agrees.

"Who do you think?"

"The bartender," she says. "Bartenders know everybody."

Mirasol gets up, goes to the bar. The bartender is serving others. She waits, looks back at me and smiles.

When he has finished, the bartender comes to Mirasol and they speak. He seems surprised. Casts a glance at me, then leans in, and they speak some more.

I look around the club. There are two hulking bouncers at the door, but their attention is on the other customers. They may be cartel, but I don't think so. They've been hired for their size, to intimidate rowdy partiers, eject them if necessary. I see other men at tables near the door and at the foot of the stairs. These guys look hard, with chiseled faces and tattoos on their arms and necks.

One of three men at the table wears a man-bun and a droopy mustache. He looks like a China seas pirate. His v-neck t-shirt reveals tattoos on his chest. At his feet is a large canvas bag. Big enough to conceal several AK47s and magazines.

My eyes flick to the men at the table near the door. Under the table, they have a similar bag. I count at least six *soldados* on the ground floor, with small arms. Two Quds in the back room behind the bar. More upstairs.

It's a hornet's nest.

Man-Bun has sharp eyes. He stares at Mirasol and the bartender. Says something to his friends, gets up and strides to the bar. I look away as he passes me.

The bartender and Man-Bun know each other. He joins the conversation with Mirasol. Looks me over, turns back to them. The bartender glanced at me. Man-Bun *looked*.

The three of them speak for five minutes. The bartender shouts for an assistant to help serve drinks. Obviously, the negotiation is more important. Finally, Man-Bun leaves them and walks to the stairwell. With a final look at Mirasol, he disappears upstairs.

Flushed, Mirasol returns to our table.

"You've bought yourself a virgin," she says. "Nine hundred dollars."

"I've never had a virgin."

"She won't be." Mirasol squeezes my arm. "These creeps sell her virginity twenty times a week."

"For God's sake."

"It's an old scam." Mirasol's air is dismissive. "We're going up together."

"You're kidding."

Mirasol grins. "I told them I was arranging a present for you. I like to watch."

I wonder how much depravity lurks in Mirasol's skull.

Man-Bun descends the stairs. He walks straight to our table, addresses Mirasol. *"Ven conmigo."*

Mirasol takes my hand. "Come on."

The stairs, covered with worn green carpet, creak underfoot. The material is worn and faded in the middle. Dark on either side. The odor of cigarette smoke clings to everything. The walls are pressed wood, painted pink.

At the top of the stairs, Man-Bun stops. Puts the flat of his hand against my chest. *"Dame el dinero."*

I take the wad from my pocket, peel off sixty dollars. Keep the sixty, hand him the rest. Man-Bun counts the money. Twice.

The corridor behind him stretches the length of the building. Ceiling lights under dirty glass domes have been set ten feet apart. The carpet is the same worn green. The doors on either side are closed. At the far end is a fire exit. It opens to the metal stairs at the back of the building.

One of the doors on the right opens, and two men step into the corridor.

Quds. The first is stocky. He wears boots, utility pants, and a loose black t-shirt. His hair is close-cropped and he is clean-shaven. His face is half-tanned.

The second man is—Hamza.

Our eyes meet across the length of the corridor. We take each other in with a single glance. He has no reason to recognize me, but he knows my bearing, my physical type. Enough to be suspicious.

Man-Bun sees me looking over his shoulder and turns to follow my gaze. Waves the money at Hamza. *"Está bien. Ellos son clientes."*

Without a word, Hamza leads the other Quds to a room at the far end of the corridor. They disappear inside.

The money disappears into Man-Bun's pocket. He opens the first door on the left. Like an obscene *maitre d'*, he steps aside and raises his arm to show us into the room.

Mirasol's grip tightens on my hand and she leads me through the doorway. Man-Bun shuts the door behind us and leaves us alone with—

The girl.

30

JUAREZ, 2330 HRS WEDNESDAY

Man-Bun leaves us alone with—

The girl.

Maybe five-four, taller than Mirasol. Young, but adolescent. Fourteen or fifteen. Wide eyes, wide mouth, rosy cheeks. Shoulder length hair and fair skin. She sits on the edge of the bed, hands clasped over knees pressed demurely together. She wears a filmy white cotton shift.

I sweep the room. It is larger than I thought. Center-fed, two blind spots, two cuts. Comfortable. I expected a hovel, a bug-infested mattress on the floor. This place is clean, with a throw-rug next to the bed. The floor bounces with the beat of music playing downstairs. There is a dressing table and chair. A mirror for the girl. A collection of combs and brushes. On one corner of the dressing table, a dish with a collection of condoms. Bottles of hand cream and lubricant. Four lengths of leather cord wrapped neatly in coils.

I look back at the girl. She tries to smile for me, but can't quite pull it off. She looks frightened, ready to cry.

Above the bed is a window. An old casement design. It has

glass panes opening inward, and heavy plantation shutters opening out. The window is shut.

I go to the en suite bathroom. Small, but a luxury in a place like this. A cheap shower stall and toilet. Plastic containers of air freshener sit open on the porcelain cistern. I smell pine and a whiff of bleach. This facility is the reason for the center-feed. The two cuts. I make certain the bathroom is empty, then join Mirasol and the girl. The two speak together in Spanish.

"I've seen what I need to see," I tell Mirasol. "How long do we have to stay?"

"We paid for an hour," Mirasol says. "Make yourself comfortable."

I pick up the chair from in front of the dressing table. Turn it around, sit down. Mirasol is sitting on the bed next to the girl. The pillowcases are white, with a simple floral design. The bedspread is white. There are a pair of towels neatly folded at the end of the bed. Imagine what they are for.

The girl looks confused. She was expecting a *ménage à trois.* Clumsily, she slips the shift from her shoulders. Embarrassed, I look away. "Oh, for... Cover her up."

"Relax, Breed." Mirasol reaches for the girl and pushes the straps back. "Nothing you haven't seen before."

"Not on a kid."

Mirasol takes the girl's hands in hers and speaks gently. "Breed, this is Nevita."

I find it impossible to generate enthusiasm. "Hi."

My mind is on Hamza and the Quds killers. How many? I consider the size of the building and the number of rooms. Perhaps half a dozen Quds and twice that number of *soldados*. The two rooms at the far end of the corridor are probably not used as bedrooms. Logistics and administration. Nevita's room must be the nicest one unless there is one like it on either end.

"There are not many whores here." Mirasol looks up from Nevita. "She says this is a VIP business. Only herself and a few other girls, all young. Only rich men and women come to see her."

"Ask her how many rooms are used for sex."

Nevita speaks quickly, gestures.

"Two," Mirasol says. "This one, and a smaller room at the other end. They keep the girls chained in another room across the hall."

"What are the other rooms used for?"

Mirasol puts the question to Nevita. I don't know much Spanish, but I understand "*No se.*"

I estimate enemy strength. Six *soldados* and two Quds downstairs. I saw Hamza and one Quds in the hall. Based on the number of rooms, I make five or six Quds, plus Hamza. Twelve or more cartel shooters.

Nevita and Mirasol are absorbed in conversation.

Mirasol translates, tells me Nevita's story. Mirasol provides context and fills in gaps from her own knowledge.

THE NORTH AMERICA Free Trade Agreement came into effect in the early nineties. It destroyed industries in two countries. One country was the United States, the other was Mexico. The United States lost its manufacturing base as factories moved south of the border. Industrialists were happy to screw the unions. Automobiles, air-conditioners, clothing. Anything that relied on labor to assemble or stitch was moved. On the other side of the border, prices for farm commodities collapsed. Mexico found its agriculture business decimated.

The result was massive dislocation on both sides. The American middle class, used to high-paying manufacturing jobs, was thrown out of work. Factories were closed. Entire towns in the Midwest were depopulated. Politicians urged men who had spent their lives building cars to learn how to write computer programs.

In Mexico, hundreds of thousands of women migrated to border towns to escape poverty. American manufacturers built factories in places like Juarez. These are the *maquiladoras*, the border factories that prove globalism works. Their products flood the United States, duty-free. In Juarez, these factories employ a quarter of a million people.

The *maquiladoras* prefer to hire women and young girls. Women are less likely to complain about low wages and poor working conditions. Less likely to unionize. Globalism works for the elites and government of both countries. But—the system is built on slave labor.

American retailers followed the manufacturers to the border towns. They went to serve the American dream to the newly employed. Walmarts and McDonald's sprang up everywhere.

There were problems.

The prosperity in the United States generated inflation on both sides of the border. America's newly unemployed middle class were crushed. Only information economy jobs could keep pace. In Mexico, an unfair economy developed. The average wage in Juarez is one-eighth the average wage in the US. On the other hand, the average cost of living is ninety percent that of the US.

Two million people live in Juarez. Unemployment is close to zero. Economists call it frictional unemployment. When an employee leaves the *maquiladoras*, another comes to take her place. This state of affairs produces a more painful consequence. The women of the *maquiladoras* are disposable. They come and go. No one keeps track.

Women who leave employment in a factory may do so for a better opportunity. Given the nature of the labor market, this is unlikely. Women and girls simply disappear.

Nevita and her mother came to this world two years ago. They lived in a rented hovel and worked in the *maquiladoras*.

The minimum working age in Mexico is fifteen. Nevita was twelve. She lied about her age. The American corporation that owned the *maquila* ignored the law. Bribed authorities to look the other way.

Together, Nevita and her mother managed to make ends meet.

Until a perverse economic development.

China had been admitted to the World Trade Organization. The global elites found Chinese workers were happy to undercut Mexican workers. Mexicans accepted an eighth of the American wage. The Chinese accepted a quarter of the Mexican wage. The *maquila* in which Nevita worked as a seamstress closed.

Thousands of jobs in Juarez vaporized. Nevita's mother clung to her employment. Nevita searched for work but found nothing.

One day, six months ago, Nevita was walking in the *Mariscal*. She was approached by a man. He was plain-looking, dressed in a clean suit. Polite and well spoken, he complimented her on her beauty. Told her he was a photographer. Would she model for him? It was humble pay, but more than she would make in a *maquila*. Desperate to help her mother, Nevita agreed. The man gave her half the money in advance. It was more than she earned in a week at the factory. She went with him to his "studio" at La Cueva.

At La Cueva, he took the money back, raped her, and refused to let her leave.

His friends raped her.

They explained what they expected. Men with money came to use her. If she did not satisfy, she was beaten. They were careful not to mark the merchandise. Nothing that would destroy her value. They punched her in the belly. They struck her on the side of her head with the heels of their hands. So hard her teeth rattled. Nevita worked hard to please.

On one occasion she tried to run away.

They bound her wrists and ankles with leather cords. The bonds were so tight she thought she would go mad from the pain. When she began to scream and beg, they gagged her. Then they loosened the cords. The return of circulation was excruciating.

When she grew quiet, they tightened the cords again. They repeated the process for two days. The process left no permanent marks, but rearranged her mind.

Nevita did not try to run away again.

"It is a common story," Mirasol says. "I have heard it many times."

Mirasol's tone surprises me. Not indifferent... Fatalistic. This is the way things are, there is no hope of changing the system.

"Do you think they'll send her across the tunnel?"

Mirasol shrugs. "Impossible to know. She is attractive. Light skinned. We do not know how well she pleases. The torture may have damaged her mind beyond repair. If they don't send her across, they will dispose of her."

I've learned enough to know what that means. If she's lucky, a shallow grave in the *Arroyo del Navajo.*

I feel sick to my stomach. "I don't want to hear any more of this."

Nevita stares at the wall with dead eyes.

Mirasol says, "This is Juarez, Breed. You wanted to come."

I look at my watch. "Not for this."

In the corridor, a floorboard creaks.

31

JUAREZ, 0015 HRS THURSDAY

In the corridor, a floorboard creaks.

It is a stealthy sound. We have only been in the room forty minutes. I have heard men walking in the corridor. Not creeping. I lift my finger to my lips, motion for Mirasol and Nevita to keep quiet.

A center-fed room. Two blind spots, two cuts. Mirasol and Nevita are close to the left-hand cut. They will naturally draw the attention of an intruder. I step to the cut between the door and the bathroom. Flatten myself against the wall.

How many? If there are two, it will be a holy mess.

Mirasol looks away from me. Takes Nevita's face in her hands and holds it to her breast.

A hand pushes the door open. The intruder leads with his pistol, a Beretta nine millimeter. Points it at the back of Mirasol's head.

We're both committed. I twist the man's wrist and bear him to the floor. I step on the back of his elbow, haul, and snap his arm like a twig. The pistol falls with a clatter.

The man's scream is choked off as I fall on him and shove

his face down. I drive my knee into his back, kick the door shut. Grab his head with both hands. Break his neck.

There is an audible crack.

"My God," Mirasol gasps. "Breed."

It's Man-Bun. He has my money. Why would he want to kill us?

I put my ear to the door. Nothing. He was alone. I reach into Man-Bun's pocket, take my money back. Pick up the Beretta, unload it, pull the slide back. A live shell rattles on the floor. I look into the chamber, slap the magazine into the grip, charge the pistol. Loaded, I decock the weapon, take the safety off, and stuff it into my waistband. I've started quite a collection.

Mirasol and I have two choices. We can either leave together, or one at a time.

Impossible to know why Man-Bun came to kill us. It doesn't make sense. Whether it was Hamza or cartel business, he wouldn't come alone.

I go to the window and open the inner panes. The plantation shutters are latched, but not locked. I swing them open wide and look out. The side street is fifteen feet below. Equivalent to a fully loaded combat landing. I can jump it, Mirasol can't.

"We have to brazen it out," I tell her. "We'll leave together. Now. Before they miss him."

"They will wonder where he is."

"But—they won't do anything. Until after we're gone."

Mirasol goes to the window and looks down. "I can't jump that."

"That's why we're going out the front together."

"All right."

I look at the young girl sitting on the bed. "What about Nevita?"

Mirasol shakes her head. "She's lost."

Mirasol steps into the corridor and I follow her. I glance

back at Nevita. The girl sits motionless, stares at me. She looks numb.

I close the door on the young girl and the corpse.

THE CORRIDOR IS DESERTED. No sign of Hamza or the Quds.

"Don't look anyone in the face," I tell her. "Especially the bartender. If anyone challenges us, say we had a good time, we're going home."

Together, we descend the staircase. The pink walls ripple with colored lights thrown from the glittering disco ball.

We reach the ground floor landing. Walk past the *soldados* at the foot of the stairs. My eyes sweep their friends at the table by the door. The bouncers. The dancers. I check out the bartender in my peripheral vision. He is staring at us.

He's suspicious. How long before he acts?

Past the bouncers, through the front door. We walk along the sidewalk toward the corner. The sentry on duty is watching the street. It's a river of red and white lights. Arm in arm, men and women make their way along the sidewalks. *La vida loca*.

We walk past the sentry. Turn toward the car. Mirasol unlocks the doors. We're almost there when someone shouts from the entrance of the club.

"*Matarlos!*"

Fucking bartender. Must have gone upstairs to check on Man-Bun.

There's a chorus of shouts. "*¿Cuáles? ¿Dónde?*"

"*El Americano y la mujer!*"

We dive into the car and Mirasol starts the engine. Through the windshield, I see the *soldado* on the corner look this way and that. He realizes we just passed him, draws his pistol as I dive into the passenger seat. I draw Man-Bun's nine millimeter from my waistband.

The windshield stars as the *soldado* opens fire. Two rounds pass between me and Mirasol. She floors the gas and the car leaps forward. He fires twice more before the Camaro plows into him. Neither shot touches the car. Instead, we're jolted by the impact, and he is thrown onto the hood. Mirasol spins the wheel and pulls into the street.

We're stuck in traffic.

I look behind us. Men with rifles are spilling out of the club.

"Go down the sidewalk."

Mirasol hesitates. "There are people."

"Do it."

Mirasol pulls onto the sidewalk and steps on the gas. It's not Formula 1, but she's doing thirty miles an hour. She crashes into one stall, then another. Pedestrians scatter in all directions. This is what it's like to part the Red Sea.

I twist in my seat. The *soldados* with rifles open fire. Bullets rip the back of the Camaro. They're falling behind. Mirasol turns down a side street.

"We need to get across fast," I say.

"They will wait for us at the bridges."

I look over my shoulder. The cartel will radio ahead, but they are also piling into cars as we speak. "Take the most direct route. When we get close, we'll check things out."

For the next twenty minutes, we drive in silence. Mirasol concentrates on the road, I keep my head on a swivel.

I begin to parse the possibilities.

"We can get across in the car, or we can get across on foot. We'll have to determine the best approach when we get there." The weight of the Beretta on my lap reassures me. "You said four dead guys rolled up to a border crossing."

"Yes. We are not safe until we are across. The approach to the border is very dangerous because one is stuck in a queue with nowhere to escape."

"And on foot?"

"They can chase you right to the inspection kiosk and shoot you on the doorstep."

"It's pretty late. What's the crossing like at this hour?"

"If no one is after you, easy. If the cartel is chasing you, there is nowhere to hide."

We approach the city center. There are many people out on the sidewalks. They take in the sights of the city at night, enjoy the street food and music.

"The Puente Rio Bravo is closed," Mirasol says. "That leaves us three options. Paseo Del Norte, The Bridge of the Americas, and Zaragoza."

"Which one is closest?"

"Zaragoza," Mirasol says. "It has two four-lane bridges, one of them for commercial traffic only. The other bridge has two walkways where one can cross on foot."

Where does a soldier begin.

"I need to see the land," I say. "Pull over, someplace dark and quiet... Over there."

Mirasol parks on a side street and shuts off the engine. I take my phone and browse to Magellan Voyager. Type in "Zaragoza Bridge, Juarez."

We are treated to a high quality map of the Mexican side of the bridge. I touch the 3D icon. In a flash, the image changes to a bird's eye view of the approaches.

Two spans, four lanes each. Viewed from the Mexico side, the span on the left is used for private traffic, the span on the right for commercial. Each has its own separate approach. The approach to the private span is Avenida Waterfill. The street is straight and a mile long. Traffic flows north and south, but once on it, there is no easy way out. Side approaches are blocked off with yellow concrete bollards. The commercial approach is at right angles to Avenida Waterfill. It runs parallel to the river, then sweeps onto the span in a smooth, sharp curve.

Everywhere, the buildings look like warehouses and customs brokerages. This is an industrial section of the city, stocked with goods from the *maquiladoras*. Trailers waiting to be shipped north. Fodder for the consumption junkies on the American coasts.

It's a death trap.

I don't want to believe how dangerous this bridge is. "Zaragoza can't be busy at this hour."

"The commercial bridge can be very busy," Mirasol says. "The private bridge, not so much."

I search for "Paseo Del Norte Bridge, Juarez." The application brings up a three-dimensional plan. The city center to the south, flanking the grand Avenida Benito Juarez. To the west, the cathedral, to the east the old bull ring. We glimpsed them on the way in.

The Bridge of the Americas approach is much like that of the Zaragoza. Multiple spans, long avenues leading to the border checkpoints. No cover.

Paseo Del Norte, Zaragoza, and Bridge of the Americas. Three very different battlefields.

"What do you think?" Mirasol asks.

I bookmark the views. Close the browser. "The Paseo Del Norte is safest. The city center is built up, with a lot of civilian traffic. Pedestrians and vehicles. We can approach on the Avenida Juarez. If there is trouble, there are more streets through which we can escape. The Bridge of the Americas and Zaragoza are closer, but more dangerous. The approaches are bottlenecks. Once on, we'll be sitting ducks unless we cross quickly."

On either side, the street is dark. Mirasol has parallel-parked in a long column of cars. I look over my shoulder at the brightly lit thoroughfare. Early morning in Juarez. The traffic, while lighter, remains substantial.

I open my phone and check the wait times at the crossings.

Half an hour for vehicles, no wait for pedestrians. "Half an hour is a long time to wait with nowhere to run."

Mirasol puts her hands on the wheel. "Okay, Breed. What do you want to do?"

The girl amazes me. Her combination of vulnerability and brass.

"They'll be looking for this car," I say.

"In Juarez," Mirasol tells me, "fifty cars a day are stolen. Junkies take them to finance their drug habits."

I rummage in the glove compartment. Empty, except for registration and insurance. "Pop your trunk," I tell her.

Inside the trunk I find a spare tire, jack, lug wrench, and a toolbox. I rummage in the toolbox, select a flat-head screwdriver.

I pocket the screwdriver and slowly inspect the column of parked cars. Mexico. Low income. These people are not in the habit of trading up their vehicles every year. Most of the cars are old beaters. In the middle of the street, I find a late eighties Ford Taurus.

The car's locked. I look up and down the street, take the Beretta from my waistband. Holding the pistol by the barrel, I use the butt as a hammer and smash the driver's side window. Reach in, unlock the door.

Once inside, I inspect the ignition. Take the screwdriver, squeeze its head into the slot. Again, holding the Beretta like a hammer, I pound the tool into the cylinder. The molding splits, but the shaft of the screwdriver is firmly seated.

I lay the pistol on the seat next to me. Take a breath, twist.

The engine roars to life.

Not just another pretty face.

I look in the rearview mirror. Mirasol gets out of the Camaro and walks quickly to the Taurus. She climbs in and slams the passenger door shut.

"Breed, you amaze me."

32

JUAREZ, 0100 HRS THURSDAY

We're two miles from the Zaragoza bridge. Behind us, a siren whoops. I swallow, check the rearview mirror. The traffic in our lane is slowing down and pulling over to the side of the road.

Three black-and-white police pickup trucks drive past in the direction of the bridge. The pickups have cages of black metal roll bars mounted on their beds. Two of the pickups have two men in front and four in the back, armed with M4 carbines. The third has two men in front and two in the back. They stand, manning an M240 pintle-mounted, belt-fed machine gun. A hundred yards back, a white civilian Impala brings up the rear.

The police are masked. They wear black uniforms and helmets, like storm troopers. Mirasol tells me police wear masks so the cartels will not know who they are. It is a fiction. The cartels know all their names. Juarez has a memorial to assassinated police officers. Killed for one reason or another. Beneath it, the cartel posts a list of police officers marked for death—"Those who do not believe."

Once the odd convoy has passed, the traffic resumes normal speed.

"What's going on there," I ask.

Mirasol frowns. "They are going to the bridge. The car behind them, I don't know."

"Unmarked police vehicle."

"Possibly." Mirasol does not sound convinced. "Breed, this doesn't feel right."

We're a mile from the bridge, approaching a three-way intersection. The traffic slows measurably. Ahead, in the direction of the bridge, the police vehicles have set up a checkpoint.

"Pull over, Breed." The urgency in Mirasol's voice brooks no argument. "This is our last chance."

Without hesitation, I pull well over to the side. Switch off the headlights, shelter in the shadow of a warehouse. The traffic stalls, bumper to bumper.

There is a wide island at the center of the three-way intersection. A gasoline station, a restaurant, and a parking lot. The gas station and the restaurant are closed, the island is shrouded in darkness.

Lights off, the white Impala is parked next to the restaurant.

"They're looking for us," Mirasol whispers.

"The police?"

"Breed, you still don't understand Mexico. The army, the *Federales*, the state police, the municipal police. All, at one time or another, perform contract killings for the cartels."

"The cartel is paying the police to set up checkpoints."

"Yes. They want to *kill* us."

"What about the white car?"

"*Soldados*. Observing the operation."

"Shit."

"They are waiting at all the crossings." Mirasol looks over her shoulder. "We have to get out of here."

The cars behind us have piled into a healthy traffic jam. The southbound lane is clear... Traffic from the American side is non-existent. It won't be easy to turn around.

The pickup with the machine gun on its bed is parked beside the road. The other two pickups are parked in a V, blocking the way to the bridge. Their front ends leave enough room for one car at a time to pass. Masked police, carrying M4s, stand in the gap. They are checking every car. Shining flashlights inside, matching faces to identity papers.

The white Impala sits in the dark. I strain my eyes. Two men occupy the front seats. They are a hundred yards away, on the other side of the queue. From where we sit, that is all I can see.

Half a mile south on Avenida Waterfill, horns blare. The long column of cars inching toward the police checkpoint ripples. Five armored Humvees are pushing past the civilian vehicles. Finally, the army column pulls into the left lane and forces southbound traffic off the road.

"Now what?"

"Anybody's guess," Mirasol says.

The Humvees halt in front of the police checkpoint. Each of the military vehicles is armed with a pintle-mounted fifty caliber. Six troopers per vehicle—a full platoon, including an officer. The troops dismount, M4s at high port.

An officer gets out and motions the civilian drivers to pull off the road. He turns to the police and shouts at them. "*Dejen sus armas! Ahora!*"

The policeman on the M240 swings the machine gun to bear on the army. Jerks the charging handle.

The soldiers open fire with everything they have. The fifty calibers rake the pickups from one end to another. The policeman on the machine gun is cut in half, blown off the truck. Heavy caliber rounds stitch the police. At point-blank range, there is no protection against half-inch armor-piercing ammunition. Caught in the hail of fire, the cops dance like puppets. Their bodies are slammed against the vehicles before collapsing to the ground.

Instinct takes over. Leaving the motor running, I get out of the car. "Come on."

Dodging between the cars, Mirasol follows me across the road. Without waiting for her, I stride to the island at the center of the intersection. At the checkpoint, army troopers inspect the policemen and their riddled vehicles.

Crack.

A trooper shoots a wounded policeman.

I take the Beretta from under my shirt. Approach the white Impala from behind.

The two *soldados* sit in the dark, observing the carnage. One of them has a handheld radio to his ear.

More shots ring out from the checkpoint. The army is not interested in taking prisoners.

I walk straight to the driver's window. It's been rolled down in the heat. I raise the Beretta to the driver's ear and blow his brains out. The passenger turns, radio in hand. I shoot him twice in the face. The driver has slumped to one side. I shoot him a second time under his jaw. The bullet blows the crown of his skull onto the passenger's lap.

More shots ring out from the checkpoint. Killing wounded, the army are having themselves a high old time.

I yank open the driver's door and haul the body out of the car. Push it against the wall of the restaurant. Go around to the passenger side. Most of the passenger's brains landed on the concrete surface of the island. Mirasol arrives in time to watch me drag the passenger around the front and lay him next to his buddy. I tear their shirts off and return to the car.

The radio, lying on the passenger seat, is crackling. Someone on the other end of the net is hollering in Spanish. I pick up the handset. It looks simple enough to operate. I make sure the radio is not in send mode and hand it to Mirasol. "Listen to what they are saying and translate for me."

"They're panicking. They want Manuel and Javier to answer."

I get in the car, slam the door, and reach over. Brush bits of scalp and brain off the passenger seat. Take one of the shirts and wipe blood from the upholstery. I fold the other shirt carefully and lay it on the seat. Sir Walter Raleigh spreading his cape for the queen. "Get in," I say. "Try not to get blood on you."

Mirasol climbs in the car and closes the door. I hand her the bloody shirt. "Do the best you can with the door," I tell her. "Throw it away when you're done."

I fire up the engine. Spin the car around, drive past the gas station pumps, and turn onto the eastbound lane.

The stream of Spanish coming from the radio continues unbroken. Mirasol listens, trying to tell the different voices apart. "They say the police are running."

"Which ones. There are no police alive back there."

"Police guarding the other bridges. They are refusing to man checkpoints."

I speed away from the intersection. We're doing sixty miles an hour in an empty lane. The long line of cars waiting for the bridge has backed up two miles.

"The cartel is recalling its men," Mirasol says. "At Bridge of Americas, Paseo Del Norte."

"We're going the wrong way. Where can I get off? I want to go to Paseo Del Norte."

"Half a mile further. Make a right."

I make the turn. "What happened back there?"

Mirasol raises the radio, still crackling with voices speaking Spanish. "When we escaped La Cueva, the cartel called the police with our description. Had them set up checkpoints. They planned to kill us when we tried to cross."

"What about the army?"

"I don't know. The president has sent the army to control violence and crime in Juarez. They might be employed by a competing cartel."

I look at Mirasol with disbelief.

"One never knows," Mirasol says. "Avoid army patrols because they make people disappear. Maybe their victims are bad guys, but—maybe not. They have detained police and policewomen. There are stories the policewomen are raped. Never written about, never reported. Reporters in Mexico are regularly executed.

"Of course, the police are no better. Three times, a town's entire police force has been arrested. Every single police officer. Once, during municipal elections. For complicity in the murder of a mayoral candidate." Mirasol pauses. "*That* is the real Mexico."

We are approaching the city center. The radio crackles again "*Manuel. Javier. Respóndeme.*"

Driving at a comfortable speed, I turn north on Avenida Francisco Villa.

The next voice that crackles from the radio speaks English. The accent is sharp, Middle Eastern. "Breed."

Mirasol looks at me with frightened eyes.

"Breed, I know you can hear me. It was a pleasure to meet you this evening. I want you to know—I am going to kill you."

A burst of static.

The radio falls silent.

33

JUAREZ, 0200 HRS THURSDAY

The old bull ring towers over our heads.

I've been to bullfights in Spain. Nowadays, the events are entertaining because of their pageantry. The organizers have the bulls' horns filed. This ensures less risk of matadors being gored. Decades ago, in the time of Hemingway, bulls' horns were not filed. The contest between man and beast was more equal.

Mexican bullfights are no different. Exercises in pageantry.

Occasionally, you hear of a severely injured matador. Wonder how it happened, because bullfights have become little more than ritual slaughter. Contests aren't exciting unless both sides bear risk.

I park the car in a dark alley off Calle Abraham Gonzalez. Shove the Beretta under the driver's seat and get out of the car. We will walk across the Paseo Del Norte.

Of course, the decision has been made for us. Well before we reached the booth, the US Border Patrol would know whether the car was stolen. Once we got there, questions would be asked about blood and brain tissue on the upholstery.

Mirasol and I check each other out—to ensure bloodstains

on our clothes are not noticeable. I put my arm around her, and we walk to Avenida Benito Juarez. Toward the bridge.

"Who was that man on the radio?" Mirasol asks.

"I think he killed my friend Keller. His wife and son."

"He's not Mexican."

"No, he isn't."

"Tell me, Breed. Have I not done enough you can trust me?"

I do trust Mirasol, though she has not told me everything.

"All right. His name is Faisal Hamza. The dark man we saw with Bledsoe the other night. He is using the tunnel to smuggle terrorists into the country. The attacks in New York and Los Angeles."

"He is working with men who traffic drugs and women?"

"Yes. Building the tunnel was expensive. Far more than Bledsoe could afford. Hamza and the cartels formed a joint venture to share the expense. Profits to share. And Hamza can get his killers into the country."

"There is no limit to the evil these men do, is there?"

"No." I stroke her arm. "They have to be stopped."

We join the flow of tourists and partiers walking toward the bridge. Like a pair of lovers, we stroll past the cathedral. Look up at the structure's illuminated facade. In the square, a tired mariachi band plays a tender song.

As we walk, Mirasol lays her head against my shoulder. My eyes restlessly quarter the ground. I sweep the street, the squares, the elevated positions. I search for any sign of *soldados* sent to kill us. I search for police and army. I am learning the border.

The song suits the procession of tourists toward the Paseo Del Norte. "That's a beautiful song."

"That is *La Golondrina*," Mirasol says. "The Swallow. It is an old song, about Mexicans who live away and miss their homeland."

"It's sad."

"We would not leave if our choices were not so terrible."

"Why did *you* leave?"

Arm around my waist, Mirasol clutches me. "I'll tell you, but not now. It's not easy."

"All right."

Two army Humvees are parked on either side of the Avenida Benito Juarez. The troops wear digital camouflage, American-supplied body armor and load-bearing vests. M4s low-ready. Soldiers stand at the fifty caliber machine guns. Their posture is casual, but their eyes are sharp.

No sign of police anywhere. I haven't seen a single policeman the length of Benito Juarez.

Mirasol's hand tightens on my waist. I grip her shoulder.

The soldiers are content to watch the procession of tourists file past. The mariachis' song is faintly audible in the distance.

We reach the Mexican border guards. Show our papers, answer superficial questions. We walk across the bridge, look down at the Rio Grande. Nothing grand about it. A mere trickle, the water glistens in the moonlight.

The Border Patrol on the US side are only slightly more difficult. I cringe as Mirasol displays her green card, but she meets only a courteous tip of the hat.

"How do we get back?" Mirasol asks.

"Find a car."

WE MAKE our way to the Greyhound bus station and find a cab. Ask the driver to take us to a twenty-four-hour car rental firm.

"Why didn't we take the taxi back?" Mirasol asks.

"Hamza's men will watch the hotel. We'll go to the Lazy K and call Stein to meet us there."

I fill in the paperwork, and we are escorted to a late-model Taurus in the back lot. In minutes, we are driving down Alameda toward Salem.

"This man, Hamza," Mirasol says. "How did he know your name?"

"We saw each other in the corridor. He called Bledsoe and described us. Bledsoe and Frank already tied us together. It wasn't rocket science."

"Now he wants to kill you."

"Now he *has* to kill me." I turn the air-conditioning on full blast. Point the vents at my face to stay awake. "Stein's management don't believe her. Don't believe a businessman would build a tunnel under an American factory. Stein has no direct evidence. She needs a statement from me to provide probable cause to obtain a warrant."

"Or me," Mirasol says.

"I didn't tell Stein you were at the lookout. I've tried to keep you out of it."

"She must suspect."

"Yes, but that's different from knowing. In any case, Hamza and Bledsoe have their reasons to kill us both."

One hand on the wheel, I take my phone and call Stein. Three rings and I'm kicked to voicemail. I can't imagine Stein turning off her phone. She might be working on her presentation, she might have gone to bed. "Stein, it's Breed. I've found the other side of the tunnel. Call me."

Mirasol gives me a skeptical look. "I thought Stein can't do anything in Mexico."

"She can't. I'll tell her I saw Hamza and his Quds in La Cueva. That will strengthen her case."

We drive in silence.

"There's one thing I don't understand," I say at last. "We should never have gotten out of La Cueva. Man-Bun should have alerted Hamza and his friends. He didn't tell the bartender. The bartender watched us leave, ran upstairs, and found the body. That's when the shit hit the fan."

Mirasol is silent. I'm wide awake now, calculating possibilities.

"Why," I ask, "did he come to kill us—alone."

"He didn't come to kill *us*," Mirasol says. "He came to kill *me*."

34

EL PASO, 0300 HRS THURSDAY

"He came to kill *me*."

I glance sideways. Mirasol's expression is serious. She stares at the string of white lines flashing under our headlights. If Man-Bun had something personal against Mirasol, it would explain a lot.

Mirasol's profile is beautiful.

"Tell me," I say.

She does.

MIRASOL'S STORY began in a manner little different from Nevita's. She was fifteen when she and her mother came to work in the *maquiladoras*. They came from Michoacán, west of Mexico City. Michoacán itself suffered a high rate of homicide and violence. Murders and kidnappings were daily fixtures. Mirasol grew up in a Catholic school, Sagrado Corazon, where she learned to speak English.

There was never a question of a father. In Mexico, men frequently marry, then abandon their families. Mirasol never knew her father. When her mother lost her job, she took

Mirasol north to Juarez. At the border, women could find jobs. Mirasol was of working age, got a job to help her mother. Together, they made a little more than Mirasol's mother had made as a secretary in Michoacán.

Mirasol was intelligent, spoke English, and was hard-working. At the *maquila,* she kept to herself. Having grown up in Michoacán, she was street-smart and knew to avoid trouble. The factory assembled laptops and personal computers for the American market.

If anything got Mirasol into trouble, it was her looks. She earned fifty dollars a week at the *maquila*, plus a production bonus. She worked twelve hours a day, the 6 AM to 6 PM shift. In the factories, line supervisors wielded arbitrary power over the workers. Her manager offered her a raise if she would sleep with him. She refused, and her life became more difficult.

The company rented US surplus school buses. To transport workers from their neighborhoods to the factory and back. The factory operated 24/7, churning out product for the Walmarts and Radio Shacks of America. The white buses, marked *Transporte de Personal*, operated to a schedule. Mirasol's supervisor forced her to work extra hours. In the evening, she finished long after the last bus had gone.

Mirasol was faced with a choice. She could find another way home, or she could spend the night at the factory. Return to the production line in the morning.

Mirasol tilts her chin at me. "I was not a virgin, Breed. But I knew if I surrendered to my manager, he would own me."

I watch the road, keep Mirasol in my peripheral vision. "Life is a string of decisions. Some are right, some are wrong, most you can't tell until you're in the shit."

"That is an interesting way to put it."

"You can't live your life hiding in a hole."

"I never have."

"You decided to go home."

"Yes, and that decision changed my life forever."

This won't end well. But—I want to know Mirasol.

MIRASOL'S *maquila* was centrally located. It was a mile and a half from the Rio Grande. In an industrial park between the Bridge of the Americas and the Zaragoza bridge. We passed it earlier, in our mad flight from the massacre.

Juarez is split in two. Most of the *maquiladoras* are located south and east of the city center. Residences are located north and west. The city center is a halfway house, a place people stop between work and home. It is where one changes buses. This makes the city center dangerous.

Those who live on the coasts cannot imagine the vastness of West Texas and Northern Mexico. Hundreds of miles of flat land. Broken by foothills and mountains further than they appear. Juarez is flat. A high plateau with the Franklins to the north and west. The *maquiladoras* stretch across the landscape in an endless sprawl. From a distance, the ground looks cramped and congested. In reality, distances are measured in miles.

The sun had gone down by the time Mirasol left the factory. The company school buses collected workers inside the *maquila* gates. Public transport was available on the city streets.

Having grown up in Michoacán, Mirasol was wary of strangers. She kept a pointed nail file in her purse. As she walked to the bus stop, she palmed it in her right hand. As much as possible, she kept to the lighted sidewalks.

I could have told her that was a mistake. Predators like their prey lit up for all to see. Standing in the light, her night vision was compromised. She should have walked in the shadows.

Reduced her profile, preserved her night vision so she could detect threats.

It was a hot evening. The wind kicked up to twenty miles an hour. It whipped her hair, blew choking dust in her face. She covered herself as best as she could. Ducked her chin against her chest as she hurried along the sidewalk.

Heart pounding, Mirasol made it to the bus stop. Stood under the light and waited for the bus to arrive. There was no shelter. She squinted in the wind, blinked dust from her eyes. Nervously, she looked this way and that, searching the shadows. She was glad when an older woman joined her. The bus arrived. Overcome with relief, she boarded and found a seat. Put her nail file back in her purse.

A two-mile ride, and she found herself on Avenida Francisco Villa. She got off and rushed to the department store on the other side of Avenida Benito Juarez. If the store was still open, she could buy towels for the kitchen. Catch a bus outside for the trip home.

The store was closed. In frustration, she turned away from the darkened storefront. Bumped into a man who casually put his arm around her. Surprised, she tried to push him away. He gripped her more tightly. She felt a hard metal object jammed against her ribs. "Be quiet," the man said, in Spanish. "I'll shoot you. No one will come. No one will care."

Terrified, Mirasol obeyed. She had always imagined a kidnapper would be oily and smelly. A hard, ugly man. This man was nothing like that. He was ordinary. He wore a clean, pressed jacket and trousers. There was nothing remarkable about his odor. The pistol was small in his hand, barely noticeable.

She didn't know where the clean man came from. He might have followed her from Avenida Francisco Villa. On the other hand, he might have been waiting near the department store. Shopping for a victim.

He guided her behind the cathedral and toward the *Mariscal*. There, in a side street, he led her to a car. It was a four-door sedan. A man was waiting in the back seat.

"Get in," Mirasol's escort said. "Remember. If you make trouble, I'll kill you."

Mirasol obeyed. She got into the car and sat in the back seat. The other man was rougher than the first. Stocky and dark, with an unkempt beard. His shirt was the color of his complexion. A shirt that had burrito stains on the front. He took Mirasol's purse and handcuffed her wrists behind her back. Then he made her slouch low in the seat and pulled a cloth hood over her head.

The darkness closed around her, and Mirasol struggled. The clean man told her to be quiet. "It's all right now," he said quietly. "It will be harder on you if you make trouble."

The man got into the driver's seat. She heard it creak as he sat down. Heard the driver's door slam and the engine start.

They drove for an hour. Mirasol couldn't tell which direction they were going. She only knew it was well past the city center because the car drove slowly at first, then sped up. They would not drive so fast unless they were free of congestion.

When they stopped, she strained her ears. In the distance, she heard gay laughter, as though men and women were having a good time. She heard muffled club music. The door was jerked open. The bearded man next to her grabbed her by the arm and pulled her from the car.

The next voice she heard was that of the man who took her from the department store. "Watch your step."

They guided her up two flights of stairs. They climbed slowly, so she would not fall. The clean man gripped her arm just above her elbow. Firm, but gentle. The street sounds disappeared. All she heard was faint music, and the thump of bass against the floor. They pushed her into a room, sat her on a bed.

With a flourish, the man in the jacket whipped the hood off Mirasol's head. She blinked in the light. She was in a small bedroom. Sitting on a single bed with a metal frame. A small dresser was pushed against one wall. The window was fastened shut with a brass hasp and padlock. The room had a small toilet.

Her captors looked down at her.

"Welcome to your new home," the clean man said.

"IT WAS A HOTEL," Mirasol says. "It could have been Hotel Verde, or La Cueva. All that matters is they had me, and there was nothing I could do about it."

"Did you fight them?"

"Not at first." In her lap, Mirasol's tiny fists clenched. "I was still thinking like a tough Michoacán kid. I wanted to learn what I could, to plan an escape."

I remember SERE training—Survival, Escape, Resistance and Evasion. Everyone thinks that way at the beginning. In the end, everyone breaks.

35

EL PASO, 0320 HRS THURSDAY

Everyone breaks.

SERE training starts like routine hazing. It gets serious when the opposing force waterboards you. Prepare for the worst. Every prisoner of war, male or female, is going to be raped. Accept it. Hold out as long as you can, wait for an opportunity to escape.

What can one expect from a fifteen-year-old girl?

Mirasol told me.

THE FIRST NIGHT, the bearded man raped Mirasol. The clean man smoked a cigarette and watched. She refused to struggle, so they demanded other services. When the bearded man sodomized her, she began to cry and scream. They found that satisfying.

With the windows shut, it was hard to keep track of time. Mirasol counted days by keeping track of her meals and activity in the hotel. Her captors' behavior toward her was structured. The clean man directed Mirasol to perform services in specific ways. Forced her to develop skills. When she failed to please, he had her beaten.

The bearded man and his friends delivered the beatings. Calculated not to mark, they were like those delivered to Nevita. Blows to her belly. The flat of the hand to the side of her head. Until she saw double. After particularly severe beatings, the clean man shone a light in her eyes. She did not try to escape, so they did not torture her. She counted herself lucky. She had heard other girls were tortured for pleasure.

Many men used her. Her captors and their friends, dozens of clients. The clients provided feedback. The clean man told her she was working in the hospitality industry. Negative feedback had to be addressed. She was beaten for lack of enthusiasm. If her skills were deficient, the clean man provided instruction. The client was invited to return. If she failed to please a second time, she received further remediation.

Always, her captors and clients used condoms.

Once a week, she was tested for venereal disease.

After a month, the clean man brought her a small suitcase and clothing. Three simple cotton shifts. Two white, one black. One of the white shifts had lace about the hem. When they took her, she had been wearing jeans and running shoes. The clean man brought her plain, flat-heeled shoes to wear with the shifts.

"Take your clothes off," he said. "Put on the white one."

Obediently, Mirasol did as she was told.

The clean man smiled and gave her a slow clap.

I look at Mirasol. "The cartel was preparing you."

Mirasol smiled sadly. "I will tell you everything, Breed. When I finish, you will not look at me the same way."

No way to avoid answering that one. "Let's find out."

. . .

THE CLEAN MAN handcuffed Mirasol and hooded her. She stood in the middle of the room, dressed in the clean white shift and flat shoes. The greasy man took her by the arm, and they led her down the stairs.

They put Mirasol in the car and drove south by west. She knew the direction of travel because it was morning. Sitting in the back of the car, she felt the hot sun on the back of her neck. For a fifteen-year-old girl who had been raped and abused, she showed remarkable presence of mind.

When she heard the sound of airplanes taking off, she knew they were near the airport. Before long, the car stopped and she was ordered to get out. She found herself standing on a concrete tarmac.

"Is everything ready?" the clean man asked.

A third voice, someone new to her, said, "Yes, we can go right away."

Bound and hooded, she was forced onto an airplane. She heard the propellers turn over. First the left, then the right. She sat in the back seat with the clean man. The pilot taxied the plane to the runway. The clean man put his arm around her and squeezed her shoulder. "Don't be afraid," he said. "Soon you will be at your new home."

The word 'home' shook Mirasol. She thought of her mother and how worried she must be. She didn't think she would see her mother again. Mirasol began to cry.

The clean man comforted her.

The airplane raced down the runway and lifted into the sky.

Mirasol became disoriented as the plane banked to avoid the mountains. It changed direction several times before settling into level flight. Mirasol could not feel the sun on her face, so she thought the airplane might be flying south by west. She could not be sure.

When the airplane landed, the clean man ushered her to a vehicle.

"There is a high step," he warned her.

The vehicle must have been a large pickup. A man in the truck reached down, grabbed her by the arms, and lifted her aboard. The clean man followed, and she was sandwiched between the two. She must have been in a four-door, because the man on her left was not the driver. The driver started the truck. With a roar, it sped off.

The pickup came to a stop. The clean man opened the door, hopped out.

It was impossible for her to get down with her hands bound behind her back. The man on her left got out, came around to the other side. Together, he and the clean man supported her by the elbows and helped her to the ground.

The clean man exchanged jovial banter with the others. Took her by the arm and guided her. "Come into the house," he said. "It is very nice. You will like it."

Mirasol heard the snorting of horses. The sound of the animals trotting this way and that. The whoops of men. The hot air smelled of dust and dung. There was an animal smell she couldn't escape.

They walked a short distance, and the clean man knocked on a door.

"Hello." A woman's voice greeted them. "I heard you land. Is this the new one?"

"It is."

"Take off the hood, Marcello. I want to see her face."

The clean man jerked the hood from Mirasol's head. She blinked in the light. Slowly, a middle-aged woman's face came into focus. She was distinguished, her graying hair piled in a bun.

"Oh, she is pretty," the woman exclaimed. "I am Carmen. What is your name?"

"Mirasol."

"A beautiful name." The woman turned to the clean man. "Take off the handcuffs, Marcello. She has nowhere to run."

The clean man shook his head. "Instructions, Carmen. Let us take her upstairs first."

"Of course." Carmen clucked. "Come this way, Mirasol. You will love it here."

They were in a ranch house. She had been brought in through the kitchen. A kitchen bigger than six Juarez apartments put together. Carmen was obviously the cook or housekeeper. She guided Mirasol and the clean man through the dining room. There was an intricately carved dining table of hardwood. Long enough to seat ten people a side with one more at either end. Cabinets with glass doors displayed expensive china. Each plate and saucer was painted with beautiful, intricate designs.

A wide staircase and foyer set the dining room apart from the living room. The banister was thick and rich. It curved gracefully to a second floor. The furniture and bookshelves in the living room looked expensive. Against one wall was a gun case, with various long rifles racked in a row. A thick chain was strung through their trigger guards and secured with a padlock.

Mirasol made a mental note of the guns.

The clean man whispered in her ear. "I saw you entertain a foolish thought. Put it from your mind, little one. Papi can love you like a daughter. He can punish you like you cannot imagine."

Heat surged to Mirasol's face.

The second floor was large, the walls exquisitely paneled. Mirasol was surprised the staircase continued to a third floor. Carmen was proud of the house. "Papi's rooms are above us," she explained. "The second floor is for girls like you."

"Are there others like me?" Mirasol dared ask.

Carmen and the clean man exchanged glances. "From time to time, there can be," Carmen said. "You will see."

Mirasol was shown to a bedroom at one end of the hall. It was surprisingly comfortable. A queen-sized bed, en suite toilet, and a dresser. The bed and dresser were of the same expensive wood as the rest of the furniture. There was a closet. The clean man put her little suitcase next to it.

The window drew Mirasol's attention. It was big, and she could see the whole world through it. Of course, it was closed so the house's central air-conditioning could work.

The view took Mirasol's breath away. She was happy to see so much, but she was depressed by what she saw.

Mirasol was held captive on a ranch. A big ranch in the middle of the Chihuahuan desert. Miles and miles of creosote and yucca. A barn, a corral, horses. Outbuildings that served as barns, workshops and garages.

The temperature outside was anywhere from a hundred to a hundred and twenty degrees. Alone in the desert, she would not survive a day.

There was no escape.

MIRASOL'S STORY has gone in a surprising direction. I expected a tale of exploitation and debauchery in the seedy whorehouses of Juarez. A trip through the mountains and across the border. Perhaps a midnight crawl through narrow tunnels. Emerging from the storm drains of El Paso to be sold into sexual slavery.

None of that happened.

Except the exploitation and debauchery.

"What was Papi like?" I ask.

"Papi was the devil."

PAPI CAME to see her that night. Sixty, fit, masculine. Light-skinned, a *mestizo* with silver hair and patrician features. He came in his finery. Dark brown jeans, cream shirt, bolo tie with a gold slide shaped like a serpent.

"Remember what I taught you," the clean man had admonished her. "Strive to please and all will be well. If you make them angry, they will be cruel."

"I'll try," Mirasol promised.

"I know you will." The clean man stroked Mirasol's hair. "You have been my best pupil."

Then he was gone. Mirasol heard the roar of an airplane's engine. She looked up and watched the twin-engine Cessna take off from the dirt airstrip.

Papi was kind and solicitous. He unlocked Mirasol's handcuffs. Put them on the dresser, sat next to her on the bed. He took her hands in his, stroked her wrists. There were no marks. The clean man had been careful not to fasten the bracelets too tightly.

"You are very pretty, my little one," the old man cooed. "Come, show yourself to Papi."

Already, Mirasol was planning her escape. She needed the keys to the gun cabinet. She needed the keys to a vehicle. She needed a map. She needed Papi's trust.

Mirasol took off her shift.

36

LAZY K, 0340 HRS THURSDAY

I spin the wheel and pull off the highway into the Lazy K's access road. Switch on the brights and race toward the ranch house. Take my phone, dial Stein.

Again, I am kicked to voicemail.

"Clock's ticking, Stein. Call me."

We arrive at the ranch house. The forensic teams have long finished their work, but crime scene tape remains strung everywhere. I ignore it, park in front of the garage. The phone number. The shell casing. The murder location. I've given Stein more hard evidence than they'll ever find here.

I get out of the car, beckon Mirasol. "Come inside," I say.

The ranch house is dark. I lead the way to the living room. Mirasol reaches for the light switch, but I stop her. "No. We don't want to ruin our night vision."

We step over the white outlines where Mary and Donnie fell. Mirasol sits on the couch.

I take out my phone and call Garrick. He should be in bed, I'm surprised he's awake. It is one of those nights.

"Breed. Where the hell are you, boy?"

"I'm at the Lazy K. When was the last time you spoke with Stein?"

"A few hours ago, after midnight. She's making an online presentation right now. Washington's two hours ahead."

Of course. That's why she was pulling the all-nighter. Probably has her phone on silent.

"Sheriff, get over to Stein right now. As soon as she's off her call, bring her here. Come together, be careful you're not followed. There's a good chance *soldados* are watching the hotel."

"What are you talking about?"

"I'll explain when you get here."

I disconnect the call.

Mary grabbed the Mossberg from somewhere. While Donnie stabbed the intruder. Where did she get it?

The living room opens to the dining room, kitchen, and Keller's study. The dining room and kitchen are open-plan. The study is closed off and opens to the living room through a door. I go inside. It's dark, but my eyes have adapted. There is a gun rack with a row of shotguns and rifles, including an M4 carbine. Mary had unlocked the chain to get at the Mossberg. The technicians neglected to secure it.

I take the M4 and check its breech. Empty. Check the bolt face. Clear. The cabinet is stacked with ammunition. I take a thirty round magazine, load the rifle. Pull back the charging handle and release it. A round chambers with a satisfying clack. I flick on the safety and go back to Mirasol.

The technicians have drawn the curtains back from the picture windows. I sit on a comfortable easy chair, kitty-corner to Mirasol. From here, I can watch for approaching cars. We sit in the dark, protected from prying eyes. I set the rifle across my knees and sigh.

"Is everything all right?" Mirasol asks.

"Yes. Nothing to do but wait." The rifle in my hands is comforting. "Will you finish your story?"

Mirasol's eyes glisten in the dark.

"You want to hear of my pain."

MIRASOL WORKED HARD to become Papi's favorite.

She lived at the ranch for months. Papi acted like a solicitous old man, but he was El Jefe. The boss of one of the cartels vying for control of the Juarez drug trade. His men trafficked drugs, women, young girls. He demanded the best for himself.

Papi had his passions. Rifles, girls, bullfighting. He loved the *corrida*. He raised his bulls, sponsored bullfights in Juarez. The Plaza del Toros. The crowds waited for Papi's events—bullfights in which his bulls performed. These events were special because the bulls' horns were not filed. That made them especially dangerous for *El Matador*. Papi sponsored the matadors. The prize money was as spectacular as the performances. The best matadors in Mexico vied to perform at Papi's events. The risks of being gored were high, but so were the rewards.

Mirasol watched Papi's men work the bulls and horses in the corral behind the big house. She catered to his masculinity. Marveled at his vigor. He had the strength of the bulls he loved. She used all her skills to please him.

Soon, Mirasol was given the run of the house. Other girls came, but Mirasol was Papi's favorite. There were times he was so vigorous Mirasol could not satisfy him. On those occasions he took Mirasol and others to bed.

The guns were locked away. The men around the ranch all carried weapons. The cowboys had pistols in holsters or stuffed in their hip pockets. Kept automatic rifles in their pickup trucks, or in scabbards when they rode horses.

One day, Papi celebrated a particularly grand bullfight with a *fiesta* at the ranch. He invited his friends and all his men.

Hired a mariachi band. While the band played gay music, Papi's men brought three steers to the ranch. They took their pistols and dispatched the animals with a single bullet each, between the eyes. Exactly the way professionals stunned animals in the slaughterhouse. The men gutted the steers, skinned them, and the women roasted the best steaks. Fed all the men, their families, and Papi's guests.

While the men celebrated, Papi's friends were invited upstairs to the second floor. There, they were free to use Mirasol and three other girls as they wished.

Mirasol worked hard to please the men. They were drunk on liquor and sex. She used her skills to coax information from them. The ranch was in the Chihuahuan desert, two hundred miles south of Juarez. It was a thirty-minute flight or a two-and-a-half hour drive from major centers.

Escape was possible. All Mirasol needed was a vehicle and a compass. Two hours in the right direction, and she was certain to hit a major highway.

She would teach herself to drive.

WHAT BALLS. Why not steal a plane?

"I made a run for it that night," Mirasol says. "If I waited too long, I might lose my nerve."

"You knew where the keys were?"

"Yes. Not to the gun rack. But Papi kept the keys to his cars and trucks in his desk. He had a red Toyota pickup that was always ready to go. I saw him drive in it with his bodyguards. To the bullring. Late that night, I took the keys."

"Didn't they hear you start the car?"

"I'm sure they did. But it was a *fiesta*. Guests came from all over northern Mexico. People had been coming and going all day and night."

"And the compass?"

Mirasol shrugs. "Cars have compasses."

MIRASOL LEFT JUST BEFORE DAWN. It was easy enough to take the red Toyota. She started the engine, checked the fuel and compass. Her plan was to drive straight north. At a speed of fifty miles an hour, she was certain she would reach a major highway in less than two hours.

She shifted the truck into drive.

An orange ball of fire, the sun rose in the east. Soon the temperature outside the truck stood over a hundred degrees. The air-conditioning worked hard, the truck swallowed fuel like a thirsty animal. Mirasol wasn't worried. There was plenty of gas.

The Toyota raced north. For the first time in months, Mirasol felt free. She allowed herself to dream of Juarez. She would walk into the apartment and hug her mother. She would forget everything that happened.

The plain was scarred by arroyos. Most were shallow enough, she could drive right across them. Down one bank, across the wash, up the other. At times, the arroyos were deeper, the banks steeper. On those occasions, she turned west and followed the bank until she found a spot shallow enough to cross. Twice, she went down one bank only to find the other bank too steep to climb. Again, she turned west and sped along the wash until she found a gentle slope.

The compass did not fail Mirasol. Her plan was perfectly sound. I might have done the same thing.

But—the lateral forays along the arroyos cost her time.

The temperature in the desert climbed to one hundred and twenty degrees. She was in the middle of a wash, racing west. The machine warned her.

Danger of overheating. Turn off air-conditioning.

She turned off the air-conditioning.

Before long, she was drenched in sweat. The red warning light on her console wouldn't stop flashing.

Engine overheating. Stop immediately.

She wondered how long she could go on. What would happen if she continued against the flashing red light.

She found out.

No water, stuck a hundred miles from nowhere.

The twin-engine Cessna saved her. The only way to spot the truck was from the air. The banks of the arroyo hid the Toyota from view. The pilot flew over her once at three thousand feet. He banked sharply, dropped to a hundred and fifty feet, and flew over her again. She stood on the bed of the wash, staring up at the plane. When the pilot rocked his wings, she did not wave. She was overcome with despair.

The fear came later.

Came with the Hummer and the big pickup trucks sent from the ranch. The Hummer looked like a tank. The pickups were monster trucks with raised suspensions and oversized tires. Banks of floodlights were lined up on the roofs of the cabs.

The men with rifles stood high on the arroyo. Waited for her to climb the bank.

They brought her back to Papi.

In the living room of the ranch, knees shaking, she stood in front of him. Two of his cowboys flanked her. One man in his thirties, with a rodeo belt and an embroidered shirt. The other a kid in his twenties. Hard, with a .380 Walther stuffed in his jeans pocket. Three girls sat together on a sofa. Other men stood along the walls.

Papi stared at her. "This is how you repay my kindness."

Mirasol said nothing.

"A man such as I survives on respect. You understand?"

Papi stood, held out his hand to the cowboy in the pretty shirt. The man had a clasp knife in a leather case on his belt.

He unsnapped the case. Flicked the knife open, handed it to Papi.

Mirasol shut her eyes. She felt the blade against her cheek. Papi traced a line from the corner of her mouth to her ear. Softly, without breaking her skin. He did the same on the other side.

"How shall I make an example of you?"

Mirasol could not speak. Tears flooded her eyes.

Papi folded the knife, handed it back to the cowboy. Left the room.

In front of the other girls, the men beat Mirasol to within an inch of her life.

"Papi cut you a break," I say. "No pun intended."

"I know." Mirasol folds her arms, shivers. "He should have cut me a smile. They beat me about the face, my kidneys, everywhere. I lost control. There was blood in my urine for a week. It took a month for the bruises to fade."

"What happened next?"

Mirasol wipes tears from her eyes.

"Next—I came to the United States."

37

LAZY K, 0400 HRS THURSDAY

"Next—I came to the United States."

Mirasol's manner is so matter-of-fact I can't believe my ears. "Papi sold you?"

"Something like that. I think he was fond of me, but could not afford to appear weak. Another *jefe* would have marked me and sent me to a whorehouse. Or had me killed. I was lucky."

Papi did not touch Mirasol again.

When her bruises faded, she was handcuffed, hooded, and put on the Cessna. It flew her to a grass airfield high in the mountains. She stepped from the plane, steadied by her escort. The air was fresh and clean, unsullied by the dust and pollution of Juarez. She could smell it through the space at the bottom of the hood. Blades of grass brushed her ankles.

The men hustled her to a waiting vehicle. Another truck. They drove her to the house. It was the same treatment she'd received when she arrived at Papi's ranch, but rougher. She missed the presence of the clean man. His manner and familiarity had reassured her. Now she was among strangers.

There was none of the activity and bustle that marked Papi's ranch. The men who handled her were silent. They took her to a room and undid her handcuffs. Made her sit on a metal-framed bed and handcuffed her to a bedpost.

The men left her alone, hooded.

She waited for hours. Finally, she tried to sleep. Slipped her shoes off and stretched out on the bed. She found a pillow on which to rest her head.

The door slammed, waking her.

"Oh my," a voice said. "Nice little package. Let's see how pretty you are."

An American accent. From the West.

The man sat her up and tore the hood from her head.

Mirasol blinked.

The old man was in his late fifties. Not as old as Papi. He wore the same western garb. His face was tanned, and he looked rough. But—he was soft around the edges. Like he was a knife grown dull from years of use.

He ran his hands all over Mirasol. Caressed her face, brushed back her hair. Stroked her knees and thighs. Her skin crawled. The old man's hands did not match his face. They were soft, like he had never done physical work. He unlocked the handcuffs. Stepped back, ordered her to strip. She had been well conditioned to obey.

He raped her.

Something snapped in Mirasol's mind. From the moment she landed at Papi's ranch, she strove to please. Here, with this rough old man and his soft hands, she lost the will to please. She lay flat on her back and allowed him to manipulate her limbs.

When he finished, he was angry.

"Do something," he said. "Goddamn you, don't just lie there."

Mirasol said nothing.

"We are going to *fix* your malfunction, girl."

The man dressed. On the way out, he slammed the door.

Mirasol put her shift back on and surveyed her room. It was smaller than the one at Papi's ranch. Smaller than the one in the hotel. The window was locked, but she could see out. She was surprised to find herself in the mountains. Gone was the dusty brown of Chihuahua. Grass and green trees were everywhere. The room was on the second floor of a sprawling ranch house built like a log cabin.

A man entered the room. He may have been the one who escorted her from the airplane, but she couldn't tell. He was in his thirties, clean-shaven. He wore jeans and a blue work shirt. She shuddered when she saw the clasp knife he wore on his belt. In his hand, he carried long strips of leather cord.

"Lie on the bed," he commanded. "Face down."

The man was American. Mirasol decided she had been flown to a ranch in the mountains of the United States.

Mirasol obeyed. The man knelt on the bed next to her. First he bound her wrists behind her back. Then he tied her feet together at the ankles. Finally, he took a long strip of leather and bound her elbows together. Her shoulders screamed.

The man left and closed the door behind him.

After an hour, Mirasol's hands, feet and arms were on fire with pain. The old man returned. Stood over her, hands on his hips. "Hurts, don't it." He smiled. "When you're ready to show me everything you showed Papi, you let me know. We'll make it stop."

"THE SAME TECHNIQUE that was used on Nevita," I observed.

"Yes. But—I beat them."

"How?"

"I found if I could bear the pain long enough, I grew numb. I felt nothing."

"There's a problem with that—gangrene."

"I didn't know that at the time, but they did." Mirasol smiled. "They loosened the cords. The old man was quite frustrated."

"Good for you."

"You know better than that, Breed."

I do know better. Everybody breaks.

"They spread me naked on the bed—used electricity."

"I don't need to hear this."

"I told you, Breed. You won't see me the same way." Mirasol looks angry. "You said we should find out."

"All right, tell me."

"The man in the work shirt brought in a heavy battery. Two long copper wires... on metal rods with insulated handles. He attached the wires to steel wool. Moistened the wool with an ointment. Then he left. The old man came in and pulled up a chair next to the bed. He spent hours with me. I screamed as much as he wanted."

"How long did they keep you there?"

"Weeks. Months. One day they hooded me again. I lay in the back of a truck. They drove for hours, took me to another hotel. I was placed with other women. Illegals from Mexico. Common prostitutes."

Mirasol leans forward. Hands clasped, elbows on her knees.

"That is what I became. In New York, we were sold over and over. One day, the FBI raided the hotel. They arrested the traffickers. Put us in custody."

"Did the FBI help you?"

"Only as much as I helped them." Mirasol looks at me like she is a thousand years old and I am a child. "To the FBI and ICE, I was also a criminal. Of a different sort.

"I testified against the traffickers. In exchange for a U-Visa. A document given to victims of crime who aid the police. In my case, trafficking a minor. Sexual abuse. A long list, I forget. The case took two years to prepare and take to trial. The FBI and the federal prosecutors helped me. In exchange for my testimony and cooperation, they got me a green card."

"Did they arrest the old man?"

Mirasol shakes her head. "No. The FBI couldn't find him. Their best guess is that I was held at a ranch somewhere in Colorado. The Rockies. They rounded up the traffickers who took me to New York. Put them away."

"And Papi?"

"The Department of Justice turned over all their information to the *Federales*. Papi is well known to the Mexican government. He finances their lifestyles.

"The authorities did nothing.

But—I am marked for death."

"Couldn't the FBI put you in the Witness Protection Program?"

Mirasol shakes her head. "No. They might have, if my testimony resulted in the conviction of a big fish. The people I put away were foot soldiers. No one higher than middle management. I was lucky to get the U-Visa and green card."

"That's why Man-Bun wanted to kill you."

"Yes. It is the only explanation. All this happened many years ago. My photograph was circulated to *soldados*, but few remember. I disappeared into the United States. Should have been happy to disappear, but could not stay away. I risked my life several times—searching for my mother. But I was careful. I think it was a coincidence Man-Bun recognized me. He did not want to share the reward, so he came alone."

Now I understand Mirasol's hesitation when I asked her to come with me.

"Did you find your mother?"

"No. The mutilated bodies of murdered girls were found in the desert. The Mexican police want to close outstanding cases. They told my mother I was dead. The body was not fit for viewing. My mother left Juarez. I searched everywhere, travelled to Michoacán. I could not find her."

I lean forward, take Mirasol's hand in mine. "When this is over, I'll help you find her."

Mirasol squeezes my hand. "Thank you, Breed. You need to know something else."

"Tell me."

"The old man at the ranch—Paul Bledsoe."

38

LAZY K, 0415 HRS THURSDAY

"The old man at the ranch—Paul Bledsoe."

I swallow hard. "How long have you known?"

"Two weeks." Mirasol shrugs. "When I saw him from the lookout, I couldn't believe my eyes. But everything makes sense."

"There are no coincidences." The diabolical web is spread before me. "Paul Bledsoe has a relationship with Papi. Papi is involved with Faisal Hamza. Papi's cartel and the Quds financed Bledsoe's tunnel."

Mirasol stares at me. Her eyes blaze in the half-light. "Breed, I want Bledsoe in prison. I want to look in his eyes when I testify against him."

I say nothing.

In the distance, a pair of headlights approach.

"Stein and Garrick are here."

Mirasol looks over her shoulder through the picture windows.

The headlights are high and closely set. I make out the distinctive outlines of the windshield and roll bar of Garrick's Jeep. He parks in the drive.

"Let's go."

I sling the rifle over my shoulder, walk to the front door. Mirasol follows me. I cross the porch and walk down the front steps to the Jeep.

Garrick switches off his headlights and dismounts. He's alone.

"Where's Stein?" I ask.

"At the hotel," Garrick says. "Doing a Q&A. She told me to get over here."

"I told you to stick together."

"There's no sign anybody's staked out the town."

I look back at the house. Mirasol stands in the open doorway, listening.

Garrick hitches up his belt. Stands with his hands on his hips. "Now what's this all about, Breed?"

"We found the other end of the tunnel. A club in Juarez."

"You have anything to do with the action over there?"

"What action?"

"Bunch of Mexican police got themselves killed in a shootout with the cartel."

"Pity."

"Yeah. Happened right at the foot of the Zaragoza bridge. Biggest bloodbath in ten years."

Mirasol cries out—a muffled sound.

I twist to see—

Hamza, standing behind her, one hand clamped over her nose and mouth. His other fist is pressed to her belly. Gripping a blade buried under her ribs.

I unsling the M4.

Behind me, Garrick's unhurried drawl. "Hold on there, Breed. Don't move."

Garrick's hand holds a Beretta Model 92. The pistol he never draws. Well, he has drawn it once before.

"That the pistol you used on Keller?"

"Put the rifle down, Breed. Slowly."

I bend at the knees and set the M4 on the gravel.

Garrick relaxes. Takes a step back. His gun hand does not waver.

Hamza extracts his knife from Mirasol's lifeless body. Contemptuously, he casts her aside.

He's dressed as he was at La Cueva. Dark shirt, black jeans, boots. He unslings an AK47, descends the front steps. He does not hurry. Approaches me with the rifle in one hand, a Bowie knife in the other. The moon is setting. Its cold light falls on the blade—black with Mirasol's blood.

My teeth clench as Hamza steps to me and raises the knife. More like a machete, it's a foot long. Three inches wide at the haft. Without smiling, he presses the flat of the knife to my right cheek. First he wipes the blade on one side of my face, then the other. Sheaths the weapon.

Hamza steps back. "The United States and Mexico are not so different," he says. "Policemen can always be bought."

I see it all, plain as day. "Is this how you got the drop on Keller?"

"Of course." Hamza covers me with his rifle. "Keller went to Garrick with what he saw. Garrick pretended not to believe the story, made Keller show him. That night, they both climbed the hill. Your friend was so trusting, he did not bring a weapon. I was waiting."

Of course. I'd wondered how his murderers knew Keller was on the hill. He wouldn't have given himself away. He was vulnerable only to betrayal.

"Garrick shot him."

"I did." The admission doesn't trouble Garrick one bit. "I always wondered what it would be like to use this popgun. Figured I should do it once in my life."

"Moving the body made sense. Taking his head was extreme."

"That was Hamza. His people have a thing for cutting people's heads off."

Hamza's voice is cold. "The prophet commands we strike their necks. To cast terror into the hearts of *kafir*. It is written—in the *Quran*."

"Yeah, never could understand that." Garrick has become jovial. "It's in your holy book, ain't it. The cartels, *they* do it for show. Arms, legs, what-the-fuck-ever. Heads. It don't matter none to them. You people have *rules*."

The Quds colonel glares at the sheriff. "And *you* have nothing. That is why your people no longer believe in Allah. That is why He, through *our* prophet, has perfected the teachings."

I tell myself Hamza is not insane. He is completely rational in the context of his belief system. That is why his fighters are committed and dangerous. I fix my eyes on him. "*You* killed Mary and Donnie."

"Yes, Breed." There is pride in Hamza's voice. How can a man take pride in mutilating a woman and her child? "They were Keller's. I should have taken them as captives of my right hand. It was not convenient."

Garrick scowls. "He wanted to kill them the night we got Keller. But the shipment had to go out. It was dawn by the time they finished. Later, I tried to talk him out of it. I knew from your friends they didn't know anything. But Hamza and the cartels don't like loose ends."

Hamza sneers. "Only a fool leaves an enemy's boy to grow into a man."

I address Hamza. "Reckon the sheriff is all about the money."

"This work sure enough does pay well." Garrick grins. Flashes two rows of perfect pearly whites. The pistol does not waver. "Everyone has their motives. Hamza here—a true believer. Bledsoe, he does like them little girls. My motives are my own. You chew on 'em the little time you got left, boy."

My phone buzzes.

Garrick's face is ghoulish in the Jeep's headlights. "Did you call Stein?"

I say nothing.

Rifle in hand, Hamza circles me. Those eyes. A snake waiting to strike.

Garrick's voice is cold. "What did you tell Stein?"

"Enough." With his rifle, Hamza clubs me. The small of my back explodes with pain. I grunt, fall to my knees. Another blow, between my shoulder blades—I pitch onto my face. Paralyzed.

Hamza throws himself on me. Crushes me with his weight, pins my arms under his knees. He twists his left hand in my hair, pulls my head back. The blade of his knife is cold against my throat.

"I killed your woman, Breed. Now *you* die."

Fucker knows what he's doing. His blade, razor sharp, cuts into my neck. Draws a trickle of blood. My head is tilted back, eyes staring into the muzzle of Garrick's Beretta. I've seen men beheaded alive. I want the bullet.

"Hold on a minute." Garrick addresses Hamza, but his eyes are fixed on me. His gun hand is rock steady. "Don't you want to know what he told Stein?"

Before drawing the blade across my throat, Hamza freezes. "I understand their silly laws. Without him, they have nothing."

"You willing to take that chance? I'm not. We're in this together, boy." Garrick looks as hardened a killer as Hamza.

Hamza takes the knife from my throat, rises to his feet.

He spits on me. "*Kafir*."

My face is in the dirt. I turn my head, look up at Hamza.

"It is almost dawn." Hamza plants his boot on the side of my face. Crushes my head against the gravel. "These vehicles will be visible from the air."

"Let's take him inside," Garrick says. "I'll make him talk."

Hamza lets out a harsh cry of frustration.

"I will dispose of his vehicle." The Quds jabs the point of his knife at Garrick. "*You* find out what he has told Stein. No mistakes, my friend. If there is *any* reason to delay the shipment, call me."

"Y'all got nothing to worry about." Garrick chuckles. "I'm going to enjoy this."

Hamza kicks me. "Get up. Give me the keys."

Awash in pain, I struggle to my feet. Hand over the car keys.

"Make him beg." Hamza turns and walks to the Taurus. He puts the AK47 in the car. Fires up the engine and drives away.

My back throbs with pain. "How did he get here?"

"Y'all are a bit slow today, Breed. I dropped Hamza a quarter mile up the road. He worked his way around while we were talking."

Garrick keeps his distance. Six feet. An easy pistol shot, far enough not to be taken by surprise. "Let's go inside," he says. "I don't want to leave a mess out here."

We climb the steps to the porch. Mirasol, tiny at the best of times, is a crumpled doll.

Garrick gestures with his pistol. "Drag her inside."

I defy the sheriff. Carry Mirasol in my arms, lay her on the sofa.

"I figured you'd be done in by a skirt," Garrick grins. "Didn't think it'd be for a beaner."

Garrick takes a step back, opens the distance between us. "You called Stein, didn't you?"

I say nothing.

"Y'all been watching too many Gary Cooper movies." Garrick shifts to a two-handed grip, a perfect isosceles. "Here's the game we'll play. One chance—a knee or elbow. Starting now."

In the half-light, Garrick raises his pistol. Points it at my left knee.

Crack.

The picture window explodes in a shower of glass.

Garrick's head jerks toward the sound.

A perfect cone of white light fixes itself on the sheriff's face. His eyes widen.

Two more shots follow in rapid succession.

Crack-crack.

Two black holes appear in Garrick's forehead. The expression of astonishment is frozen on his face. He crumples to the floor.

The light remains fixed on the sheriff.

A figure in black raises a leg and steps over the low windowsill. It's a woman. Careful not to cut herself on the jagged glass.

Cautiously, Stein steps around the sofa. She holds the SIG in her right hand, supported on her left wrist. Her left hand holds a flashlight.

"Breed, get the lights."

Not bad, Stein. Where'd you learn those moves?

I flick the light switch at the entrance. Blink as the lights come on.

Stein stands over Garrick. With the toe of a perfectly polished dress shoe, she slides the Beretta away from his body. Turns off her flashlight, holsters the SIG. She drops to one knee, turns the dead man's pockets inside out. Recovers two mobile phones.

Broken glass litters the floor, lies on Mirasol's body.

"We have to get back to Salem," Stein says. "You can thank me on the way."

"Give me your jacket, Stein."

Stein shrugs off her suit coat.

Gently, I cover Mirasol.

39

LAZY K, 0500 HRS THURSDAY

Stein's Civic is cool and comfortable. I like the new-car smell. In the east, the sky is lightening. The dashboard thermometer reads ninety degrees external temperature. The SIG P226 Legion is holstered at Stein's hip.

Sexy and stylish. She knows how to use it.

"There's Kleenex in the glove compartment," she says.

"What?"

"Your face, Breed." Stein's voice is gentle. "You can lose the war paint."

Hamza wiped Mirasol's blood on my face. I open Stein's glove compartment. Tear fistfuls of Kleenex out of an open box. Scrub my face.

Stein glances at me. "Let me see."

I turn my head to look at her.

"It's dried." Stein shakes her head. "Leave it. You can wash in the hotel."

I'm not too concerned about my appearance. "It was Garrick all the time."

"Yes."

"How did you find out?"

"Everything came together at once." Stein hands me one of the cell phones she took from Garrick's corpse. "That's the burner. An hour and a half ago, it came alive."

I suck breath.

Stein smiles. "Can you remember what happened an hour and a half ago?"

"I called Garrick."

"You called Garrick. And he used that burner to call Hamza. I had my phone on silent. You're lucky my team messaged me online. Pulled me out of my presentation."

"You couldn't have known it was Garrick using the phone."

"No. But—the burner was active. My team used active cell towers. Triangulated it real time. The transmission originated from Salem County's sheriff's station. I rushed over, but Garrick was gone."

Stein's eyes are fixed on the road. Once more, she is all business. "I commandeered Garrick's office. Instructed my team to track the phone. They were already spinning up all its previous contacts."

"You got in your car and peeled rubber."

"Not yet. Nothing was conclusive. It would have helped if you'd told me where you got the damn number."

Stein's tone is accusatory. I refuse to be baited. "So. You sat and waited."

"My team was collating intel. All we had were pieces. I sat behind Garrick's desk. Kept myself awake by rocking and making his stupid chair squeak. Then—I saw it."

"Come on, Stein. Don't keep me in suspense."

"Shoe's on the other foot now, isn't it? I'll trade you."

"What do you want?"

"Where did you get the number?"

"Two *soldados* sent to kill me, after we visited the plant. They coordinated with Garrick. That's why he helped arrange the tour. They planned to kill me afterward."

"Figures. Where are they now. No—don't tell me."

"I told you last night, you didn't believe me. They're vulture food."

"How many people have you killed in the last twenty-four hours, Breed?"

"Personally?"

"Do you miss Afghanistan?"

Need to think about that one. "Yes. I miss the clarity. Your turn."

"Jesus. That's why they put war dogs down." Stein fishes in her shirt pocket. Hands me a black-and-white photograph. "Recognize this?"

"I don't have NODs, Stein. Do you have a light?"

The sky behind us glows salmon pink. Stein's still driving with brights. She flicks a switch and the ceiling light comes on.

I stare at the photograph from Garrick's trophy wall.

High in the Rockies. Two hunters posing at the gate of a ranch. Stetsons, rifles, long sheepskin coats.

Doug Garrick and Paul Bledsoe.

STEIN TURNS off the ceiling light.

"I can't believe I missed it," I say.

"Don't feel bad. We both stared at that photograph. The significance didn't sink in because we hadn't met Bledsoe."

"Find out who owns that ranch. El Diablo."

"My team is working on it. There is so much intel now, we are stretched thin. I expect the prints from the shell casing soon. We're checking Garrick's finances. He lives closer to El Paso than Salem. Probably to conceal his lifestyle."

"You know Mirasol was trafficked from Mexico. She was held at a ranch in Colorado."

Stein looks at me. For the first time, her eyes show empathy. "Yes. I read her file, her statements. I was prepared to share that with you last night. Of course, there is no guarantee she was held at El Diablo."

"She told me Bledsoe was the man who tortured her."

Stein raises an eyebrow. "I'm sorry, Breed. Mirasol wasn't involved. I didn't try to involve her."

"No." Now I understand why mourners rend their clothes. "I did."

Stein's voice goes cold. "Square yourself away, soldier. Mirasol Cruz involved herself."

We ride in silence.

"Thank you, Stein."

Stein acknowledges with a curt nod. "My team tracked Garrick. He picked up Hamza at the plant, then doubled back to the Lazy K. I called El Paso for reinforcements. They were half an hour away, so I drove out myself. I tried calling you, no answer."

"I was otherwise occupied."

"Obviously. I parked off the road in a gully. A car ripped past, so I started running."

"How fast do you do the mile?"

"Five minutes. What did they say before I got there?"

Not a hair out of place. Not a drop of sweat.

Stein isn't human.

"Hamza killed Mirasol," I tell her. "Garrick told him to get rid of my car. The one that passed you on the way in. Hamza and Bledsoe are arranging a shipment for early tomorrow morning. Quds, women, drugs. Garrick was going to kill me, then make sure there were no roadblocks in Hamza's way."

"Cocky bastards."

"With me dead, you wouldn't have enough for a warrant."

"The United States will kill the Iran nuclear deal as scheduled," Stein says. "Our sources in Caracas indicate Colonel Faisal Hamza is in Chihuahua. He is preparing to move on

Monday or shortly thereafter. You are the only person who can confirm Hamza's presence in Juarez."

I slump with physical exhaustion, and the loss of Mirasol. "What do you want from me, Stein?"

Stein pulls off the highway and turns toward Salem. We drive past the Dusty Burger. "As soon as we get back, you're going to give me a signed statement. That you saw Hamza at the Bledsoe plant and La Cueva. That you saw them loading girls into that truck. As soon as I get the green light from Washington, we'll go to federal court in El Paso. I'll get that damn warrant. When they try to move the Quds tomorrow morning, I'll hit them with an army."

The woman's ambition is demonic.

"Why don't you send a Hornet. Drop a couple of GBU-28s on Bledsoe and La Cueva," I tell her.

The GBU-28 is a five thousand pound, laser guided bomb. A "bunker buster" designed to take out hardened underground command and control centers. It's the perfect weapon with which to seal a tunnel.

Stein's forehead furrows. "Management will never let me wipe out five square blocks of Juarez."

My God, she took me seriously.

"All right," I say. "I'll give you a statement."

"Hamza thinks you're dead, yes?"

"Yes."

"Turn that burner off. You're going to stay dead."

40

SALEM, 0600 HRS THURSDAY

We pull into the hotel lot, and Stein parks next to Keller's truck. I get out of the car, notice the absence of Mirasol's Camaro. The urge to tear at myself overwhelms me. I force myself to straighten and follow Stein into the hotel.

I must be a sight. At the front desk, the blond girl's eyes widen.

"Meet me in the dining room," Stein says. "Half an hour."

In my room, I refuse to look in the mirror. Go straight to the shower. When I am clean, I dry myself and pull on fresh clothes. I reach into my duffel bag and retrieve the Glock. It's been out of my sight, so I check its load. Stuff it into my waistband, straighten my shirt.

My phone's battery is low. I plug it into a wall charger and collapse into a chair. Outside, the sun's rays bathe main street in a warm glow. The shadows are long, there is little traffic.

I dial a number.

The voice on the other end is familiar. I feel like I'm calling home. "Lenson."

"It's Breed."

"What's up?"

"I know where they are."

No elaboration is necessary. "Where?"

"A hotel in Juarez. Half a dozen Quds, twice as many cartel shooters. Suicide vests, small arms. They plan to infil early tomorrow morning."

Lenson doesn't hesitate. "Roger that. I'll call Hancock."

"I will send you a link and photos of the ground floor. I will call again in a few hours."

The photographs I took of La Cueva pack a single email. I type in Lenson's address and click send. Message him, "You've got mail."

I return to the gallery and swipe through the photos. We can breach La Cueva.

The last photographs are the selfies I took with Mirasol. I'm smiling. My mind is on the background, the bouncers and Quds who are my subjects. Next to me, Mirasol looks shy. Her hand is on my arm, her eyes on my face. She looks like the fifteen-year-old girl Papi stole from the *maquila*.

Hamza is a walking dead man.

I check my phone. The battery is half charged. I set the alarm to wake me in an hour. Stretch out on the bed, close my eyes.

CAN'T SLEEP. I swing my legs off the bed. It's still early. The sun's rays shine through the window at a flat angle. Like a prism, the glass casts the light against the wall. Bands of copper, bronze and gold.

Barefoot, I step into the hall.

Quiet. No one about. With a measured step, I walk to—

Room 210.

I push the door open, step inside. Swing it shut behind me.

Mirasol is sitting on the edge of the bed. Her legs and feet are bare. Smooth skin, the color of milk chocolate. Long black hair, a fan about her shoulders. Her lips part, a hesitant smile.

She wears only a loose t-shirt. Eyes all pupil, she stares at me. Slowly, she rises. Folds herself into my arms. I am dizzy with her coconut scent, the hard-soft feel of her flesh against mine.

"Breed," she says. "Breed."

THE BUZZ of my phone wakes me. "Breed."

It's Stein. "Breed, where are you? It's eight o' clock."

Shit. "Good morning to you too, Stein."

"I need your statement. *Now*."

"I'll be right down."

I disconnect the call. Phone's charged. I unplug it from the wall, put it in my pocket. Go to the sink and splash water on my face.

Mirasol's scent is still with me. The sensation of holding her in my arms. The taste of her kiss.

I'm dreaming again.

The girl at the desk greets me as I step out of the elevator. "Is everything okay, Mr Breed?"

Innocence should be rewarded. There is so little of it these days. I smile. "Everything's fine, just needed some sleep."

"A whole hour and a half?"

She cares.

"Better than nothing. Any breakfast left?"

"Buffet closes in an hour. You have lots of time."

Stein is at the window table with three men. They are clones. Short hair, dark suits, jackets draped over chair backs. Their laptops are open on the table. I wave to Stein, go to the buffet, and load up a plate.

Breakfast in one hand and a pitcher of orange juice in the other, I find a table for one. Kitty-corner to Stein and the clones.

Stein sighs, gets to her feet. Motions to a blond kid with red suspenders and a Cross pen in his shirt pocket. The SIG P226 on his belt is *not* a Legion. He does not have Stein's panache, her sense of fashion. The pair come to my table.

"Breed, this is Agent Collins. He'll take your statement."

Agent Collins has boyish good looks, a solid jaw, and a cleft chin. He holds his hand out to me.

The agent's grip is firm. I release his hand. "Can it wait till after breakfast?"

"Afraid not." Stein treats me to a sweet smile. "Breed, I am going in front of management at ten o'clock. You owe me."

Stein *did* save my life. "Okay. Let's do it."

"Agent Collins will record your statement and type it up. You can sign it."

"Fair enough."

Collins pulls up the seat opposite, sets a digital recorder on the table. He checks the sound level, records the preamble. His name, the date, our location. Then he asks me to state my name, military rank, MOS, and current status.

"Let's begin with what led you to the hilltop," he says. "Tell us everything, and what you saw occur at Bledsoe Meats."

I tell Agent Collins almost everything. He asks a few questions at critical points. How many girls did I see board the truck. How old. How many men.

When we get to the part about La Cueva, he asks me about the premises. "Describe the building."

"Two floors. Old."

"Did you see the entrance to the tunnel?"

"No."

"How do you know it is there?"

"Logical inference. La Cueva is clearly a cartel logistics base. It is the right distance from the Bledsoe plant. Everything fits."

"Where is the entrance to the tunnel?"

"It will be in the cellar. Accessed from behind the bar. Perhaps from the room I saw the two Quds enter. I did not see them come out."

"For all you know, those two Quds might have been shipped north."

"It is possible," I admit. "Trucks leave Bledsoe every night. They are shipping drugs, women, Quds. Not necessarily at the same time."

By the time I finish my story, it's oh-nine-hundred. Collins goes back to Stein's table. Plugs the recorder into a USB port, adjusts a set of earbuds. Stein gets up and comes to me.

"Do you have enough time?" I ask.

Stein sits with me. "Plenty. Software will automatically transcribe the recording. The software transcription isn't perfect, so Agent Collins will edit the result. That won't take long. When he's finished, he'll print it out. You can read and sign it."

The blond girl brings me another pitcher of orange juice. It looks heavy, rattles with ice.

"You're thirsty, Mr Breed. Let me take that for you."

The girl takes the empty pitcher and sets the new one on the table. "I put ice in it," she says.

"That's sweet." I peer at the nameplate pinned over her shirt pocket. "Thank you, Tara."

The girl blushes. "Oh, it's nothing. You looked so tired this morning."

"Let me see." I pour Stein a glass of juice, then serve myself. "Your mother's favorite movie is *Gone With The Wind*."

"It is." Tara beams. "How did you know?"

"Wild guess."

"You remind me of Rhett Butler."

Stein rolls her eyes.

When I look in the mirror, I do not see Rhett Butler. I promise you. "Tara, you are too kind."

"I'll leave you to finish breakfast." Tara bends close and

whispers conspiratorially. "The buffet's closed, but the kitchen leaves food in the warming trays. For another half hour. If you want more, let me know."

Tara walks away. Stein watches her go with an expression of incredulity. "As though we don't have enough cradle robbers involved in this case."

"Oh, *please*." I stare at Tara's retreating bottom. "She's at least twenty-four. Got breasts and everything."

Stein grimaces. Opens her leather notebook and takes out the Montblanc. "Okay. Here is how things are going to go down."

"This is cozy." An agent stands over us. He looks forty, older than Stein and Collins. Dark hair, face twisted into what looks like a perpetual sneer. "Mind if I join you?"

I *know* I'm going to hate him. "Yes. I mind."

The agent does a double take. Stein inserts herself smoothly. "Breed, this is Agent Harris. You've met Agent Collins. Over there is Agent Wilson. Agent Harris is the senior at El Paso station."

"Congratulations."

"Pull up a chair," Stein tells the agent. She flashes me a warning look. "Agent Harris needs to know this. He will be involved in the takedown."

Harris borrows a chair from another table and sits between us. I pour orange juice for Stein and myself, set the pitcher down. Far away from the agent.

"All right." Stein consults her notes. "I'll meet with management at ten o'clock. I will request approval to go to federal court. Prosecutors from El Paso will be on the call. They have booked time with the judge for thirteen hundred hours. We think we can get a warrant to raid Bledsoe Meats."

"How specific will the warrant be?" Harris asks.

"Specific enough to target key items of interest. Generic enough to allow us to capture incidental materials. We will be authorized to confiscate desktop computers, laptops, mobile phones, storage devices. We will be authorized to search any vehicles on the premises, vehicles arriving, and vehicles that have left during the period specified. We will open packages of meat that have been palletized. We will be specifically authorized to search the US Department of Agriculture Retain Cage for a tunnel entrance. Once we find that, we can do anything we want."

Stein's eyes meet mine. She is gambling everything on my theory.

"The strength of the raiding party will be in the Border Patrol and ATF contingents. They will bring dogs trained to sniff narcotics, firearms, and explosives. BORTAC will have armored vehicles capable of breaching the perimeter fence."

BORTAC. The Border Patrol's tactical unit.

"We are authorized to arrest any illegal aliens on the premises. We have Border Patrol officers trained to take charge of underage illegals. We have covered everything."

Harris folds his arms. "What about the Quds?"

The tunnel, the drugs, the illegals are one thing. Quds Force terrorists are something else. Whoever gets the Quds will have the thickest dick in Washington.

"This unit," Stein says, "will go in with TAC gear. It will be our job to take the Quds."

The first flaw in Stein's plan. I've fought jihadists my entire career. Whatever training Stein and Harris have received, they do not have the training to take on Quds fighters.

I say nothing.

"I'd like to attend the meeting," Harris says.

"No." Stein's voice is firm. "I'm gambling on this. If I burn, I'll burn alone."

And if she's right, the greater share of glory.

. . .

Harris doesn't like it. Bites back a protest. The three of us stare at each other in silence.

Without a word, Harris gets up and returns to the window table.

"Isn't he a ray of sunshine," I say.

"Harris was my senior back east." Stein closes her notebook. "He kept one foot on my neck the whole time. Two years ago, I got a counter-terror assignment overseas. Harris got a narcotics assignment in El Paso. On the organization chart, we are now peers, and he doesn't like it."

"He feels like he's being passed over."

"I give a shit how he feels."

"How are you going to get the timing right?" I ask her. "You have to strike when the Quds are on the US side or you'll miss them. Bledsoe may hide out in Mexico, where you can't touch him."

Stein smiles. "I'll have someone on that hill. When Bledsoe and Hamza load up that truck, BORTAC will breach the fence with armored vehicles. Round everybody up, hold them in the yard. Then we'll go into the plant and search."

"You've thought of everything, haven't you?"

"No one can think of everything. I try."

"Can you get the *Federales* to take down La Cueva?"

Stein shakes her head. "Impossible to coordinate. The fact is, no one in Mexico can be trusted. If I tried to arrange that, the cartel would be tipped off."

"Send in a US hit squad."

"And create an international incident. Absolutely not. The most I can do is send a US team to gather evidence *in partnership* with a Mexican contingent. But as you pointed out, timing is everything. A joint US-Mexican force can only go in *after* the major engagement. Otherwise, the bad guys will be tipped off."

Can't argue with that. "Where were you assigned overseas?"

Stein smiles. “Everyone has a story, Breed. You’re not ready to hear mine. Ah—Collins has your statement.”

The blond agent borrowed the hotel printer. Sets a thin sheaf of papers on the table. “Here you are, Mr Breed. Please read and sign it. I’ll witness when you’re done.”

Stein gets to her feet. “We’ll leave you alone for a while.”

I pick up the statement. “The clock is ticking.”

41

SALEM, 1015 HRS THURSDAY

I sign the statement.

Slide the paper across the table to Stein. "Good luck."

"Thanks." Stein examines my signature. "I have more than enough now to establish probable cause."

"The fingerprints came back?"

"The prints on the shell casing were Garrick's—as expected. My team in Washington uncovered tons of circumstantial evidence. In Colorado, Garrick and Bledsoe jointly own the El Diablo. Garrick's house in El Paso is worth one-point-two million. That's why he keeps it far removed from prying eyes. Nothing compared to the waterfront property he owns in Corpus Christi. And a boat."

"For God's sake. How long has *that* been going on?"

"Ages. Garrick and Bledsoe have been partners for a long time. Bledsoe leveraged his relationship with Papi. Garrick provided law enforcement cover. In the last two years, events gathered momentum. Bledsoe formed a joint venture with Comida Del Sol, a Mexican food processing company. Comida Del Sol provided financing for extensive renovations to Bledsoe Meats. Upgraded their property, plant, and equipment."

"Let me guess—Papi owns Comida Del Sol."

"Yes. The ownership structure of Comida Del Sol is complicated. My team have uncovered evidence Comida Del Sol is involved in money laundering. But—that's not all. Iran's Islamic Revolutionary Guard Corps, the IRGC, has an ownership interest through a series of Cayman Islands shell companies."

The scope of the enterprise is breathtaking. "Another joint venture."

"We gave them one-point-eight billion in cash as part of the nuclear deal. Some of us expected them to finance terrorism. We never thought..."

"We never thought they would *invest* it," I finish for her.

"It was a no-brainer," Stein says. "The IRGC isn't using the one-point-eight billion to finance terrorism. They're using the *returns* on the one-point-eight billion to finance terrorism."

"How could our government have fallen for Iran's bullshit."

"The last administration wanted the nuclear deal for its legacy. That doesn't matter. We have to stop the Quds."

Stein slaps her laptop shut. Folds my signed statement, goes to her room. I watch her leave, finish my coffee. Get to my feet.

Harris steps in front of me. "Where are you going, Breed?"

"Back to my room. Stein's court appointment isn't till thirteen hundred."

"You are not to leave the hotel." Harris stands with his feet spread, hands on hips. "Stein's instructions."

"I'm glad those mean so much to you, Harris. Stein's instructions. You'll get used to them."

Harris's face slowly turns purple.

"I'm going to my room," I tell him. "Get out of my way."

I walk away from bar fights. Some asshole pushes me, I buy him a beer. It's too easy to kill some fuckwit and end up in jail. Especially when the other guy doesn't know what he's doing. Truth is, the more killing you've done, the less you want to do.

The agent outweighs me by thirty pounds. He's ready to

make a move. I should hit him first, but I won't. Deflect or absorb the first shot. Incapacitate him. I have a menu of options.

Harris steps aside. "When this is over, Breed."

I walk out of the dining room. There are at least six Quds fighters going out early tomorrow morning. Hamza intends to hit between three and six targets. High concept, mass casualty attacks.

Stein plans to take Hamza with three men. Harris's team will be outnumbered and outgunned. The encounter will be a bloodbath. These guys won't be at breakfast tomorrow.

It's not about numbers. The end state of any training program is defined by an operator's mission and likely opposition. If the mission is to neutralize the most committed killers the enemy can field, you select Deltas. If the mission is to arrest narcotics smugglers, FBI training may suffice. If the mission is to arrest gangbangers on inner-city streets, police training is appropriate.

Personnel are not interchangeable.

Stein knows this. She told me she wanted to go in with a hit squad. Harris and his men don't qualify.

Not my problem. I shut the door behind me and collapse into a chair. Take my phone and dial Lenson. "It's Breed."

Lenson cuts to the chase. "We can't breach this objective from the ground floor—too many civilians."

"Agreed. There is a metal staircase bolted to the rear wall. We will breach the second floor, clear downward."

"How do we get weapons across?"

"I have reconnoitered Puente Rio Bravo. We will conceal weapons under a vehicle. M4s, shotguns, handguns. Spare shells and mags. Break everything down, reassemble on the other side."

"That will not be a problem."

Lenson has all the weapons we need in his store's inventory.

M4s, which are illegal for civilians to own. The carbine's 14.5-inch barrel is shorter than the 16-inch legal limit. Civilians often add a flash suppressor to the M4 to legalize the weapon.

Delta gives operators latitude in weapons selection and maintenance. Early in my career, I used an older variant of the M4, with a 10.5-inch barrel. The muzzle flash was blinding, but at close quarters the weapon was lethal. In the end, the short barrel caused reliability to suffer. Delta standardized on 14.5 inches.

"Is Hancock with you?"

"Yes. Good to go."

"Where are you?"

"My store."

I remember Stein told me Lenson's store was close to bankrupt. It's a converted warehouse off Alameda Avenue. Near the El Paso Skeet and Trap Club. Lenson sells sporting goods, guns, and ammunition. The front room looks like an arsenal. A gun show, with weapons of all types covering the walls. Fifty caliber sniper rifles on display tables. He had a tripod-mounted Ma Deuce. I thought the store would be ideally located to attract business.

Maybe he borrowed too much money to finance the inventory.

Borrowed to finance his hobby rather than a business.

Who knows what Lenson keeps in the back room.

The best thing about the army is its simplicity. You train and you fight. Your food, lodging, expenses are all handled for you. You don't need to worry about a budget, or paying bills, or anything like that. The army allows you to drop out of the real world.

Six months out and the phone company still has to chase me. Not that I don't have the money. I don't have the organization to handle the logistics. Lenson and Hancock are probably not that different.

Keller was the only one of us who ever amounted to anything.

"You'd better close the shop early."

"I didn't open."

"Good. We have one more problem."

"Tell me."

I tell him.

42

SALEM, 1145 HRS THURSDAY

Stein walks into the lounge, wearing a triumphant expression. "We've got a green light."

I've been sitting at one of the circular tables, chatting with Tara. She's standing behind the bar, polishing glassware. I'm drinking a beer, enjoying the light conversation, her pleasant company. For the past half hour, I've switched off from the darkness that envelops the border.

"Congratulations, Stein."

Dressed in another all-black pantsuit, Stein flops down across from me. I wonder how many copies of the same outfit she carries.

"All we have to do now," she says, "is get that warrant."

"What charges will you bring against Paul Bledsoe?"

"Depends on what we find. Harboring illegal aliens, trafficking illegal aliens, sex trafficking, trafficking minors for the purpose of prostitution, trafficking narcotics. I could go on."

"Not murder?"

"There is no evidence Paul Bledsoe was involved in any of the killings."

Bledsoe tortured Mirasol. What punishment does such a man deserve.

"Hamza?"

"Murder, terrorism. We'll throw the book at him."

I saw Hamza kill Mirasol. I am not certain justice will be done.

Stein straightens, prepares to leave. "Don't worry, Breed. We'll get them."

I hide my skepticism. "Sure."

"You mustn't leave the hotel. So long as Hamza thinks you're dead, so long as he doesn't hear from Garrick, they'll go ahead as planned. Where's Harris?"

"In the dining room with his team."

"I'm going to El Paso. He'll stay here, make sure no one takes a shot at you. Right now, you are the only person who can testify to Hamza's presence in the United States."

"I don't need a babysitter. Especially not that dick."

"Harris is a good agent."

"Agent of *what*? You're a spook, so is he. None of you are agents."

"What's in a name, Breed? Live with it." Stein gets to her feet. "Come on."

I catch Tara's eye. "I'll stay here, thank you. Tara's nicer company."

"Breed, are you going to make a career busting my balls?"

"Stein, I love to hear them clank."

"Fine. Harris will keep an eye on you from the dining room."

Stein turns her back on me, crosses the foyer. She's changed from flat dress shoes to dressy ankle boots. The heels add an inch and a half to her height.

Harris and his team move their laptops to a table from which they can see me. Through the window, I watch Stein climb into her Civic. Reflexively, I scan the 7-Eleven and the gas station for suspicious vehicles.

Nothing.

Stein pulls onto main street and heads for the highway.

I SIP MY BEER.

Stein's detective work was impressive. She has everything she needs to crack the case wide open. The problem is, most of the pieces are overseas. Comida Del Sol, the IRGC shell companies. She can shut down the Bledsoe operation, but the cartels and the Quds are a hydra. I'm sure Papi is not Iran's only partner. The IRGC and Quds have certainly formed joint ventures with other cartels. The Tijuana sector. The Gulf of Mexico.

How long will Stein be in court? An hour maybe. She'll be back by fifteen hundred.

"Who are all the people with guns, Mr Breed?" Tara asks. "They look so... square."

I stifle a laugh. "They're FBI types—But not."

"I don't know what that means."

"It means they're play acting."

"Pretending to be FBI?"

"Yep."

"You're helping them?"

"You could say the lady and I are helping each other."

"It looks that way. Those men don't like either of you."

"They don't?"

"I heard them talking." Tara hangs a wineglass on an inverted rack. Begins polishing another. "Nobody ever thinks I hear anything."

"Tara, I would never underestimate you."

"You're too nice, Mr Breed."

"They don't like her because she's their boss." I sip my beer. "A lot of people hate their boss."

"Why don't they like you?"

I never thought I would say it. "I guess it's because I get on with their boss."

"Well, *that* makes sense." Tara glances at Harris. "That one man never smiles, always looks like he's pissed off."

Harris returns her glance with a sneer.

"I have some business to take care of, Tara. I have to go out, but I need to go without those men seeing me. Can I get out the back way?"

Tara stops polishing the glass. Looks at me, a wicked smile on her face. "See those two doors at the back of the lounge? The one on the left goes to the bathroom, the other to the kitchen. You can get out the kitchen."

I glance at Harris. He has turned back to his laptop. His team are pounding away. The table at which they sit is far removed from the front window. It's perfect.

"I'm going to go to the bathroom for a minute. Okay, Tara?"

Tara winks at me. "I'll be here when you get back, Mr Breed."

I get up and stride quickly to the kitchen door. Turn the knob, pull it open. I'm through in a flash.

Empty. Noon, but no one's ordered lunch. The back door is shut, fastened with an old-fashioned barrel bolt and hasp. I slide the bolt free, open the door, and step out into the furnace of a West Texas high noon.

I'm facing the back lane. I look up, see Mirasol's window. Dodge around the side of the building and find myself at the end of the parking lot. Go straight to Keller's truck, start it up, and peel out of the lot.

I RACE DOWN main street toward the highway.

Check the rearview mirror. Harris, Collins, and Wilson are piling into a four-door Caprice. One of the models that replaced the venerable Crown Vic as the standard police workhorse. The Caprice has whip antennae mounted between the rear window and the trunk hinge. I smile to myself. By the time I pass the Dusty Burger, the Caprice is tailgating me.

Objects in mirror are closer than they appear.

No shit. Collins at the wheel, the Caprice's image fills the mirror. Every line of Harris's face is visible in sharp relief. Any closer and we'll have to get married.

I slow down, turn onto the highway. Collins tries to pass me, and I accelerate to sixty miles an hour. I'm flying, but this is hardly a high-speed chase. Texas 20 is not built for the Indy 500. I want to take care of Keller's truck.

The Caprice pulls up next to me. Harris yells, but I can't hear him. Not through two side windows. He gestures at me to pull over. I ignore him.

Collins drops back, gets himself into position. He's going to ram the left corner of my rear bumper, push the truck into a spin. A standard police interception technique. When he makes his move, I speed up, overtake three cars, and settle back into the right lane.

The Caprice races up the left lane, tries to pass me. They're going to cut me off. I speed up to seventy-five miles an hour. Fly past the Skeet & Trap Club. The arid fields and grassland of Salem County are behind us, we're in Socorro, approaching the built-up areas of El Paso. On our left, the Franklin Canal. On either side, broad subdivisions, strip malls, community centers.

The highway sweeps north by west in a broad arc. I slow to forty miles an hour. The Caprice slows with me. For the moment, Harris and Collins are content to see what I'm going to do.

I slow further. Drop to thirty, then twenty. Pull off the highway into an industrial park. A long, low building two football fields long. Smaller buildings, densely packed, with narrow spaces between. Arranged perpendicular to the long building.

The spaces look like alleys. I turn left into one of them, drive until I can go no further.

It's a dead end.

I stop the truck, look in the rearview mirror, and wait for the Caprice to catch me. Collins parks ten yards back. The three men get out.

"Come on, Breed." No triumph in Harris's voice. He's tired and pissed. "What the fuck are you trying to pull. Get out of that truck."

I open the pickup's door and step into the heat. Turn to face Harris and his team. Three clones in a row. Collins and Wilson look nervous. They're not used to being pricks.

"You're coming back," Harris snaps. "Right the fuck now."

"I don't think so, Harris."

"What do you mean, you don't think so? Get in this car. Wilson will drive the truck back."

"He means," a voice calls out, "he's not going with you. *You* are coming with *us*."

It's Hancock, standing on the roof of the building to my right. He is covering the clones with an M4. Lenson stands on the roof of the building across the street, similarly armed.

The men look bewildered.

"Harris." I step to the rear of the truck. "You are on the X. Covered from an elevated position. Lie face down, hands behind your head. Right now."

"You son of a bitch."

"Just do it."

The clones get on the ground, clasp their hands behind their heads.

Lenson tosses a package to me. It sails through the air and lands on the asphalt at my feet. I pick it up, tear it open. A knife, zip ties and duct tape. I step to Harris, bind his hands behind his back, bind his ankles, and slap gray tape over his mouth. I do the same for Collins and Wilson.

One at a time, I search them for guns. Each has a SIG P226. Harris carries a Smith & Wesson Bodyguard in an ankle holster. It's a nice personal protection revolver. Five shots, .38 Special, a shrouded hammer that won't catch on clothing. I stick the Bodyguard in my hip pocket and throw the SIGs into the pickup.

"Hot damn." Hancock steps from a doorway. He's come down from his perch, the M4 slung over his shoulder. "Hog-tied like steer."

I collect phones from Harris and his team. Pull the SIM cards.

"Let's go," I say.

Lenson puts up his rifle, turns away from the edge of the rooftop.

I take cloth hoods from Hancock and bag Harris's head. He makes muffled noises as I cinch the drawstring under his chin. I turn and hood Collins and Wilson.

Together, Lenson and I sling the men over our shoulders and throw them onto the bed of Keller's truck. We take a heavy canvas tarp and spread it over them. "We're saving their lives," I say.

"How do you figure that?" Lenson asks.

"Stein was going to send them up against Hamza."

"Huh." Lenson grunts. "We're saving their lives."

Hancock gets into the Caprice. Lenson and I get into Keller's truck.

"Where are you parked," I ask.

"Just around the corner."

Hancock and I back up the length of the alley, pull into the street. Lenson points to his SUV parked at the end of the long building. I drive him over to it and he gets in. Together, the three of us make a little convoy.

We make our way to Lenson's store. He's renting more space than he needs. Not sure what rents are like in Socorro, but he could certainly save by moving someplace smaller. The back of the warehouse doubles as a garage. We park the three vehicles inside.

Lenson switches on the lights and lowers the roller doors.

I get out and drop the tailgate. Together, we drag Harris and his team out of the truck and dump them on the floor of the garage. They're struggling. Jerking against the ties.

"Be still." I kick Harris. Not hard.

It's not quite thirteen hundred.

Stein is going to court.

43

SOCORRO, 1400 HRS THURSDAY

Lenson's garage makes a great workshop. There is so much space it feels like an airplane hangar. Our voices and the sounds we make as we work echo from the walls. The smell of grease and gun oil is familiar and comforting.

After I called Lenson, we took the SIM cards from our phones. I deactivated Harris's at the industrial park. Should Stein trace us, she will find nothing.

We go into the store's front room, where Harris cannot hear. I marvel at the arsenal Lenson has on display. He has set out the weapons we will take to Mexico. For himself and Hancock, two M4 carbines, two 12-gauge Benelli automatic shotguns, and two Glock 21 .45 caliber pistols. I will take Keller's Winchester 1897 12-gauge and the Glock nine millimeter. Lenson and Hancock will each pack a Bowie knife.

Lenson has piled ammunition on the counter. Sixteen thirty-round magazines for the M4s and boxes of two-and-three-quarter-inch, 12-pellet shotgun shells. Double-ought buck. Four magazines for each of our pistols.

I vetoed the fragmentation grenades.

"There will be civilians on the second floor," I say. "Girls the cartels are trafficking."

Lenson closes his fist around one of the grenades. "That makes the floor harder to clear."

No way will we frag kids. "Then it's harder."

Careful not to damage the molding, we unscrew the front interior door panels on the SUV. Wrap the magazines and shotgun shells in plastic bags and pack them in. When we are finished, we replace the panels and screw them tight.

The pistols and knives take less room. We remove the interior panel on the left side of the passenger compartment and conceal the weapons in the dead space.

The rifles and shotguns are the most difficult to conceal.

We break them down separately and package them in large plastic garbage bags. Bind them tightly with duct tape.

Lenson throws two wooden creeper trolleys on the floor of the garage. Together, we lie flat and slide under the SUV. The long sills between the wheel wells are perfect for concealment. We tape the packages securely. Slap black grease over the plastic bags.

I doubt the border guards will check under the vehicle. If they do, the camouflage will pass a cursory inspection.

We store flashlights, screwdrivers, and mat knives in Lenson's toolbox. Everything we need to reassemble the arsenal on the other side. Canvas haversacks to carry magazines and ammunition look innocent when empty. We fold and lay them under the toolbox.

The process takes over an hour. We go back into the store. In the bathroom, we clean the grease from our hands.

Lenson takes two six-packs from his fridge. We sit behind his laptop and use Magellan Voyager to review the geography of Juarez. We familiarize ourselves with each of the bridges, the major landmarks, and the roads to and from La Cueva.

When we reach the La Cueva neighborhood, Lenson flies

down and surveys the street in front of the club. Turns to the river and scans the back.

"The image is digitally rendered," I tell him. "It is not accurate."

We switch to the link I sent him. The photographs Mirasol showed me. The front of the club. "There are two sentries at the front," I say. "One on each corner. Here—and here."

From the counter, I snatch a pen and pad of paper. Sketch the club, the street in front, the lane at the back. Side streets connecting the two. I place an X on each front corner of the building, facing the street.

I draw an X next to the back lane. "There is one sentry watching the fire stairs."

"No pictures of the lane?" Hancock asks.

"No. The lane will be the most difficult part of the infil. It's dark, the sentry was inexperienced. There is a ditch—here."

A thick line between the lane and the river represents the ditch.

"We will approach as close as we can under cover of darkness," I tell them. "I will cover the remaining ground by crawling in the ditch. When I reach the club, I will neutralize the sentry."

"If there's more than one?"

"We improvise."

I take another sheet of paper and draw a rectangle. I sketch the street in front, the back lane, the fire stairs. "This is the second floor plan."

A corridor. Rooms on either side. The fire door at one end, stairs leading to the ground floor on the other.

"That," Lenson says, "is a bitch."

Corridors are killing fields. For both sides. Anyone sticking his head into a corridor is likely to have it blown off. Anyone standing in a corridor has nowhere to run.

"No way around it." I draw rooms on either side of the corridor. "I saw Quds in these two rooms at the end closest the fire stairs. *This*—is a fuck room. Center-fed."

"The others?"

"There is another fuck room by the fire escape. Smaller, probably corner-fed. One of these others holds the girls. Not sure which one. The rest could be Quds and cartel quarters, armories. We have to see when we get there."

We have spent thousands of hours in shoot houses, training for hostage rescue and close quarters combat. I estimate six Quds and as many *soldados* occupy the second floor. A challenging exercise.

I raise my eyes to Lenson's. "You and I will clear the rooms."

"Roger that."

Together, we turn to Hancock. "You have to dominate the corridor," I tell him. "As we clear the rooms, we will leapfrog each other."

"At least another six cartel downstairs," Hancock observes.

"If anyone comes up the stairs, kill them."

Once the shooting starts, the battle will turn fluid. Some will race into the corridor, others will be more cautious. There is no way to determine ahead of time how individuals will react.

"We will proceed surreptitiously for as long as we can." I trace our path with the point of my pen. "Once shots are fired, we have to roll."

Two operators are required to clear a center-fed room. Fine when you go in with overwhelming force. In La Cueva, we will be outnumbered.

I have only seen the interior of one room. The others are question marks. Once the shooting starts, we will have to clear the second floor as quickly as possible.

Lenson's tone is grim. "Each of us takes a room."

"And Hancock covers the hall."

There is no other way.

"All right," Lenson says. "We've cleared the top floor."

I take a third sheet of paper. Sketch the floor plan of the ground floor, including the staircase. "Civilians will scatter. That leaves at least six *soldados* with rifles on the ground floor. Quds. They will zero in on the staircase."

"We dominate with volume of fire."

"Give them gas," I tell them. "Be proactive, force them into *reactive* mode."

"Attack down the stairs," Lenson agrees. "Kill them all."

"Wish we had armor," I say.

Hancock looks up, a strange light in his eyes.

"Nobody lives forever."

44

SOCORRO, 1700 HRS THURSDAY

I stand over Harris.

Stare at his bound, hooded body.

Prod him with the toe of my boot. "Hey."

Harris's head turns in my direction.

Wilson, Collins, and Harris. Three bundles, all in a row. Lying on the concrete floor. Soaking up the smell of axle grease. Damn, those Brooks Brothers suits will never be the same.

I grab Harris's ankle ties with one hand and drag him. Between the garage and the front room, there is a three-inch sill in the doorway. Harris's head bumps over the sill and he grunts. I should have dragged him by his necktie.

Lenson and Hancock watch me take Harris to Lenson's office behind the counter. I sit the agent up in a straight-backed chair and close the door. Reach behind him, lift his wallet.

A Texas driver's license and credit cards. No other identification.

There's another chair in front of Lenson's desk. I set it in front of the bound man. Sweep the room visually for anything that could identify our location, the owner of the premises.

Satisfied, I sit down in front of Harris and take off his hood. Set his wallet on the desk.

Behind the duct tape, Harris's face is contorted with rage.

"Calm down," I tell him. "We got time to kill."

Harris screams into the gag.

I lean forward, elbows on my knees. "Listen close, because you need to hear this."

Red faced, Harris sits quietly.

"My friends and I are going to leave in a few hours," I say. "We will not be coming back."

Harris's eyes widen.

I smile. "That's right. We are going to leave you here. If I'm in a good mood, I *might* drop Stein a note.

"We'll turn off the air-conditioning. Have you ever walked into a death house? Smelled corpses rotting in the heat? I don't like you, Harris. I'll enjoy leaving you to die."

Fear grows in Harris's eyes.

"I'm going to take the tape off. I expect you to answer my questions."

I grab a corner of the duct tape and peel the patch from Harris's mouth. Leave it hanging from his right cheek.

"All right. You're not FBI. You carry no government ID. What are you?"

Harris mumbles something.

"I didn't hear you. Speak up."

"CIA."

"Fucking spooks. You're not supposed to operate inside the United States. What is Stein's status?"

"CIA. Attached to the Department of Justice. So are we."

"I believe Stein has been seconded. Not sure about you guys."

"She called us in."

"Means exactly nothing. What military training have you had?"

"Collins and I are ex-Marines. All of us have had CIA TAC training."

"What about Stein?"

Harris shrugs.

"Tell me about Stein, Harris—or I'll leave you here."

"Harvard Law, FBI. She transferred to CIA five years ago."

"How long with the FBI?"

"Five years."

Stein is thirty-four. Older than she looks.

"Why did she transfer?"

"Ask her. She never told me."

"She worked for you. You asked at the interview."

"I didn't hire her. She was a mediocre case officer."

"Really. Did you inherit her, or was she assigned to your team?"

"Assigned."

Someone senior at the CIA wanted Stein to spy on Harris. Maybe he was a fuckup and she was told to babysit him. "What happened two years ago?"

Harris looks miserable. The man's shoulders slump, his whole frame seems to dissolve into the chair. "Stein was recruited for a counter-terror assignment."

A plum assignment. The kind you give a superstar. I'm impressed Stein didn't badmouth Harris earlier. She must find him contemptible. Treats him with respect regardless. A political animal, navigating her bureaucracy.

"Because she was mediocre." I smile. "Where was she assigned?"

"Breed, we operate on a need-to-know basis. I did not need to know."

Admitting that had to hurt.

"You kept your ear to the ground, didn't you."

"You want me to make stuff up?"

"I want the truth. If I don't get it, I'll cut you before we leave." Harris stares at me with a blank expression. "I'll open the garage door—enough to let animals in."

Harris shudders. The weasel's imagination starts working overtime. I stretch, cross my legs at the ankles. Yawn.

"I *heard* she worked all over." Harris's voice trembles. "She put out fires. Afghanistan, Iraq, Ukraine, Colombia."

"Go on."

"Management considers her expendable. If she fucks up, they'll dump her. It's her attitude. She'll do anything to get ahead. Went on patrols with SEALs in Afghanistan. Responded to Troops In Contact when HVTs were involved. Anything for a splash. If you want something done, give it to Stein. Don't ask how she made it happen."

"She looks more like an analyst than a field operative."

"That's Harvard Law. Don't let it fool you. That woman is as cold-blooded as they come. A real bitch."

There's a recommendation if I ever heard one.

"What do you think Stein will do when she gets back. Finds you and I aren't there?"

Harris frowns. He has trouble thinking ahead. "Look for us."

"She might look for *you*. If she sends up flares looking for me, Hamza will realize I'm not dead." I smile. "The question is —how *hard* will she look for you?"

"Hard. This city will be crawling with agents."

"Because you're her elite TAC squad. Does that sound like the woman you just described?"

I slap the tape back over Harris's mouth.

Hood him.

"I don't think so."

45

JUAREZ, 2200 HRS THURSDAY

For the second time in twenty-four hours, I approach the Puente Rio Bravo. I wonder if I'll draw the same border guard. I sit in the passenger seat of Lenson's SUV. Hancock sits directly behind me. We are sitting on a small arsenal.

South Stanton Street is narrow. Compared to the wider avenues that dominate the Bridge of Americas, Zaragoza, and Paseo Del Norte. The Puente Rio Bravo is intended for south-bound traffic, the Paseo Del Norte northbound. Both service the center of Ciudad Juarez.

A short line. Two cars in front of us.

Beside the road is a large wooden sign.

WARNING
ILLEGAL TO CARRY
FIREARMS / AMMUNITION
INTO MEXICO
PENALTY — PRISON

Lenson and I exchange glances. Smile.

Guns are getting through. Not long ago, cartel shooters attacked the Mexico City police chief with three Barrett fifty caliber sniper rifles and M16s. The HVT took three hits and lived. Two bodyguards and a woman were killed. All those weapons came from the United States.

The Barrett is a prestige weapon. In Mexico, shooters assume the size of a man's dick is proportional to the size of his gun. In practice, we use Barretts to take out Scuds and tanks. Not people. For human targets, we prefer .308 Winchester or .338 Lapua rifles.

I remember the slack Mexican border guards. If the Mexicans don't care, why should we? Maybe they care, but are too corrupt to be effective. The end result is the same.

Guns get through.

"Why do they call it Rio Bravo?" I ask Lenson. Small talk. To keep my stomach from fluttering.

"Don't know," Lenson says. "It's a Mexican thing. This bridge is also called the Friendship Bridge, or the Stanton Street Bridge."

"*Boring*." Hancock twists sideways in the back seat, stretches out his right leg. "Puente Rio Bravo is a great name. Has character."

Tonight the border guard is a woman. Mexican descent, fortyish. She looks like the kind of person who is proud to be American. Takes her job seriously. Pays her taxes. I hope she does not use us to exercise her *diligence*.

"How you gentlemen doing tonight?"

"Just fine, ma'am." Lenson flashes her a charming smile.

The guard's eyes flick to her screen and back. "Documentation, please."

We hand over our passports and Department of Defense identification.

"What y'all up to in Juarez tonight?"

"Just a bunch of gringos out for fun, ma'am."

I pray Lenson doesn't ham it up too much.

"You guys serve overseas?"

"Yes, ma'am. Afghanistan and Iraq."

The woman smiles. "I served in Iraq. Oh-three and oh-four."

"No shit. What outfit was you with?"

"512th Maintenance Company."

"Hot damn. Nasiriyah. See any action?"

"Not as much as you boys." The woman passes back our IDs. "You gringos got a designated driver?"

Lenson grins and jerks his head at Hancock. "Our buddy back there likes to keep us honest."

"Don't let *la vida loca* do you in," the women advises. "You gents have yourself a good time."

The Mexican border guards are lazy. They check our papers, ask Lenson to pop the hatchback. One guard opens the toolbox, lifts out the tray, and rummages inside. He doesn't bother to put everything back. Slams the hatchback and waves us on.

"Do they ever do it right?" I ask.

Lenson laughs. "Are you kidding? They're *terrified* they'll find something. The cartels know where they live. All these guys want to do is take bribes and wave people through."

The SUV noses out of the border checkpoint. Mirasol turned right to show me the city center. Tonight, we want to get to La Cueva's neighborhood early. Lenson turns left on Avenue Heroico Colegio Militar. We cruise south by east in the direction of the Zaragoza. Before we reach the bridge, Lenson turns right and we lose ourselves in a maze of *maquiladoras*.

"It's like I've been here before," Lenson says.

"It's the simulation," I tell him. "In most cases, realistic enough to put you on the ground."

I guide Lenson to a factory. Surrounded by a chain-link fence, topped with razor wire. The streets are dark, illuminated by the orange glow of sodium lights. The air is thick with dust. I direct him to the back of the factory, the cluttered alleys of an industrial park.

The windows of the factory are brightly lit. There are not many. Most of the buildings are black. I know how the *maquilas* operate. 24/7. Twelve hour shifts at minimum wage, five dollars an hour. In that building, women and girls toil to assemble vacuum cleaners and electric fans. Toasters and microwave ovens.

Mirasol worked at this *maquila*. Walked down the road we just passed, on her way to the bus stop. The night she was taken.

I curse my sentimentality. Cannot help myself. Cannot.

Lenson parks on a dark side street.

The first thing we do is remove the door panel in the rear passenger compartment. Extract our knives, pistols and pistol mags. Lenson and Hancock strap on pistol belts with holsters and scabbards. I stuff the Glock into my waistband and cram spare magazines into my hip pocket.

Hancock and Lenson unscrew and pry loose the door panels in the driver's compartment. I toss them the haversacks folded under the toolbox. Together, they unpack the magazines of five-five-six ammunition and shotgun shells. Strip them of their plastic wrappers and stuff the haversacks.

I drop to the ground and crawl under the SUV. Rip the plastic-wrapped rifles and shotguns from behind the sill. Lenson joins me on the other side. In ten minutes, we have arranged the components of the weapons on the ground and unpacked them. In the darkness, Lenson and Hancock assemble the rifles. They have trained to do this blindfolded.

When we are finished, we replace the panels and shove the trash under the car. Climb back in, load the weapons, breathe.

Lenson stares at the dark streets. The lonely *maquila*. "Have you done anything to let Stein know where those boys are?"

I shake my head. "We'll be back. If we're not, who gives a shit."

"Stein will find her hit squad someplace else."

"I don't think she ever intended to use those clowns."

Lenson looks puzzled. "Why involve them in the first place?"

"Someone in management wanted their El Paso station involved. Perhaps someone sponsoring Harris. It's like any company. Stein and Harris. Two peers, each has a mentor. A patron."

"You think she used you to clean up some office politics?"

I smile. "The thought crossed my mind."

Hancock raises the lid of a Styrofoam cooler. Inside, packed in ice, two six-packs. He opens three cans and distributes them. "Doesn't it bother you?"

I accept a can. Drink. "No. Stein has another hit squad lined up. That's why she didn't want Harris at the management meeting. She told them his guys were good, but not good enough."

Lenson grunts. "Crafty bitch."

"I think her heart is in the right place." I drain the beer, motion to Hancock for another. "She wants Hamza and Bledsoe as much as we do."

Lenson switches the engine on. Runs the air-conditioning. "But—she wants them alive."

I adjust the SUV's side mirror so I can watch the street. We are used to waiting. Remaining alert. "Stein *has* to want them alive. Her management wants to preserve plausible deniability."

"Don't you hate dealing with bureaucracy."

I press the cold beer can against the side of my face. Close my eyes.

"That's why I'm using Stein. She'll take out the Bledsoe plant."

46

JUAREZ, 0300 HRS FRIDAY

Shotgun clutched to my chest, I roll into the ditch bordering the back lane. The ditch is dusty and carpeted with litter. Flies buzz over half-eaten food. I wrinkle my nose at the smell of rancid fat. Careful to avoid making noise, I crawl the sixty feet to La Cueva. Head to toe in dust, I blink sweat from my eyes.

A shoe crunches on gravel.

The guard is walking toward me. I freeze and try to make myself part of the ditch wall. The footsteps stop and the man unzips his fly. I close my eyes and lower my face.

The sharp stink of ammonia floods my nose.

Piss.

The stream passes over me, gurgles against the far side of the ditch, and runs into a puddle under my belly. The man finishes, and his last drops dribble across my back. He zips his fly and his shoes scuff as he turns away. I count to three and rise to my feet.

The man is six feet away with his back to me. I climb from the ditch and close the distance with one stride. Smash the butt of the Winchester into the back of his skull. His occiput cracks, and he pitches forward onto his face. I whack him again, and his head comes apart. Scallops of bone and brain, held together by loose membranes of flesh.

I kick the body into the ditch. Walk deliberately to the steel fire stairs attached to the back wall of La Cueva. Lenson is there, M4 low-ready. A haversack of M4 magazines and shotgun shells hangs at his left hip. A Benelli automatic riot gun is bungeed on his right.

Similarly armed, Hancock limps forward.

Single file—first Lenson, then Hancock follow me up the stairs.

We are about to breach the objective.

THE PAINT on the fire exit is cracked and bleeds rust. I point the shotgun with my right hand and test the handle with my left. To my relief, the door is unlocked.

The corridor is deserted. My stomach muscles tighten.

Left and right, the doors lining the corridor are closed. I turn to the first on my left and push the door open. Come face-to-face with a Quds gunman. I push the muzzle of the Winchester against his chest and pull the trigger.

The gunman's body acts as a silencer. With a thump, the contact shot punches a bloody hole in his sternum. The muzzle blast sets his cotton shirt on fire and throws him on his back. I pump another round into the shotgun and grind my heel into the dead man's chest. Stamp the flames out.

A bomb factory. Two tables pushed against the wall—stacked with canvas vests. Explosives. On the tabletops sit tools, wires, and makeshift detonators. Contrived from burner cell phones.

Lenson and Hancock cover the corridor. The sound of bedsprings bouncing comes from the room on the right. I turn the knob and push the door open. Paul Bledsoe, buck naked, is sticking it to Nevita. His jeans, western shirt and rodeo belt hang across a chair back. His Stetson lies on the dressing table, his crocodile boots on the floor.

He has a bald spot, a pink circle of flesh in the center of his silver mane.

Nevita's chin is tucked against Bledsoe's shoulder. Her cheeks are rosy and flushed with heat. Eyes squeezed shut, she whimpers. Her legs are wrapped around his hips, and her heels are braced against his buttocks. The girl opens her eyes, stares into the muzzle of my shotgun, opens her mouth to scream.

I lift a finger to my lips and the scream dies in her throat. I draw the Glock from my waistband, step close, and bring the butt down on the back of Bledsoe's head. The skin splits across his bald spot, and blood trickles down his neck. Lenson pulls him off the bed.

Nevita scrabbles at the sheets to cover herself. Sits in bed with her back to the wall.

I cross the hall to the bomb factory. Select a suicide vest with a mobile phone trigger. The number four has been Scotch taped to the back. A trigger linked to a speed-dial. I turn the phone on, ensure it is charged, slip it into my hip pocket.

A spool of insulated wire sits on one table. I tuck the suicide vest under my arm and grab the roll.

Bledsoe is coming around. Hancock holds him up while Lenson fastens the suicide vest around him. I pick up Nevita's and Bledsoe's underwear. Ball them up, stuff them into his mouth. Strap the gag in place with my belt.

I signal Hancock to give me his belt. Bledsoe is wide awake, eyes staring in terror. Lenson draws his Bowie knife and cuts a length of wire from the spool. Binds Bledsoe's wrists behind his back. I loop Hancock's belt around Bledsoe's neck, pass the free end through the buckle, and cinch it right up to his throat.

Now I have a leash with which to lead him.

I hand the leash to Hancock. Nevita is crying softly. I motion for her to stay quiet.

Lenson follows me into the hall. Bledsoe in tow, Hancock brings up the rear.

I approach the next room on the left, motion Lenson to cover the door on the right. My heart pounds like a jackhammer. I turn the handle, push the door open, and go inside.

Three Quds at a table. One in the middle, facing me. Two on either side. Examining bus and train schedules. Rifles and pistols are scattered about the room. The men stare at me and suck breath.

Lunge for their weapons.

I shoot the one facing me in the chest. Twelve pellets of double-ought buckshot blow him apart and rock him back. The chair goes over and he crashes to the floor. The man on the left reaches for a nine millimeter on the table. I point the Winchester at his ear and pull the trigger. The blast rips his head off and the corpse pitches sideways.

The third man goes for an AK47 hanging from a peg. Before he reaches it, I pump a shell into the Winchester and shoot him in the back. A cluster of holes erupt between his shoulder blades. The force of the blast throws him against the wall. Arms flung apart in an attitude of crucifixion, he slides to the floor. Ears ringing, I jack another shell into the chamber.

I step back into the hall. Lenson has moved up, M4 raised to his shoulder.

Two shots left in the Winchester's tube. I throw my shoulder into the next door. The slab of plywood bursts open.

A Quds steps into the corridor, raises his rifle. I dodge into the room. Behind me, the earsplitting crash of a shotgun. Hancock's semi-automatic Benelli. Five shots, as fast as he can pull the trigger.

Clutching the Winchester, I sweep the room.

Mexican girls. Four of them. All pretty, all in their early teens. Handcuffed to iron beds.

"*En el piso*," I tell them.

I snap-load shells into the Winchester and turn back to the hall. Hancock leapfrogs me, dragging Bledsoe. The Benelli's empty, and he's switched to his M4. Hancock forces Bledsoe to the floor and kneels on his back.

Winchester raised, I step past Hancock and Bledsoe. M4 raised to his shoulder, Lenson moves up on my right.

Two more rooms. A dead Quds on the floor, blood pooling in the corridor. I roll him over with my boot. Not Hamza. Pulp. Hancock pumped sixty balls of double-ought buck into him.

Lenson takes the room on the right and kicks the door open. Goes in with M4 raised. Inside the room, Mexicans with rifles. Lenson and the Mexicans fire simultaneously. Lenson jerks as their rounds slam into him. He holds the M4 on them and fires until they're down. Staggers and props himself against the door frame.

I barge into the room on my left. A Quds and a Mexican open fire. A burning knife cuts my right side. The impact of the round slams me against the door jamb. Half my shot pattern hits the Quds in the face. He cries out, drops his rifle. I rack the Winchester and shoot him again. The gut shot puts him down.

A round snaps past my ear. I rack the Winchester, fire again. The pattern catches the Mexican high on the chest. He pitches backward. The Quds lies on his back like a squashed cockroach. The room reeks with the stench of his guts.

The windows stand open. Outside, people from the club are spilling into the street. Hancock has leapfrogged me again. He's pushed Bledsoe to the floor and is covering the stairs with his M4.

"They got Lenson," Hancock says.

Chin on his chest, Lenson sits lifeless in the right-hand

doorway. The M4's pistol grip is clenched in his right hand. His torso is a mass of blood.

I reach out and close his one eye.

My shirt is soaked with piss and assorted crap from the ditch. I find the entry wound in my side. The slug went in and out. I tear my shirt tail, wad up the fabric, and plug the hole. Tear more off, stuff cloth into the exit wound. Pray I don't die from infection.

Winchester in one hand, Glock in the other, I run to the stairwell.

Gunshots ring out from below. I squat to one side of the landing, brace my back against the wall.

Two Quds left, including Hamza. Half a dozen *soldados*. I wave Hancock over. He gets up and drags Bledsoe behind him.

"Give me the leash."

I take the leash and jerk Bledsoe to the floor beside me. He crosses the stairwell and the brief glimpse of his naked white legs and dangling privates drives the *soldados* crazy. Rifle fire sprays from the foot of the staircase. Half naked, choking on the gag, Bledsoe weeps shamelessly.

Hancock snap-loads shells into his Benelli.

I take the mobile phone from my hip pocket. Run my thumb over the keypad. Press 4. Now all I have to do is punch the green call button.

Leaning into the stairwell, I fire the Glock. Mexicans with automatic rifles force me back. I pull a full mag from my pocket. Slide the half-empty mag out of the pistol, reload.

I shove the Glock into my hip pocket and jerk Bledsoe to his feet. Pull him close and look into his eyes. Ignore his tears, the muffled, keening sound that comes from behind the gag.

This is for Mirasol.

Holding Bledsoe in front of me, I push him to the head of the landing. He shrieks into the gag. I plant my boot on his ass and kick Bledsoe down the stairs. The Mexicans riddle him with bullets. I squint as the rounds impact his body. Caught in the hail of gunfire, his body jerks like he's having a fit. My thumb hovers over the keypad.

I punch the call button.

La Cueva heaves with the force of the explosion. The walls shudder and plaster dust showers down from the ceiling. Hancock and I are knocked flat on our asses. A cloud of dust and smoke billows from the stairwell.

Move.

I charge down the stairs, leading with the Winchester. Hancock follows, dragging his bad leg.

Bledsoe has disappeared. His remains are splattered over the ceiling and walls. Like shreds of wet toilet paper, blood and bits of flesh stick to the plaster.

Soldados on the ground floor have been slaughtered by the shock wave and shrapnel. Body parts and viscera are scattered among shattered tables and chairs.

There is a gaping hole in the staircase where the last four treads and risers used to be. Half the banister has been splintered and blasted into the club. A million wooden needles. I hurdle the gap and throw myself onto the ground floor landing.

Wounded *soldado*s struggle to their feet. Ponderously train their weapons on me. The Winchester bucks in my hands. I take one man out, then another.

There—behind the bar. Hamza.

Eyes like black marbles. A doll's eyes, set in a mask. Standing, he fires his rifle. I crawl into the abattoir. Use corpses for cover.

Hancock fires his Benelli. Hamza dives behind the bar. Cones of buckshot smash shelves of liquor. Glass bottles explode in glistening showers of glass and whisky. Hancock can't navigate the hole in the staircase with his bad leg, so he dives head first across the space. Lands on his shoulder.

A Quds behind the bar fires his AK47. Hancock cries out. I

get to my feet, raise the Winchester, and pull the trigger. The blast of buckshot hits the zinc bar top, ricochets, and blows the gunman's face off.

I drop the Winchester and draw the Glock. The club has gone quiet.

Where is Hamza?

I cover the length of the bar with my pistol.

"Hancock," I call.

"You're covered."

I switch to a Weaver grip, dip my left elbow. Cautiously look behind the bar. The Quds is sprawled on his back, choking on his own blood. I shoot him twice in the forehead.

No sign of Hamza.

The dead man is lying on something. Heavy wooden slats, an iron ring. A trapdoor.

The tunnel.

47

JUAREZ, 0335 HRS FRIDAY

"Tunnel," I yell.

I look back at the stairs. Hancock is sitting on the landing, his shirt brown with blood. He has set the Benelli down, covers the club with his M4 carbine. "Go," he says. "I'll hold."

I kick the corpse aside, lean down, and grab the metal ring. Raise the trapdoor.

The effort sends a bolt of pain through my body. I grope for the makeshift plugs. They are still in place. I'm functioning. Alert.

I let the trapdoor fall on the dead man. I step back, pistol trained on the opening.

Hamza is not the type to run. He must be waiting for me.

My gaze sweeps the floor behind the bar. One dead body. One AK47. Hamza is still armed. Standing in the dark, waiting to shoot anyone who starts down the ladder. I grab the dead man by his collar. Lever him into a sitting position on the floor, legs splayed on either side of the opening.

I push the man forward so his face and shoulders block the light for anyone staring up from the space below. He'll look like a live man sneaking a peek. I jerk him back, hold my breath.

Nothing.

Hamza's not stupid.

He might be waiting to blow me apart.

Or he might be halfway across the border.

The space below must be a basement. Within that chamber, a seventy-foot vertical shaft will lead to the tunnel.

The dead man's heavy, but I stand him up next to the trapdoor. Hands under his armpits, I hold him over the opening and drop him into the hole. Follow him down, bracing for the impact.

We fall twelve feet together. The corpse hits the floor with a thud, and I land on him. Feet together, knees bent. I roll to one side. There's a blinding muzzle flash as Hamza cuts loose with his AK47. The burst rips the corpse apart, reaches for me. I twist on my side, raise the Glock, fire at the winking light.

A cry of pain. The rifle clatters to the floor.

A black figure scuttles crab-like across the basement. Disappears into a dark corner. I fire again and again.

I drag myself to the corner, all knees and elbows. Plant my hand on something hard and metallic. Hamza's AK47, wet with blood. I hit him.

He's climbing down the access shaft. Trying for the tunnel.

The shaft echoes with a low thrum. An engine.

There's a wooden ladder fastened to the wall. Next to the ladder, running the length of the shaft, is a wide-gauge rubber hose. Hamza is descending, his figure silhouetted by light from the chamber below. I aim the Glock just as he reaches the bottom and disappears from view.

Fuck.

I stuff the pistol into my hip pocket, swing onto the ladder and slide down. I clench the vertical rails of the ladder between my knees and feet. Control the drop with my hands. Ten feet from the bottom, I hang by one hand and draw the pistol. Let go and jump the rest of the way. I land on bent knees and swing the Glock to bear.

Hamza grabs my wrist with his left hand, pushes the muzzle of the pistol away. In his right hand is a Bowie knife. The one he used to kill Mirasol. The one he used on the Kellers. I grab for his wrist and miss. My fingers close around the blade and I grip it with all my strength. I shout with the pain.

Hamza tries to jerk the knife out of my hand. He's holding the knife blade-down, the cutting edge buried in the meat of my palm. I squeeze the blade harder, trapping it in my fist.

Teeth bared, the killer slams my gun hand against the ladder and I drop the Glock. He lets go of my wrist and punches me.

Right in my fresh wound. A red wave of pain crashes over me.

I reach up and dig my thumb into the inside corner of his left eye. Rip the eyeball out.

Hamza's scream is inhuman.

I butt him in the face with the crown of my head. He rocks back on his heels and I twist the knife from his grasp. Blade up, I thrust the weapon into his belly.

My body is awash with pain. None of it matters. I thrust the blade up under Hamza's sternum and lift him off his feet. I impale him on the knife and carry him across the chamber. Slam him against the wall. His hands grip my shoulders, his legs kick like those of a pithed frog. I watch him die.

The stench from Hamza's corpse is nauseating. My nine millimeter round hit him in the belly. Wounded, he fought. I draw the knife from under his rib cage and throw the body face down on the floor of the chamber.

I slump against a wall of brown bricks. Thousands of kilos of cocaine. Plastic bags wrapped in brown paper.

The chamber is larger than I imagined. It's fifteen feet wide and maybe thirty feet long. At one end is the horizontal tunnel, burrowing under the Rio Grande. Half of this chamber has been devoted to a chemical toilet, a diesel generator, and a ventilation device that pumps fresh air into the tunnel. The rubber hose from the access shaft is connected to the engine's exhaust. The chamber is lit by naked bulbs strung along the ceiling. Seven feet high and five feet wide, the tunnel looks like it has been shored up with timber and cement.

I stare at the knife in my hand. The knife this animal used on my friends.

Slowly, I kneel on the small of Hamza's back. Twist my fist in his greasy black hair. Bare his throat.

I CLIMB from the basement and stagger around the side of the bar. Hancock sits on the landing where I left him. His face glistens silver and I fear he is in shock. He is staring at the eight-pound ball of skull, matted hair and blood I carry in my right hand.

Exhausted, I set Faisal Hamza's severed head on the zinc bartop.

Hancock says nothing. I go to him and examine his wounds. He's been hit twice, high on the left side of his chest. His left arm is limp. It looks like his clavicle has been broken, but there are no jets of arterial blood. I check the exit wounds. Bloody holes, bone visible in the openings. A shattered scapula. No blood in his mouth or nose.

I take Hamza's Bowie knife and cut Hancock's shirt away. Bind his wounds.

"Breed, this is getting to be a habit."

"Shut up, you lazy bastard."

I get to my feet. Hancock takes my hand and throws his good arm around me. Together, we lurch toward the front door.

Federales burst into the club and fan out, automatic rifles trained on us.

"*No te muevas, pendejo!*"

"*Manos ariba! Ahora!*"

I raise my right arm. My other is supporting Hancock.

"*Está bien.*" a woman calls out. "*Ellos son mios.*"

The *Federales* put up their rifles and sweep the battlefield for wounded *soldados*.

Anya Stein steps forward. Dressed in a black catsuit and tactical gear. Full body armor, front and back plates. An H&K MP5 is slung across her chest, low-ready. A nine millimeter in an open holster, Velcroed to her right thigh.

"Stylish," I tell her. "Very. I pictured you exactly like this."

She steps forward, bends at the waist, and peers at Hamza's head. "Is it him?"

"Of course."

"I remember him with two eyes."

"And a body."

Stein's long brown hair has been bound into a severe bun at the back of her head. She sniffs. "I don't suppose you could have just shot him."

"What are you doing here, Stein?"

"My team has been tracking your phone since you and the girl crossed into Juarez the other night. When you took the SIM card out yesterday, a drone was tasked to cover you."

I'm not surprised. "You've been following me the whole time."

"Did you think it was a coincidence the Mexican army saved you? They practically escorted you and the girl across the Paseo Del Norte."

Mirasol and I crossed the border under the eyes of soldiers. Not a single policeman in sight. "How did you manage it?"

"I pulled strings, spun a story. Told the Mexicans two

undercover DEA agents were trying to cross. The cartels and police were going to kill them."

The *Federales* are picking through body parts and debris.

"I thought you couldn't mount an operation this side of the border."

"Not this hard-core. We took out the Bledsoe plant. Left this to you."

A dozen hard men with M4s and full tactical gear enter the room. Stein turns to them, barks commands. "Sweep it," she says. "Laptops, hard drives, memory sticks. I want photographs, DNA. Especially *that* one."

Stein points to Hamza's head. A bearded operator whistles. "We'll bag it."

"No." Stein's tone is abrupt. "Leave it there. I want those Hajjis to think long and hard about what it means to fuck with the USA."

Stein must be a delight in bed. "We need a medic."

"We don't have one. Sit down, we'll take you back with us."

There isn't an intact piece of furniture left in the club. "Stein, you're going to hurt my feelings."

"Don't fuck with me, Breed. I could let you rot in a Mexican prison."

"You used us."

Stein shrugs.

"Everybody uses everybody. Don't they."

48

EL PASO, SIX WEEKS AFTER

Stein had the decency to take Lenson back with us.

She brought a dozen operators with her to La Cueva. I didn't recognize any of them. Their manner and weapons discipline showed they knew what they were doing. Contractors, or special forces without insignia. Not Deltas. Deltas like two-point slings, these men used one-point slings. They wore SIG sidearms in drop leg holsters, low on their thighs. Lots of Velcro. Deltas prefer 1911s or Glocks, worn higher. Subtle indicators of a different close quarters combat culture.

They bagged everything of value they could find. Went into the tunnel for Hamza. Fingerprinted him, took DNA samples from his head and body.

The team that hit Bledsoe's plant must have been equally capable.

Hancock and I were helped to the street. There were a dozen police pickup trucks. *Federales* manned the machine guns on their beds. The vehicles were arranged in a cordon—to keep people *away* from La Cueva.

Stein's team had arrived in four up-armored Chevy Suburbans. Black. Tinted glass, opaque from the outside. Bulletproof.

The operators helped Hancock into the back seat of a Suburban. I climbed in beside him. Stein got into the front passenger seat. They carried Lenson's body to another Suburban, laid it on the cargo bed.

We drove in silence to the Zaragoza. Four Suburbans in a column. Two *Federales* pickups, one in front and one at the rear. Neither the Mexican nor the American border guards stopped us. We had a clear lane. The *Federales* peeled away at the approach, the Suburbans raced across the border.

Next thing I knew, we were at William Beaumont. Medics and nurses rushed out, laid Hancock on a gurney. Set up IVs of plasma, rushed him to the operating theatre.

They did the same to me. A doctor took one look at the torn shirt I'd used to plug my wounds and swore. They rushed me to another operating theatre. Pressed a mask to my face. The world went black.

I SIT with Hancock in his hospital room, watching television. He's propped up in bed, his shoulder and chest covered with bandages. Next to him, I lean back in a wooden side chair. Cheap hospital furniture. The chair legs wobble.

Stein took care of the funerals for Lenson, Mary, Donnie and Mirasol. Hancock and I were laid up. My wound wasn't bad, but the infection I picked up was. Delirious, I ran a fever for days. Mainlined antibiotics for longer.

The images streaming from the old television set are scenes from Teheran. The streets are awash in a mob of thousands. They are burning American flags. Burning effigies of the US president.

"Nothing new," Hancock says.

"I get a glow of joy every time we piss them off."

"Have there been further attacks?"

"No, but they'll try again. It's only a matter of time."

The United States filed its embargo motion at the UN Security Council. The effect was predictable. Other parties to the Iran nuclear deal protested. Tabled a counter-resolution, promptly vetoed by the American ambassador. The US threatened secondary sanctions against any country trading arms with Iran. The Europeans grumbled, but complied. Russia announced it would sell arms to Iran regardless.

The camera cuts to a press conference held by Iranian officials. The man on the screen sits behind an ornate desk. He is in his forties, with a neatly trimmed black beard. A touch of gray. He is simply dressed, in an open-collared dress shirt and linen sport jacket.

The Iranian press secretary.

"The United States is isolated," he says. "The international community no longer cowers before its bullying. The Islamic Republic of Iran has many friends. We will respond to America's treachery in an appropriate manner, in our own time."

The usual veiled threat.

Hancock's voice drips venom. "Motherfucking Hajji-beard."

"Bring them on," I say. "We'll kill them till they stop coming."

We're unhappy we missed the funerals. Lenson's parents came to William Beaumont to visit Hancock. I was still delirious, fighting off infection. They live outside Dallas. I'll stop by to see them on my way to Fayetteville.

I've killed more people than I can count. Only a few faces stand out. The Iraqi kid who ran at us with an IED in his arms. Cut in half with a machine gun. He sat up, clutching his stomach. I could see he was suffering, so I shot him in the face. The Afghan women dragging our flayed POWs through the streets. The heat I felt as I pulled the trigger.

We have lost many of our own. They all knew the score

when they gunned up and went into battle. Each man a brother. You grow close, but not too close. When they are killed, you feel hollowed by the loss. But you do not feel grief.

It is like that with Lenson and Keller. Hancock and I are saddened by their loss. Now they are gone, there are holes in our lives. But we will not sob and rend our clothes. We killed Hamza and his Quds because our friends' ghosts demanded justice.

Hancock shakes two pills out of a bottle and fires them down with a gulp of water.

"Go easy on that shit," I tell him.

"Can't seem to get enough." Hancock sets his glass down on the bedside table. "What are you going to do?"

"Go back to Fayetteville. Private companies are hiring operators."

Hancock grins. For a moment, he becomes the cocky young man I used to know. "You gonna grow a handlebar mustache? Walk around in a biker vest and carry a 1911 in your hip pocket?"

We laugh together.

"Maybe." I get to my feet. "Listen, I'll see you later."

"Where are you going?"

"I have an errand to run."

I PARK my rented Taurus off Montana Avenue. Evergreen East Cemetery. I get out of the car, walk to the office. The lady at the desk lays a map of the grounds on the counter. Draws an X. "Here it is," she says. "Next to the Garden of the Cross."

"Thank you."

"Are you Breed?"

"Yes, I am."

The woman takes an envelope from her desk and hands it to me. "I was asked to give you this."

The envelope is plain white, letter size. I slip it into my back pocket.

I walk across the cemetery. The sky is blue, the breeze is fresh. The amount of greenery surprises me. There are gravel sections, and patches of brown grass. Sprinklers work overtime watering the lawns. Most of the grounds are green, and there are trees everywhere. A plot in this cemetery must be expensive. I wonder how Stein managed it.

The grave lies under the shade of a tree. The wind is kicking up, ruffling blades of grass. The headstone and plot are small. She was a small girl. There is a cross chiseled into the stone, and Mirasol's name.

I take the envelope from my pocket. Open it. A note, addressed to me. The handwriting is careful, precise.

Breed.
I think Mirasol would like it here, don't you?
Stein

Yes, Stein.

I think she would.

ACKNOWLEDGMENTS

This novel would not have been possible without the support, encouragement, and guidance of my agent, Ivan Mulcahy, of MMB Creative. I would also like to thank my publishers, Brian Lynch and Garret Ryan of Inkubator Books for seeing the novel's potential and taking a chance. Thanks also goes to Claire Milto of Inkubator Books for her support in the novel's launch.

Not the least, I wish to thank members of my writing group, beta readers, and listeners, who support my obsession with reading every word of a novel out loud in pursuit of that undefinable quality called voice.

If you could spend a moment to write an honest review on Amazon, no matter how short, I would be extremely grateful. They really do help readers discover my books.

Feel free to contact me at cameron.curtis545@gmail.com. I'd love to hear from you.

Best wishes,

Cameron